BLOWOUT

BLOWOUT

SUSAN VAUGHT

BLOOMSBURY

First published in Great Britain in 2006 by Bloomsbury Publishing Plc
36 Soho Square, London, W1D 3QY

First published in the USA as *Trigger* in 2006 by Bloomsbury
Publishing,
Children's Books, USA
175 Fifth Avenue, New York, NY 10010

A CIP catalogue record of this book is available from the British
Library

ISBN 0 7475 8284 X
ISBN-13 9780747582847

Digitally printed in Great Britain by Clays Ltd, St Ives plc

1 3 5 7 9 10 8 6 4 2

www.bloomsbury.com

For Kathleen, Dorothy, and Jeri.
I don't have to tell you why.

chapter 1

*I have this dream where both legs work and both arms
work and I don't have any scars on the outside . . .*

Dreams, no dreams, more dreams. On August 2, a Friday a
few weeks after my seventeenth birthday, a little less than
a year after I took a bullet in the head, I finally got to go
home. Dreams. Good old Carter Brain Injury Center, my
fourth and last hospital, was about to be history.

Carter wasn't much to look at, just five brick buildings
in a circle around a paved driveway. There was a pool behind the therapy building (tiny) and gardens by all the front
doors (neat). It was clean (sometimes), the rooms were
white (usually), we got to have our own bedspreads (anything but white), and the therapists were perky.

Perky. That was a Dad-word.

Mom probably agreed about the therapists, but I didn't
know for sure. Perky. Mom wasn't big on words. Bank
presidents focused more on numbers, according to Dad,

1

who wasn't a bank president. When my parents came to pick me up, Mom didn't say much except *proud of you, honey*.

Example:

Hi, Mom. I got married.

Proud of you, honey.

She's a bank robber, and she has nine tattoos.

Proud of you, honey.

We're planning a crime spree, starting with you, Mom. Hand over that purse.

Proud of you, honey.

Sometimes she said it louder than other times, and sometimes she even looked at me. Just try talking to Mom. I guarantee she'll be *proud of you*, too.

The day we found out I was getting discharged from Carter, Mom was proud of me for completing the program. Proud. I'd been excused from outpatient treatment, too, because I'd done so well. Proud. We'd have to go to counseling, but our first appointment wasn't for six months. The nearest outpatient doctor who took brain-injured patients was a hundred miles away with a long waiting list, but the Carter shrink thought we could handle the break. Shrink. Handle it. Proud. Like there was a choice. We were good to go. We could handle it. Proud, proud, proud. There was a big yellow banner over my door to prove it.

UP AND FORWARD, JERSEY!

I kept staring at the banner like its green letters might turn red, but they didn't. If they had, and if I told somebody, I probably would have earned myself a few more weeks of rehabilitation. Red. Proud. Up and forward. Or at least a bunch of tests and studies and stuff, to make sure

2

the bullet didn't take more than my smarts, the vision in my right eye, and the strength on the left side of my body.

You're a lucky boy, Jersey Hatch.

To my doctor, everyone was lucky. I had nightmares imagining a conversation between the doc and my mom.

Your son's lucky, ma'am.

I'm proud of you, Doc.

Yep, he's a lucky boy, Ms. Hatch.

I'm proud of him, too, Doc.

Lucky.

Proud.

Lucky!

Proud!

Figured my dad had a great time at all those team meetings to review my progress. Never mind all the meetings deciding stuff about school and what kind of classes and help I'd need. I knew Dad had a great time getting Mom to visit me. She didn't much like coming to Carter. Even on the afternoon of my release, she came in for maybe ten minutes, then went to wait in the car until it was time to leave.

You've got to give her time, Jersey, the Carter shrink insisted. *She's still distant because she needs to heal. So does your father.* Lucky. He wanted me to work on insight, that shrink. Lucky. Proud. Said insight would be my biggest problem, except maybe paying attention to how other people feel, since the right side of the brain did all that, and the right side of my brain had a big hole in it.

Insight. *You're like a five-year-old genius.* The shrink always tapped the side of his head when he said stuff like that. *Your intelligence—it's all there, but you don't have*

3

the social skills to use it. Pragmatics, Mr. Hatch. Focus on pragmatics!

Insight. Pragmatics. Proud. Lucky. A hand patted my shoulder.

"You ready, son?" Dad's voice seemed loud in the hallway.

Pragmatics. I'd looked up that word a bunch of times. Facts. Actual occurrences. Practical stuff. I managed a smile, but kept an eye on the green letters in the UP AND FORWARD, JERSEY! banner, hoping they would turn red after all.

No such luck. Practical pragmatic fact. Insight.

Dad and I loaded my stuff in the car without too much trouble, and quick as that, I was in the backseat, strapped in tight. Mom started the car without revving the engine like Dad usually did.

"Is the house okay?" I asked as we drove away from Carter. Couldn't help asking even though I'd asked a hundred times, because the worry wouldn't leave me until I spit out the question. I hadn't seen the house in so long I was afraid it would be gone.

"Yes, Jersey." Dad sounded annoyed, but he flashed a giant grin. He was sitting directly in front of me in the passenger seat. If I turned my head and leaned a little, I could use my good eye to see his brown hair and brown beard stubble in the side mirror. His eyes—they were brown, too—darted from his window to the mirror. When he noticed I was staring at him, back to the window he went.

Mom, of course, said nothing as she drove. If she had, I was sure it would have involved the word *proud*.

I tried to stop thinking about the house so I wouldn't ask again. When I got nervous, it was harder to keep my mouth shut. The therapists all warned me about that, over and over. How much harder it would be outside of Carter. How much harder I'd have to try just to talk and think. Whatever. I'd try harder. But the house might have been gone, because lots of things were gone. Like Todd Rush. He'd been my friend since third grade and he lived next door to us, but I hadn't seen him since . . . well, since Before. I forgot stuff, so I asked Dad again, to be sure Todd hadn't visited.

Dad said Todd and I hadn't been close for several months Before, but I couldn't remember that no matter how hard I tried. My fifteenth year got blown right out of my head, along with a lot of the time After—the time during my sixteenth year, when I'd been in rehab. Sometimes I dreamed things and thought they were memories. Other times I thought I was dreaming and it turned out to be real. Like the house. Had something happened to the house?

"Is the house okay?"

"The house is fine." Dad's teeth clenched in a pretend smile. Silence from Mom. She might have been an automated Crash Test Dummy, except that she was driving.

Had she always been so quiet? Crash Test Dummy. I didn't remember her being quiet. I remembered her being real funny and telling lots of jokes, but she hadn't done that in a long time. Dad and the Carter shrink kept telling me she got quiet when she found me.

After, I mean.

I didn't get that, because I wasn't dead and I didn't die, but to Mom, it must have been a big deal, walking in on After.

Only I still wondered about Before and After. I wondered if I really got shot in the head. Maybe I was in a car

5

wreck like most of the guys at Carter, the poster cube. When I first heard the nurses say "poster cube," I couldn't figure out what a poster cube was, but I kept looking for one, even after they told me to sit down, until the doctor gave me a shot because I couldn't quit looking for that dumb cube, and trying to go home, to make sure the house was still there. Later on I found out they meant "post acute." Post-acute hospital, another kind of rehab. But I still didn't know if the house was there and I kept worrying even though I didn't have to find a poster cube.

"Is the house okay?"

Dad let out a groan, then pasted on his smile again. "It's fine, Jersey."

Poster cube.

"Oh." I rubbed the scar on my right temple. "Sorry."

"In the brain, out the mouth, I know, I know." Dad glanced at me in the mirror. "You've got your memory book, right? Want to write it down?"

I picked up the white binder off the car seat beside me, the one with *Hatch, Jersey* written in purple letters down the spine. Without much thinking about it, I flipped to a blank page, took the pen tied to the book by a dirty white string, and wrote, *HOUSE IS FINE MORON QUIT ASKING.* Then I left it on my lap without closing it. Didn't do me much good closed. A memory book was one of the things I had to deal with after getting shot in the head. If I got shot in the head.

It could have been a car wreck. Most of the guys at Carter had been in wrecks, and lots of them had been drinking. Maybe I was drinking, and got in a wreck, and—did I wreck the car into the house?

Before I opened my mouth, I glanced down at my book. *HOUSE IS FINE MORON QUIT ASKING.*

"The house is fine." My head tingled with relief. "The house is fine."

Mom coughed. Dad coughed louder. Some sort of parent-cough Morse code. I rubbed my scar and wondered why they didn't just tell me to shut up like the Carter therapists did. Fine. Whatever. Harder on the outside. Harder out of the hospital. I had to try harder, so I told myself to shut up. Morse code. In fact, I pretended to stuff a sock in my mouth so I'd shut up. The sock usually lived in my head, right between my ears, muffling ideas when I tried to remember.

For example, we were on the road home, and I already couldn't remember everything about leaving Carter. Only snapshots. This and that, and not always hooked together. I wrote most things down in my book like I was supposed to, so I turned back a page and squinted at the pen scrawls.

It was my To-Do List. My Carter shrink made me do it.

1. *See Mama Rush and give her all the presents I made her.*
2. *Talk to Todd and find out why he hates me.*
3. *Pass the adaptive driver's evaluation.*
4. *Make decent grades.*
5. *Take the ACT.*
6. *Get a girlfriend.*

Beside "Pass the adaptive driver's evaluation," my occupational therapist had written *Ha, ha, ha. Good one.* She wasn't being mean. She just didn't think I could handle being on the road with an occupational therapist and a physical therapist taking notes to make sure I had brain enough to drive. Besides, I'd failed it three times already, and now that I was out of Carter, it would cost five hundred dollars to take it again. Harder on the outside. Harder out of the hospital. I figured I'd get a chance once a year if I was lucky. Proud. Lucky. Proud. Lucky. House is fine moron quit asking.

Oh, and some of the guys wrote on Number 6, too, stuff like, *You're so dreaming, Hatch*. I probably was, but I figured dreams were okay, so long as I didn't think they were real.

I looked at the opposite page, at the most recent entry before *HOUSE-MORON*.

August 1, 3:00 p.m.: Said bye to Hank and Joey. Said bye to Alicia. Alicia gave me her ceramic duck. I made her take it back since it was her good luck charm.

Lucky. Proud. Lucky. Proud. Pragmatics, pragmatics, pragmatics.

The duck had felt cool and smooth in my hand.

I balanced the book on my knees and studied my fingers, remembering. Alicia held onto it all the time. It made her feel safe and happy. Would I have gotten shot in the head if I'd had a duck like that one? If I got shot in the head, I mean.

Did it hurt? Because I had this dream . . . no. Only a dream. But did I feel the bullet slam into my brain? In the dream, it burned and it hurt, so much. So, so much. Just a dream, right?

I gripped the sides of my memory book and squeezed. If I got shot in the head, I bet nothing went through my mind,

8

and it did hurt.

Maybe I had time to think, "Oh, shit."

My shrink told me I *shouldn't dwell on trauma like that*. And Carter taught me I wasn't supposed to curse under any circumstances.

Watch your mouth, Hatch, the occupational therapist would say. *That shit's in the past.*

Did I mention the occupational therapist could curse? Only the OT called it swearing. And she said I was supposed to do what she told me to do, not what she did. *Pragmatics, Hatch. Don't forget pragmatics.*

Quit goofing off, Jersey. Grip that ball if you want any of that hand back. Squeeze. Squeeze harder.

The brain has no sensation. That's why they keep people awake during some brain surgeries. After they saw through the skull, it's no big deal. Now squeeze the ball before I cram it up your nose.

Curl those fingers! What are you waiting for, an invitation? Up and forward, Hatch! Get with the program. The least you can do is get better so your parents don't have to wipe your butt.

Curl 'em, or I'll break your good hand. Squeeze that ball like it's a hammer about to fall on your nuts.

The hand-Nazi. I'd never forget her. Hell, she did a lot for me. Oops. Not supposed to curse. Up and forward. No swearing. Harder on the outside. I didn't need an occupational therapist anymore. I'd get to see a psychotherapist, but that wouldn't be for months. Waiting lists. It was time to do things for myself. Proud. Lucky. I could have had a very good duck. Curl those fingers. Duck balls and hammers. Pragmatics.

I was still thinking about hand-Nazis and nut hammers and wondering why my parents didn't talk to me like the therapists did when Mom drove up to a take-out window and bought us all an early supper. She drove us to Lake Raven, really close to my house, and we sat there in the car at the wide end of the lake to eat. I turned my head to the right a little, so I could see the water, all blue with ripples and sunlight on top. There were some benches close by, and a little two-rail safety fence. I'd been there a lot. I knew I had, only I couldn't really remember when, except for when I was lots younger, so I just stared at the water.

It took me forever to eat hot wings with one hand, and I couldn't really taste them that much, but I managed—and I didn't ask about the house a single time, not even when Mom started the car and got back on the road. Not even when she hit the blinker and steered the car into our neighborhood. Right away I noticed all the lawns were mowed up and down, like baseball fields. Neat, like our four-house cul-de-sac. Neat, like our two-story white house with black shutters.

HOUSE IS FINE MORON QUIT ASKING.

Proud. Lucky. Very good duck balls.

In a few seconds, I'd see the house for myself. I touched the messy circular dent in my throat. Tracheotomy scar. That's what happened when I couldn't breathe for myself. Some doc cut a hole in my neck and stuck a plastic tube through my trachea. The tube was hooked to a machine, and the machine pumped air into my lungs. In and out. Beep, click, hissss. Beep, click, hissss. I didn't remember that, but I learned about it at Carter. One of the therapists made me sit by a ventilator so I'd know what my parents had to go through the whole seventy-one days I wouldn't wake up. Beep, click, hissss.

You need to spend more time thinking about other people, Hatch. It's not all about you.

Beep, click, hissss.

Can you imagine this day after day? Seventy-one days? Can you?

Beep, click, hissss.

Focus on what I'm saying, what you're hearing. I want you to remember this. You can if you try. Apply yourself, Hatch. It's gonna be harder on the outside.

I rubbed a hand across my close-cut hair and fingered the upside-down C on the left side of my head, where they cut open my skull and took out the bullet and a bunch of blood. The craniotomy scar had lost its swelling—gone pale—but it was still there, like the entry dent in my right temple.

You're a lucky boy, Mr. Hatch. It's a miracle you're blind in only one eye. A little higher, a little lower . . .

It's a wonder you're alive, Mr. Hatch. An inch. Just an inch . . .

Must have a purpose . . .

Up and forward . . .

God must have his eye on you . . .

"God?" I laughed.

Dad stared at me in the mirror. Mom got stiffer behind the wheel.

"Oh. Sorry. Don't worry." I gave them my best half-grin, which was all my mouth could do. Seeing myself in the rearview wasn't fun. "He didn't say anything. God, I mean. At least not that I heard. I was just thinking about proud and lucky and ducks and stuff. But not the house. Honest."

Mom sighed as she pulled onto our short street. I let out a breath, too, because I was glad to see the house. It was still there, and I hadn't been talking to God.

As we parked in the driveway, my fingers went from scar to scar. Did I really get shot in the head?

Would God care if I had?

The scars—but I didn't remember anything.

Why? Dad had asked a thousand times.

We'd covered it in family therapy at Carter over and over, the not remembering. The shrink explained I'd never remember getting shot—and probably not the year leading up to it, either. He said the gunshot wound was an open head injury, that it damaged my brain. Getting shot in the head was like unplugging a computer with nearly twelve months of data unsaved. The entries for those fifty or sixty weeks got fried. Gone. Poof. Most of my summer before my sophomore year, and the year itself. Fried.

Then I'd done eleventh grade in the hospitals, and now it was the end of summer before my senior year. Fried. Nobody from my school came to visit, so they didn't ask how I got shot. Nobody from outside school came to visit, so they didn't ask, either. My parents finally quit asking. Fried. Oh, yeah, wait—Mama Rush, Todd's grandmother, came once during the third hospital, and she asked. But I don't think she believed me when I told her I didn't remember. Fried. In three weeks, I'd go back to school. Somebody probably would get around to asking that one question I couldn't answer, even for myself. Fried, fried, fried.

I struggled out of my seat belt, opened the car door, and got out, and I stood in our neat yard, which had been mowed up and down like a baseball field. The house stared at me. I figured if it had eyebrows, the one above my window would have gone sliding halfway to the roof. Even the house wanted to know the answer to that one question I couldn't answer up and forward, down and backward, proud or lucky, very good duck or not.

Jersey Hatch, why did you shoot yourself?

chapter 2

I have this dream where both legs work and both arms work and I don't have any scars on the outside. I'm sitting on the edge of my bed in dress blues holding a pistol. Sunlight brightens the dust in my room and darkens all the places where I've nicked the walls and doors. My fingers tingle as I lift the gun to my mouth. It tastes oily and dusty as I close my lips on cold gunmetal—but I can't. Not in the mouth. I'm shaking, but I lift the barrel to the side of my head. The tip digs into my skin. I'm thinking nothing but how it feels, and that my hand's shaking, and that my room has so much dust in places I didn't even know. Then I'm squeezing the trigger and looking at the dust and feeling my hand shake and thinking nothing and there's noise and fire and nothing. Nothing at all.

Only a dream, something I made up because I never remembered and not remembering almost made me crazy. I had the dream every night. Crazy. But I didn't tell anybody.

I wasn't sure why I didn't tell anybody, but there were lots of things I didn't talk about, not even to the Carter shrink. Crazy. But now I was home and the dreams were right here and I had to go inside or I'd be stupid and unpragmatic and a big crazy baby. The five-year-old genius sucking his thumb.

Mom went inside before I even got to the door. Dad followed behind me lugging my bags. I got my memory book, but I couldn't carry the suitcases myself because of my balance. My left leg—it pulled. Sometimes I tripped on my foot. And my left arm, I kept forgetting it. Always bashing it into doorframes and chairs, which helped me trip over my foot a lot. That's why the pictures made me cry.

They were hanging right inside the front door, first thing, in the foyer. There was a boy in the frames, standing at attention in a marine R.O.T.C. uniform. He was dressed in football pads, going long. He was standing with a set of clubs on a green with a guy who stopped speaking to him long before he even pulled the trigger. The boy in all the pictures had wavy brown hair and no holes in his head and no holes in his throat, and I knew he was me—but he couldn't be. So I held on tight to the memory book and my stomach hurt and I cried.

Dad came up beside me and put down my bags. For a second or two, he pushed the first button of his sweater vest in and out of its hole—something I couldn't do on purpose with lots of help. After a while, he put an arm around my shoulders.

"Let's go on upstairs," he said in his I-support-you voice. "Be careful and use the rail."

I nodded and wiped my face off with my shirt. Tears

smeared across the cover of my memory book, but the inked name on the spine didn't run, not even a little. The pen on the dirty white string swung back and forth, back and forth.

Dad looked like he wanted to say something, but he bit his bottom lip before picking up the suitcases and starting up without me. I stood there for a while, staring at the pictures and trying to breathe.

The last time I had been here in this house, I shot myself.

I actually . . . but no. I didn't know that for sure. I *might* have shot myself. Still had my thoughts about that, but I sort of believed it. Dad believed it, because he said I used his gun, his pistol, from his bedside table, the one he kept to deal with thieves and murderers.

Maybe Dad thought I was a thief and shot me. I could believe that easier than the story about me coming home from school, dressing in my uniform, loading a single bullet in Dad's gun, sitting down on my bed, and blowing my brains out.

I mean, a person would have to remember *something* if he did all those things, right? And he'd have to remember why. All I had were my dreams of sitting on the bed and feeling nothing at all.

My eyes drifted over pictures. Before-boy. Jersey Hatch, prior to cleaning his own clock. Jersey-Before. J.B. I remembered him well, at least up until ninth grade. After that, things got a little patchy. R.O.T.C., golf, football . . . me. I did them all. And school and girls and everything. And these pictures, these were J.B. from two years ago. Do-everything J.B. I-want-to-be-a-lawyer J.B. Straight-A J.B.

I was him. He was me.

Not real, but he was real. Wasn't he? I could see him, coming right out of the pictures, floating down, standing beside me, dressed just like me, only with no scars.

My teeth hurt when I clamped them on my lip. I thought about my socks. Wished I could stuff a sock in my brain so it would shut up. The more nervous I got, the more I thought about socks. Socks and ghosts. Ghosts coming out of pictures.

J.B., he sure looked like a ghost. Socks. His eyes seemed wide and bright and focused. The line of his jaw gave him a set, determined expression. J.B. was not a guy to give up. I couldn't believe he'd put a bullet in his own head.

"So why'd you do it?" I asked. "Socks."

"Do what?" Dad called down from my room.

"Not you." I pointed the memory book at J.B. even though Dad couldn't see me do it. "I was talking to the ghost. Socks."

"Go upstairs, Jersey." Mom's quiet voice startled me out of the ghost-pictures. She was standing right in front of me, eyes wider than usual, holding a Diet Coke. "Help your father unpack." Then, like she forgot the important part, "I'm proud of you for working hard to get home. Try to enjoy the day."

"Um, okay. Sure." Sweat broke out under my shirt. I felt clammy and cold. Socks. It was time to go upstairs, to J.B.'s room, to where he tried to kill us. Why hadn't I asked them if I could move into the guest room? I couldn't ask them now, could I? Not with them acting so nervous and freaky. That might blow their minds. They might think I wasn't ready and send me back.

But going back might not be so bad. Socks. The

therapists told me it was easier at Carter. Easier. Probably was easier.

Before Mom could tell me to go up again, I faced the stairs. They looked really steep.

Steps were hard for a one-footer like me, but I could hear the therapists in the back of my mind.

Wah, wah, wah. It's hard. So what?

So what.

The memory book tasted all plastic and salty when I crammed it between my teeth. I knew I'd need my hands. Strong one for the rail, weak one for the wall. Balancing as best I could, I moved my good leg up, then made my bad leg follow.

Behind me, Mom walked away. I heard her footsteps, but they sounded like whispers, like she was tiptoeing. Or maybe it was the ghost in the air in front of the pictures. J.B., coming with me. Socks. I tried to go faster. Up, and up. Each thump sounded like an earthquake. Up, and up. Maybe I could outrun him. If I went fast enough, the ghost would have to stay downstairs.

"Do it like the therapists said," Dad yelled from the bedroom. "Good boys go to heaven. Bad boys go to hell. Good leg going up, bad leg after."

That's how I remembered it. Good leg leads going up the stairs; coming down, bad leg leads. Up, up, up. Heaven, hell. Heaven, hell. Heaven . . . hell. I made it. Socks. Socks. The landing at the top of the stairs seemed like paradise, no matter which word got me there. Up and forward, and all that rehab perky stuff. Socks. I went fast, so maybe I left the ghost downstairs after all.

"You did great." Dad was standing in my doorway, too-big smile blazing.

I pulled the memory book out of my teeth and tried to smile back, but I froze. Seeing him there, framed by that familiar wood facing, cedar against the white walls, it felt all wrong.

No way that door was mine. Even though I could remember how the room should look inside, with trophies and posters from pee-wee baseball all the way through high school golf . . . one bed, blue spread . . . a rug with a big knit football—no. No! It wasn't my room. It was *his*. It was J.B.'s.

My breath came short and sharp. My body didn't want to move. Maybe if I went in there, J.B. would be waiting on that bed, holding the gun. He might kill us, and this time, he'd do it right.

"Need help?" Dad sounded like a therapist. His whopper smile faltered, and I imagined the hospital van swooping down to pick me up and cart me straight back to the brick buildings and the OT and the big yellow banner.

Up and forward. Up and forward.

I slowed down my breathing and paid attention to everything around me, just like I had learned from the shrink at Carter. Familiar smells. Perfume, from my parents' room. And aftershave. And leather, like footballs and golf bags and everything but socks. I didn't think they made leather socks, at least not for regular people. Leather and footballs and aftershave with no socks. My room. J.B.'s room. He wouldn't be waiting. J.B. was dead. Socks. The gun was gone, except for my dreams and the scar from its bullet

19

on my right temple. Socks. The gun was gone. I wobbled down the hall using the wall until I was almost nose to nose with Dad.

"Welcome home," he said as he grabbed me into a hug. The floor creaked like it would break and drop us all the way back downstairs.

Dad's voice seemed strained, but the hug felt real enough. I hugged him back with my good arm, taking care not to whack him with the memory book. My bad arm was sort of crushed between us. I nearly lost my balance when he turned me loose, but he let me use his shoulder until I got steady.

Still giving me that bizarre over-smile, he moved aside and I stepped into ghost-boy's lair.

The first thing I noticed was the bedspread. It was green, not blue. There was no J.B. ghost-boy wearing socks and no gun. Just a green bedspread. It should have been blue. Blue, not green. Why was it green?

Dad must have seen where I was looking because he said, "Old bedspread was a waste. We had to chuck it. Sorry about this one. I tried to get your mother to buy something psychedelic, but she wouldn't go for it. Do you like this one? Is it okay?"

"Yeah. Sure." I wondered why Dad was so jacked up about a bedspread. I wanted him to relax, to quit with the freaky smile. Socks.

"We even got you a new mattress. But the rug, the football rug beside the bed, that was clean. You folded it and set it on the dresser, so it wasn't—um, messy." He scrubbed his hand across his beard stubble. "I'm sorry. I guess I shouldn't be talking about that right now. It's your welcome-home day."

Air faded from my lungs as if sucked by some beep-click-hissss machine gone insane. The rug on the dresser. I didn't know that. No one had mentioned that before, ever, I was sure of it. Why would I—no! Why would J.B. do a thing like that? I mean, if he planned to die, why'd he care about some stupid rug?

Because Mama Rush got it for us, whispered that Before voice, from way down in my mind.

Oh, God. Socks and footballs.

J.B. was real. He was upstairs and he was talking to me. The sweat came back double under my shirt, and I got so cold my teeth started to chatter. There was a ghost in my room, and it was going to kill me again, I just knew it.

Dad put his arm around my waist and I jumped. "Jersey, are you okay? If this upsets you, you don't have to stay in here." He was talking so fast. "We can move you to the guest room. I guess we should have asked. I'm really sorry we didn't think—"

"No. I'm fine. Fine socks." Except a ghost just whispered in my head, and that ghost, he used to be me, and he was going to kill me right next time, and I wanted my dad to shut up more than anything and go back downstairs and leave me alone. I felt like if I told him that, he'd break into twenty pieces.

Jersey Hatch, J.B. called in a mean, mocking tone. *Why'd you do it? Why'd you shoot yourself?*

I looked to my left and right really fast, but I didn't see any ghosts. Great. J.B. was in my brain. I'd brought the ghost with me in my head.

Why'd you do it? he taunted as my teeth clicked together.

Of course, the answer to that question was the million-

21

dollar prize, the whole contest give-away, the biggest of the big sock enchiladas. Why, exactly, did I put my father's gun against my head and pull the trigger?

It was a robbery, maybe. Or an accident. Maybe I had a car wreck.

Bright sun through the window made me blink to be sure the scene was real, since "real" often turned left when I chased it. My life After reminded me of a bad geography video. North African deserts and stuff, with all the wind. I saw or heard something, finally got a fix on it, but siroccos blew sand across the landscape until everything got hidden again. Buried under two tons of yellow white dunes.

Yellow white spots flashed in the eye that didn't work anymore. Ghost spots, ghost sand. Just brief pictures in the dunes, like the ghost pictures on the wall downstairs and in the ghost in my head that had come upstairs to kill me. Pictures of sand dunes danced in my brain. Yellow mountains. Ripples and blowing clouds. God, first the house and socks, now sand dunes. I'd probably be thinking about sand for a month. The therapists told me it would be harder to think in the real world. That I'd have to try harder. Sand. I didn't believe them. Sand. I wished I had.

"Would you like me to stay, or would you like some time to yourself?" Dad let go of my waist and stepped away from me. He looked like he wanted to snatch me up and hug me all over again.

"Uh—well." My stomach heaved. Why did he want me to pick? Why was he acting so weird? "Sand. Some time to myself would probably be good."

I braced myself and stood still as a sand dune with no wind blowing.

To my great relief, Dad didn't touch me or fall apart. He just nodded and backed away until he reached the steps. It sounded like he ran down, I swear. For a full minute, I just stood there feeling like the man was scared I had a guillotine in my closet or something. Like I was the king of France waiting to chop off his head the first time he said something wrong. King Jersey. I snorted. What a joke. Sand dunes didn't have crowns. Sand dunes didn't have guillotines. Were there any sand dunes in France?

My bad leg and arm started to ache, along with my head. Scar to scar, like always, the pain stabbed like knives, then spears. I lurched to the green-that-should-have-been-blue bedspread and sit on the edge.

When the headaches came, the pain was awful at the start. The worst would pass if I relaxed. It would fade into a dull pounding and finish in a few hours and leave my head and neck sore. Nothing helped the headaches, and pain medicine made me fall and vomit, so that was out.

God, my stomach hurt as bad as my head.

I bent forward and held the memory book against my chest.

This is where you did it, whispered J.B.

My teeth clamped together.

Want to write that in your stupid white book so the wind doesn't blow it off your stupid yellow sand dunes? Go ahead and lie down. You probably fell sideways with your head on the pillow, since it's to your left. Don't you think that's how you fell?

"Shut up," I mumbled. It was all I could do not to hit that pillow headfirst.

What was I doing here? Why had I come back to this

place? I should have stayed at Carter. No way was I ready for this.

Lie down in the sand, King Jersey. The voice in my head was mine, but not mine. I blinked hard. The headaches always blurred my vision. Usually, I didn't notice not being able to see out of one eye. Only sometimes, when I turned my head and saw something I didn't know had been there. But now I noticed, since my good eye was blurring. The sun was going down, I could tell—but the light, it was still so bright. Like hammers against my eye. It made the dust bright. Dust and sand, sand and dust.

My fingers tingle as I lift the gun to my mouth . . .

I had folded the rug first. The rug Mama Rush gave me. I put it on the dresser so it wouldn't get messy—

"Stop it," I said out loud, whacking my forehead with the memory book once, twice. The pain echoed between the scars. Those weren't my memories. The dust and tingling fingers, those were from a dream. The rug being folded, Dad had told me that a few minutes ago. I was filling in holes again, making dreams real and turning words into pictures.

"Up and forward." I lowered the memory book and held it tight against me. For a while, I rocked back and forth, feeling the football rug move back and forth under my sneakers. "Up and forward, up and forward, lucky proud king moron who could have had a duck. Socks and sand, sand and socks."

It was like a chant. I sang it to myself until the sharper pains got better and the toothache-throb started at my right temple. That I could stand—except I was so tired. I felt like I'd run home from Carter. Ignoring the whispers in my broken brain, I kicked off my shoes and let myself lie down, head on the pillow. My feet stayed on the floor because I didn't have the energy to move them.

When the pain let up enough, I opened up the memory book and stared at the To-Do List, letting the gray light show me my goals one more time.

1. *See Mama Rush and give her all the presents I made her.*
2. *Talk to Todd and find out why he hates me.*
3. *Pass the adaptive driver's evaluation.*
4. *Make decent grades.*
5. *Take the ACT.*
6. *Get a girlfriend.*

I repeated them three times, until I at least remembered the first one without looking. *See Mama Rush.* That was easy enough. She was right next door. All I had to do was knock and ask. If Todd answered, I might take care of the second one, too. Creak, creak, the floor was creaking. I could talk to Todd and ask—

"Jersey!"

Mom's shocked gasp made me slam the book and sit straight up.

My head hurt so sharply I thought it would explode.

She was standing in my doorway like an ice statue, pale white, both hands against the side of her head. Sand and socks. Socks and sand.

"Mom?" I felt dizzy, and I really wanted to throw up. What was wrong with her?

Slowly, she seemed to come back to herself and thaw a

little. The hands came down. "I—I—," she started, but she didn't finish. Her lowered hands shook as she twitched her head from side to side once. "Nothing. Sorry I disturbed you. Do you want the light on?"

"No, thanks. I've got a headache right now. Sand."

"Okay." And she was gone. Poof. The wind blew her away. The sand wind melted the ice. Socks on the sand wind.

Frowning, I eased myself back down to my pillow. Numbers. Mom was good at numbers. Numbers—the list. I had been trying to remember the list without looking. Making plans for crossing off numbers. I had been trying to get started. Lucky proud king ducks in the sand. At least I didn't hear the ghost-voice. J.B. had gone to sleep or died or whatever. Maybe the headache killed him before he could kill me.

My eyelids closed against the pound-pound-pound of my scars, my teeth, my eyeballs. My good arm draped across my stomach. Getting started with my list should be easy enough. I'd use what I learned at Carter. Eyeballs. Envision, then implement. Up and forward. Imagine what I would do, then do it.

Eyeballs. Sand and socks.

I was mentally chanting about the sand eyeballs and socks, mentally heading back down the steps and next door to see Mama Rush, when I fell hard, hard, hard asleep.

chapter 3

I have this dream where both legs work and both arms work and I don't have any scars on the outside. I'm sitting on the edge of my bed in dress blues holding a pistol. Sunlight brightens the dust and sand in my room and darkens all the places where I've nicked the walls and doors. The football rug, the one Mama Rush gave me when I made the team my freshman year, is folded neatly on my dresser so it won't get messy. I give it one last look before I turn back to what I'm doing. My fingers tingle as I lift the gun to my mouth. It tastes oily and dusty all at once as I close my lips on cold gunmetal—but I can't. Not in the mouth. I'm shaking, but I lift the barrel to the side of my head. The tip digs into my skin. I'm thinking nothing but how that feels, and that my hand's shaking, and that my room has so much dust and sand in places I didn't even know. Then I'm squeezing the trigger and looking at the dust and sand and feeling my hand shake and thinking nothing and

27

there's noise and fire and pain and I'm falling, falling, my
broken head smashing into my pillow . . .

Dad made oatmeal for breakfast, which struck me weird because Dad was a cold cereal sort of guy, or at least he had been Before.

"Everything changes," he said when I asked, then talked about reading articles on nutrition and how nutrition really helps people not be depressed and stuff. Dad was worried I'd get depressed now that I was out of the hospital, because of pressure. Too much pressure. Depressed. Dad reading articles. That was another weird thing, because Dad usually read articles in his law enforcement journals to help him out at work, not articles about food. A probation officer, my dad. Cold cereal, long hours, lots of worrying about all his "other kids." Now he was staying home to look after me, I supposed. He offered to take me to the movies. Everything changes.

Mom, who used to get up before dawn, run a bunch of miles, and keep her blond hair tight and pulled back and her clothes perfect even on the weekend, she was still in bed.

"So, about the movies?" Dad's über-smile filled up his face.

"No, thanks." I looked away. My parents. I had no idea what to do with them now. "I have this list from Carter I need to start working through—and it's stuff I kinda need to do for myself, for independence and up and forward and all. Everything changes. Carter. Stuff."

When I looked back at Dad, his expression had changed to one that might have been disappointment, then he found one of those weird smiles again and wandered off to his study to make phone calls.

My parents.

Everything changes. Except Mama Rush. She always told me she was way too old to change, and at the moment, I was glad. Dressed in jeans and a short-sleeve shirt she had sent to me while I was in Carter, I picked up my memory book and the plastic bag of presents, and I headed out the front door without looking at the pictures of J.B. I made sure to check back with my good eye, but I didn't see any ghosts following me out of the house, and I figured I was safe the minute the front door closed.

It was warm outside. The sunlight made me blink really fast, and it hurt in my blind eye. At Carter, they told me to wear a patch or sunglasses, but I thought that looked stupid, so I just dealt with it. I didn't wear my hand brace either, or the foot brace. Too uncomfortable. I was supposed to sleep in those stupid things so my foot wouldn't turn in and my hand wouldn't curl up. No way. They sent the braces home with me, but when I unpacked this morning, I put them in the closet.

The oatmeal—one ounce of butter, no sugar—churned in my stomach as I tried to forget Dad's strangeness and the dream I'd had. The folded rug. The stupid folded rug.

I covered my right eye with my memory book. The sun felt hot on my fingers even though the breeze was cool. Rug. Fall was coming. Fall and school and my life and I had a To-Do List, and Mama Rush was first, and she was too old to change. Rug.

Todd's house seemed a lot farther from my front door than I remembered, but I made the hike without even losing my breath even though I was carrying a plastic bag that

29

had to weigh ten pounds. Bad boy going to hell down the front steps, then good boy going to heaven as I climbed up to Todd's porch.

Reality check: Todd would probably slam the door in my face if he answered.

Rug.

I needed to be ready for that, but I didn't feel ready at all. I felt scared and clumsy and ugly, and like I was eight years old again, running over the day after he moved in to see if he wanted to come out to play.

Rug.

For a few seconds, I chewed on my lip. My teeth punched hard on the right side, but I couldn't really feel them on the left. The doorbell was right there in front of me, but I didn't want to push it. That oatmeal—I should have stopped after a bite or two. Rug.

BELL'S FINE MORON START RINGING.

"Bell's fine." I lifted my chin like my speech therapist taught me to do.

Pragmatics, Hatch. You can recite the whole Bible and nobody will hear a word if you don't raise your head.

Back to pragmatics. This time the nonverbal aspects of speech. I had tons of words, but my social skills sucked. That's what the therapist meant, that five-year-old genius problem again. That's what a bullet in the head did for you, assuming it left any words at all.

Bell's fine, moron.

I pushed it.

From the other side of the door came long, slow chimes I remembered. I closed my eyes and listened. Couldn't help smiling. Not everything changed. Not everything.

The door opened.

A beautiful girl dressed in blue warm-ups was standing a foot from me.

Her black eyes went wide and her mouth opened, revealing perfectly straight, perfectly white teeth. She had her hair on top of her head in a knot like Mama Rush wore, but pretty ringlets hung down on either side. Never mind any of that, though. She was built. Like, way, way, built.

Had the Rush family moved away?

"Who are you?" I blurted, clutching the memory book to my chest. The present bag felt heavy in my hand. Sometimes I forgot I was a guy since so much of me didn't work— but at that moment, I knew for sure I was a guy. Broken in a few places. Scarred in lots of places. But yeah, a guy.

The knockout girl looked back over her shoulder, like somebody might catch her talking to me.

"You shouldn't be here, Jersey. My parents will throw a fit."

Then I knew her.

"Leza?" I shook my head. "No way. You're—I mean— middle school, all short, with braids and braces, and—"

"I'm a sophomore now. You've been . . . um, gone for a while." Leza sure sounded older, and more like Todd than I remembered. That made me sad all of a sudden, sad enough to feel tears in my eyes. Crying in public in front of pretty girls. Pragmatics, Hatch. Thanks a lot, bullet. Why did I have to be a guy, anyway?

"I don't want to bother anybody." My words tried to jumble up, but I slowed myself down, relaxed, and squeaked out the next sentence. "I want to talk to Mama Rush."

Leza's mouth twisted like she might be chewing the

inside of her cheek. She let out a breath, glanced over her shoulder again, and whispered, "Didn't you know she moved? It's been about a year, over to The Palace. That place in all the ads, you know?"

I did know. I had seen the ads everywhere.

"Mama Rush is in a place for old people?" I scratched my half-moon scar. "That can't—I mean, why did she go there?"

The sparkle left Leza's eyes. Her long, dark fingers tightened against the yellow door. "Lots of people changed after what you did." Another glance over her shoulder. "You should go now."

I started to ask her what she meant when somebody pulled her out of the way. It was Todd. Just like that, he was standing in front of me.

He seemed . . . taller. And his hair was buzzed against his head, making his ears look taller, too. His skin, which had been dusky, looked smooth as black marble. He was dressed in shorts and a T-shirt, both black, and he was all muscle, like he'd been in a gym every day for two years.

"Hi," I said. *Talk to Todd and find out why he hates me.* My chance. Here it was. "I came to—"

Todd's eyes blazed. "Get away from my sister, you freak."

"Todd, I want—"

"Man, I don't care what you want!" He looked like he wanted to shove me, even jumped forward like he was going to. At the last second, he pulled up and brought his fists down hard, knocking the memory book and Mama Rush's presents out of my hands.

The snap-crunch of pottery breaking made my stomach

32

roll. At the same time, the book flipped open. Pages tore out and blew off the porch. Four or five at least. A chunk of my days and hours, tumbling across grass, heading for the road.

Todd hesitated, fists still balled and raised. His gaze flicked from me to the dancing memory book pages. For a second, he looked uncertain, maybe even sorry. Then he backed into his house, frowning. "If you come back over here, I'll mess you up."

Before I could say anything else, he slammed the door and left me standing on the wide front porch all alone. I didn't move even though I was scared of him. I had no idea what to do next.

Freak. Yeah, well. Freak. I was a freak. And I knew he'd mess me up if he wanted to.

Todd never bluffed, at least the Todd I knew Before. Freak.

I glanced down at Mama Rush's gift bag. Lots of stuff in it probably broke. Tears trickled out of my eyes. Freak. Lots of it was stupid junk, anyway. What would she want with pottery flowerpots and ceramic trivets at a place like The Palace? The Palace in all the ads, with the old people smiling and riding around on mobility scooters and taking buses to get ice cream.

My bad leg dragged as I edged over to the bag. It took me a long time, but I finally got in the right position, did my balance check, and carefully bent down to snag it with my right hand. It still weighed the same—almost pulled me over as I straightened back up. The freak trying to stand tall. Pragmatics, Hatch. Freak.

Pragmatics. Nonverbal aspects of speech. Todd said a

lot with how he looked, with what he did. Freak. Nonverbal and verbal, too, really. Did I have snot on my face? I probably had snot. After I wrapped the gift bag around my bad wrist so nobody could knock it out of my hands again, I wiped my face with my shirttail. No snot I could see at least.

The memory book was trickier because I couldn't snag it like the bag handles. If I got down on my knees, I might not be able to get back up, so I kept trying. Up and forward. The nonverbal aspects of speech. Pragmatics. The pragmatics of notebook retrieval. Hatch, Jersey. Memory book. Pages of my life blowing across Todd's yard, blowing down the street in the neighborhood with all the baseball field grass. All the way to the Sahara with sand and more sand and fine doorbells I should get to ringing. Freak.

Tears dribbled down my chin. I was probably making snot. I stood up, wiped my face again. Checked my balance. Bent down for the notebook. My back hurt. So did my neck. I felt like I was hauling my left side around like some big, heavy backpack—and it was trying to make me fall. I grabbed at the top cover and got it, started up with the book. More pages tore out. My tears plopped on the paper, smearing words, but I got it up. I finally got it up. Only, it seemed like half the pages were leaving me, dancing, cartwheeling, hopping up and down like little mice on sand in a big green desert.

Banging Mama Rush's already crunchy present bag, I bad-boy-to-helled off Todd's porch and started after the first page. At least my eyes were drying up. Maybe I had snot on my face. I stopped to wipe off my nose with my shirt, and the first page I was chasing took off.

I sighed and dragged my weak leg across the yard. One at a time, I could do it. Up and forward, and ringing doorbells, and sand, and all. I could catch the pages. When I finally drew even with the sand-doorbell-page-from-bad-boy-hell, I stepped on it with my good foot. Balance check. Deep breath. Bend and grab. Freak.

The page tore in half under my foot.

"Don't curse." My lip throbbed from where I bit it. "Don't curse. No swearing. Pragmatics. Sand. Ding-dong-doorbell."

I tried to lift my foot off the torn piece and fell to my left so fast the sky and road and grass blurred past in a flash. Mama Rush's bag dug into my hip and side, smashing more stuff, including me maybe, I couldn't tell. Doorbells. Doorbells.

"Doorbells!"

"Are you all right, Jersey?"

The voice was soft, whispery. I managed to roll to my good side, sit up, and blink into the bright sunlight.

Leza was standing right beside me holding a fistful of pages. She had picked them all up. She bent and retrieved the torn piece, too, and held out her free hand.

I couldn't get a good breath from the fall. I still had tears on my face and probably snot, too, and I was an ugly freak on top of everything else. In spite of all that, I handed her the piece I had managed to grab, then my book, too. After examining the notebook and the holes, she shook her head.

"Can't hook them back in." She shuffled the loose pages around and folded them together, even the torn piece. "They'll go in this pocket, though. I tried to put them in order."

Had she read anything? God, I hoped not. I probably wrote about snot and sand. I probably had snot on my face. Pragmatics. The nonverbal aspects of being an ugly freak. King Jersey of Desert Nothing at All.

"Thanks." My voice sounded like I'd been in a desert.

Leza stuck out her hand again while still holding my memory book. It struck me weird, but then I remembered she had two good hands, not just one. Face burning, I let her help me to my feet. It was easy to get up with a little help. Mama Rush's presents felt like a bag of pulverized junk.

"Thanks," I said again, holding back sand-doorbell rattling. Leza didn't want to hear about sand, I was sure. Pragmatics. Don't curse. She's pretty. Doorbells.

Leza reached up with the sleeve of her blue warm-up jacket and wiped both of my cheeks. "I'm sorry Todd got so angry, and I'm sorry he tore up your book and stuff. If I were you, I'd stay away from him."

"Why does he hate me?" I blurted. "I mean, Before. Dad said he hated me Before."

She gaped at me like I was an uglier freak than usual. Doorbells. Sahara. Don't curse. Don't say something stupid out loud, like doorbells.

"Doorbells," I muttered. "Pretty doorbells. Football rugs."

Leza gave me a longer, stranger look. "You don't remember? Elana Arroyo and all that?

I shook my head.

She studied me for a few seconds. "Well, that was you and him. I wasn't there. I just heard about it."

"What? Heard doorbells? I mean, heard what? Why? Why did we fight?"

More studying me. She bit at one of her nails. "That was a long time ago. And like I said, it was him over that girl. That's all I really know. Now—well, I think he can't stand what you did. Kind of like my parents."

I looked at the ground. It was easier than looking at Leza. "Doorbells."

"You can't help that, can you? Saying stuff."

"No. Well, a little, but not all the time."

"And you can't help turning your head funny, to the side so you can see better." She picked at her palm like she might have a callus. "I read about that in a pamphlet Mama Rush brought home from one of your hospitals. It's because your brain is broken, right?"

"I'm a five-year-old genius," I offered.

"Okay, yeah." Leza actually smiled. "I've got to get to the track, and you need to go home before Todd comes back outside. Mom and Dad are down in the basement getting ready to go to Lake Raven, so—"

"I'm gone. Thanks for helping me."

"Welcome." Leza turned and jogged toward her house.

I wondered if I had snot on my face.

chapter 4

My father overreacted when I got home from my Saturday morning in Todd's front yard, all because my book was torn up, and my bag had grass on it, and I told him I fell. He dragged Mom out of bed and hauled us to the emergency room to have my bad hip checked out, and my ribs and arm and leg and whatever else he could think of asking them to examine. Fell. I just fell. Fell down.

Mom didn't say much, ate a pack of peanuts for breakfast, and somewhere between the fourth X-ray and the orthopedic consultation, she left for the bank "to catch up on some work while nobody could interrupt." I fell down. I just fell down. But Dad had to have X-rays, and Mom left.

After Dad and I got home with a prescription for really strong aspirin, something for my stomach so I could take the aspirin, and a diagnosis of "multiple bruises," Dad told me I had to stay home for the next week. I fell down! Just a fall. A little fall. X-rays. I tried to argue, but it did no good. I was there, trapped in the house with Dad, J.B. the homicidal ghost, the football rug, and sometimes, late at night or early in the morning, Mom.

"Use the time," I told myself Wednesday afternoon, repeating something the hand-Nazi from Carter had told me over and over again. "No such thing as downtime if you use it to get stronger. Time."

So, I avoided looking at the devastation of Mama Rush's presents by studying the driver's manual, doing hand exercises with a tennis ball, and repairing my memory book as best I could. Time. Time and more time. After a while, I sat down on my bed, looked up the number in my memory book, called Carter, and asked for Alicia. She was in occupational therapy and couldn't come to the phone. Time. Hank was seeing the shrink, and Joey had been discharged. No forwarding number. His parents wanted him to "go back to his real life." Probably didn't want him talking to the kid who shot himself. Me. If I shot myself. Whatever. Time. When I got to talk to Hank, I'd ask him about Joey's number.

I had to dig out a school directory to look up numbers from people I knew Before. People other than Todd, anyway. Guys from football. Guys from the golf team. The first one I tried was Kerry Brandt. Time. I used to know him from golf. I used to like him. At least I thought I did. And I wasn't nervous. Time. Not nervous at all. I made myself quit rocking on the bed.

The phone rang three times before a guy answered with, "Loooo-ooove shack, may I take a reservation?"

"Time!" I blurted. Coughed really fast. Shook my head. "I mean, hello. Kerry?"

Silence. A lot of silence. Then, "Hatch. Is that you?"

Surprised, but mean-sounding, too. Not friendly.

I coughed again. "Yeah. I just—"

"What are you doing calling me?" A snort, kind of like a laugh. "Don't waste my time."

I just sat there holding the phone. I didn't have a clue what to say, but I didn't have to say anything, because Kerry hung up.

Okay.

I took a deep breath.

So guys from school didn't visit me, and now one of them didn't want to talk to me. But that was just one person. I looked up another name. Just one person. A guy I knew from football. I punched the number, got it wrong. Stopped. Took another deep breath and punched it again. Just one person. Just one.

This time, a woman answered. "Hello?"

"Person. One. Hello." Another breath, but a fast one. Focus. "Mrs. Janson? May I speak to Alan?"

The woman took a few breaths, too. "May I ask who's calling?"

"Jersey Hatch."

"Oh." More breathing from Mrs. Janson. "Jersey, I—I don't think this is a good idea. I don't want to upset you, but I'd rather you didn't call here."

This time, it was me who hung up. I don't know why I did it, really. It was rude not to say good-bye. But for a second, I felt rude.

"Good-bye." I slammed the school directory. "Rude."

More deep breaths. My heart thumped faster and my jaws hurt. I realized I was grinding my teeth, so I stopped. Then I opened the book again and looked up *Arroyo, Elana*.

I squinted my good eye at the printed name like it might make a picture pop into my brain, but it didn't. I couldn't see her in my head. Maybe if I heard her voice, I'd remember something.

"Rude." I dialed the phone. "Rude. Good-bye."

One ring.

Two.

A click. Recorded voice. "The number you have reached has been disconnected or is no longer in service . . ."

I hung up. Started to throw the phone. Stopped.

"Rude."

Pictures. I wanted to see her. Talk to her. Remember something—anything. So I put the phone down and got busy digging out my yearbooks and stacking them on my bed. One at a time, I went through them. I found *Arroyo, Elana* in the last three, but I couldn't tell much. Dark hair, dark eyes, a dimple on her right cheek. She looked Spanish or Egyptian or something exotic. I remembered her a little from when she started at our school, but after that, nothing.

By the time I found Elana's picture, J.B. and I were on conversational terms up in that room on that bed where I shot myself—if I shot myself instead of having a car wreck.

"I lost my best friend over her?" Shaking my head, I closed the book. "Time."

Maybe she was Todd's girl and you took her away, J.B. suggested. I wasn't as scared of him as I should have been, being that he was probably ectoplasm or whatever, and could have killed me if he wanted to. Maybe.

"Yeah, right. Time. Stronger. Even without the Franken-stein scars, Todd's always been the movie star, not me. Ectoplasm."

You're talking worse. Those calls made you upset and you're not focusing, so you're worse.

"Am not. Ectoplasm."

Don't say ectoplasm.

"Ectoplasm."

See? Getting worse.

"It's harder in the real world. Time. They said it would be. Therapists, I mean. More pressure. Time." I didn't say ectoplasm. It wasn't easy.

J.B. made a snort-noise in my head. *Maybe you went out with Elana and ignored Todd, and he got mad about it.*

Todd, jealous. Ectoplasm. Ectoplasm, ectoplasm. I traced the raised cover of the yearbook. Green to gold, gold to green. The Green Rangers. Todd, jealous. That just didn't make sense no matter which way I traced the words. Todd was straightforward and honest. If he'd been jealous or had a problem with me, he would have said so, and we would have worked it out.

Maybe Todd changed. You don't really know him now, After, do you? Maybe he even changed Before.

"Ectoplasm. You talk too much, chump."

The floor creaked.

"Jersey?"

My head jerked up and I snatched my hand off the yearbook cover like I shouldn't have been touching it. "Mom? You're home. Time—it isn't. Ectoplasm. I mean, I didn't know it was time for you to be home."

She stood in the doorway and glanced around my room. Her eyes lingered on the bed, the pillow, the football rug I was keeping spread out where it was Before. She seemed to be studying everything but me. "Who were you talking to?"

"Um, I—myself, I guess. Bored, looking up faces in the yearbook, and . . . and stuff." I felt like a big idiot, and I couldn't tell her about J.B. No way. Besides, the ghost seemed to have taken off the minute she made a noise.

"Where's your father?" She glanced around the room again, like Dad might be hiding somewhere in a corner.

"I think he went to the ectoplasm. I mean, grocery store. Something about getting a bunch of boy food—easy food— for after he starts back to work next week."

Mom jerked like I had hit her. "Did he actually say he was going back to work next week and leaving you here alone?"

"I didn't—I didn't write it down." I had made a big mistake here, but I had no clue what it was. "But, I think he said that. Food. Boy food. It'll be fine. Really. Boy food."

Mom's eyes closed. I realized that her normal banking suit, the blue skirt and jacket with the white shirt, was wrinkled. Her pantyhose sagged like they were too big for her.

"How long have you been here? How long has he been gone?" Her voice came out murder-quiet. It gave me chills.

"I didn't write it down."

When Mom opened her eyes, she stared at where I was on the bed, but I didn't think she was seeing me. Not now, not in the present, anyway. "Have you been okay alone?"

"Sure." I shrugged. "I'm seventeen."

"No thoughts about . . . what happened?"

I think about what happened all the time. Every minute. The words wanted to rush down from my brain into my mouth, but in an unusual fit of pragmatics and social awareness, King Jersey the five-year-old genius figured this was the wrong answer. Do not pass doorbells. Do not collect deserts.

"No thoughts," I lied. "Pragmatics. I've just been trying to figure out who this girl Elana was. Ectoplasm, and stuff."

Mom stiffened and hardened, turning into that scary ice statue with moving lips. "The girl you dated?"

All thoughts of pragmatic deserts dropped out of my head. "You know who she was? I dated her? When? Ectoplasm!"

Mom's mouth opened and closed, opened and closed. "You said you were bored, right?"

"Well, yeah. Dated. Dad said I had to stay here until at least Saturday, so I've been trying to find things to do, and—"

"Clean up and come downstairs. I'll call a cab to take you over to The Palace to see Mama Rush." She closed her mouth again. Took a deep breath. "Can you handle a cab, Jersey?"

"Sure, practiced at Carter. I can handle it."

"You positive?"

"Sure. Cab."

Mom sighed.

Pay the driver. Pay the driver. I could do easy math. I could count change and money and stuff. If I remembered to pay the driver. If I walked off and forgot, he'd call the police and send me to jail. Pay the driver. I clung to my memory book and the bills Mom had given me. The plastic bag with Mama Rush's presents felt heavy on my weak wrist. Don't forget to pay the driver. Jail. Don't forget to keep enough money to get home. Jail. Don't forget to pay the driver.

The taxi pulled slowly to a stop beside a long sidewalk. A bunch of flower bushes lined the sides of the white concrete.

Pay the driver.

"Pay the driver," I echoed as I got out of the cab. The present bag smacked my leg.

The cabbie, who had hair redder than apples and strawberries, couldn't quit staring at me as I forgot how much to pay him and just held out my fistful of money. His eyes went from my scars to the money, from the money to my scars. He glanced once at my weak, limp side. Once at the memory book tucked under my bad arm, and once at the plastic bag full of presents looped around my bad wrist. Then he took the cash, thumbed through it, and started to put it in his pocket. He stopped, gave me a guilty look, thumbed through the bills again, and handed me some of the money back.

"For the ride home," he said.

"Pay the driver." I nodded, grateful, mad I forgot to keep some on my own. "Thanks."

The guy sighed and shook his head before he pulled away. I crammed the money in my pocket.

When I turned around and gave the place a good look, The Palace reminded me a lot of a hospital, even though commercials said it offered "The latest in independent living for seniors." It was sad that I had seen those ads so many times I remembered them word for word. Must have taken at least a thousand times. White walls, white floors—but at least The Palace had carpet. The carpet was royal blue just like on television. When I turned my head a little, I could see it through the open front doors.

I limped up the flower-bush walkway, passing between brick columns topped by gold lions. My left foot dragged along as usual, bumping every crack in the concrete. My left arm felt tight against my belly as I worked not to drop the present bag. Stupid arm always tightened up when I was nervous. I shifted the memory book to my good hand. It helped me feel more balanced.

If Mama Rush remembered me, would she talk to me? She might be mad at me, too, and I couldn't say I'd blame her. Of all the people in the world, Mama Rush had the most right to slap me in the face. A lot of things in my past might be blank, but I knew one thing for sure. Mama Rush wouldn't have run out on me even if everyone else did. My best friend's grandmother—well, Todd used to be my best friend but now he hated me—never let me down. I'd known her since I was five, about twelve years if you count the one or two I don't remember. She would be mad I didn't talk to her before I did it. If I did it. Before. After. Everything changes.

The Palace was bigger than I thought. Lots of hallways. Lots of people in wheelchairs or using walkers or canes. The blue rug made swishy-scrunch sounds as I walked, and the whole place smelled like cleanser and muscle rub. I started to sweat. Walk faster. Was that the fireplace in the Carter great room? No. Jesus. I wasn't at Carter. This was The Palace.

My hand hurt. My head started to hurt.

I turned another corner. People sitting in doorways staring out at me. Bathroom stink. I *was* back at Carter. Why did I have to go back?

Chewing my lip, I hurried around another corner, and another.

A woman with very black hair emerged from a crowd of people in bathrobes. She was wearing a bright red dress, and she held up her hand to stop me. A silver headset with a blue button on the earpiece made her look like those people on television commercials taking phone calls about credit cards. I couldn't help noticing the button was the same shade of blue as the carpet, but I didn't think it had anything to do with credit cards.

"May I help you?" she asked. Perky. Definitely Perky. Her name tag said MEKI SHANSU RESIDENTIAL DIRECTOR. Her smile said, *You're some kind of thief or murderer, aren't you?*

"No," I answered without being able to stop myself. "Thief or murderer. Credit card blue."

This wasn't Carter. This wasn't Carter. It wasn't.

Meki Shansu Residential Director stared at me, mouth slightly open. Like the cabby, her eyes went from scar to scar to my weak side and back to the scars. Her right hand twitched as she lifted it toward the credit card button on her headset.

"I came to see Mama Rush," I blurted before the woman could push the button. It might bring a bunch of guys with guns or something. "Guns," I echoed helplessly. "No, wait. Credit cards. Royal blue." I bit my tongue to shut myself up and decided I should carry an actual sock for times like this.

Meki Shansu Residential Director lowered her hand a fraction, eyes now fixed on my memory book. "Do you know her apartment number?"

"Um, I—no." I lowered my head, but lifted it again in a hurry. Pragmatics, Hatch. "Credit cards. I came to see Mama Rush. I need to talk to her, please?"

"I'm sorry." Her fingers were moving toward the button again. "Without an apartment number, you can't visit a resident. You'll have to leave and come back when you know it."

"Please?" My face heated up. Part anger, part frustration. "I've got to talk to her to see if she remembers me, to find out if she's mad at me. It's the first number on my list, and the second number's already blown to hell—oops, sorry I cursed. Desert credit cards. I mean, thieves and murderers. I need a sock."

Meki Shansu Residential Director's fingers were millimeters from her blue button when a deep, scratchy voice behind me said, "Back off, Attila the Red. This one's okay."

The woman with the headset frowned, but she once more lowered her hand. Without comment, she strode away, probably to find some other thief, murderer, or credit card fiend.

I turned around.

Mama Rush was sitting behind me on a bright purple mobility scooter. Her right hand rested on the controls, and she had a half-smoked stubbed-out cigarette in her left hand.

"You finally got around to showing up, huh?" Her voice rasped like an old movie actress, but her fuzzy white hair and bowling-pin shape didn't look so Hollywood. She had big black eyes, huge eyes, framed by gold-rimmed glasses, and when she blinked at me, I knew I was supposed to answer.

"Yeah. I mean, no. I mean, credit cards." I fidgeted, clutching my memory book.

Mama Rush's lips were as red as that blue-button woman's dress had been, and when she smiled, she looked friendlier. The smile vanished as quickly as it came and the grumpy old general on the purple scooter returned. I adored her. It was nice to find familiar feelings in the middle of all the strangeness.

"Well, come on back outside. If we're gonna talk, I want to smoke." She rubbed knobby fingers over her chin. Her gold and green robes whispered with the scooter's movement, and the scooter barely made any noise at all. Just the softest hum against the royal blue carpet. I followed as fast as I could, noticing that I could still smell her. Smoke and apples, and something spicy I couldn't name—except it lingered, even if she left. Just like Before. When I was little, I used to think she followed Todd and me everywhere we went. Smoke and apples. Something hadn't changed. Thank God. Something was the same.

"Apples," I muttered as we headed out side doors that swung open without us having to push a button or anything. Mama Rush was here, and she was on a purple scooter, and she was driving to a patio with lots of metal tables and metal chairs and stand-up ashtrays.

"Slow down, Apple Boy," she called over her shoulder. I could see her big eyes in the rearview mirror of the scooter. "The way you're hopping, you're gonna fall."

I did what she said. She was right, too. King Jersey the Apple Boy was about to fall right on his ugly freak face. Slower. Slower. Balance check. The present bag crunched and rattled as it swung back and forth. Slow. Slow. Slow steps over to the metal table Mama Rush had picked. She parked her scooter with a jerk, switched it off, eased up from the seat, and stood. By that time, I had reached the table.

All I could do was stare at her. Mama Rush. I was really looking at her, and so far she was talking to me.

"Go on," she finally said, pointing her unlit cigarette at one of the metal chairs. "Sit."

I put the memory book on the metal mesh of the table, started to sit, and remembered the bag.

"Here." I thrust out my bad arm, bag dangling from my wrist. "I made you some presents. Only, I think some of them are broken. Apples. I fell on them and they got banged on my leg and stuff and I haven't looked and—"

"I know. Leza told me." Mama Rush sighed, tucked her cigarette behind her left ear, and worked at untying the bag from my wrist. She had long fingers like Leza, and her skin was the same perfect ebony, smooth and silky looking, except it had a few wrinkles. Funny. I always thought Todd looked more like her than Leza did. But that was Before and this was After and lots of things had changed.

"After," I muttered. "Credit card apples."

Mama Rush finished untying the bag and put it on the table. She didn't react to what I said, not even a glance up to stare at my scars or anything. Instead, she yanked her cigarette out from behind her ear, fished a lighter out of her pocket, and settled herself in a chair. The green and gold robes cascaded like a waterfall between the arms and the seat. "Well, we'll see what's salvageable, you and me. Now sit down like I said, boy."

"Waterfall," I said, and I sat.

chapter 5

Mama Rush lit her cigarette and smacked her yellow lighter down on the table, all the while keeping her gold-rimmed eyes trained directly on mine. I felt like she was staring into my busted brain, counting how many cells I had left.

"You look better than you did last time I saw you." She took a drag, then pointed to her throat. "Got those tubes out and everything."

"Yes, ma'am." I squirmed in my chair, pressing my good hand against the cover of my memory book. I was keeping it in front of me on the table, a white shield with my name down the spine.

"You stupid, or you got some smarts left?"

I smiled. My muscles relaxed, even on my bad side. Something hadn't changed. Mama Rush hadn't changed. She wasn't talking to me like I was an alien or a freak. "Freak smarts. I mean, I've got some smarts. My words get messed up. Stuck on things, like waterfalls and credit card blue. It's harder in the real world. Waterfalls."

She nodded, taking another slow draw on her cigarette. "That's what all the pamphlets said. Stuff about how thoughts and words keep running through your head, and how you'll say them whether or not you want to." Drag, exhale. "I've been reading a lot about brain injury. And Leza pretty much gave me a blow-by-blow of your fight with Todd, before you ask." Drag, exhale.

Smoke swirled around her, making her look like a gold and green djinni rising out of the metal chair. A djinni with white fuzzy hair and a low scratchy voice. It would have been cool if she could grant wishes, but then, she sort of was granting a wish just by seeing me.

"Djinni," I said, then put my good hand over my mouth.

"I don't care what you say, so long as I can understand you when it counts. Put your hand down."

I put my hand in my lap. She fiddled with her cigarette, then stared at me in that brain-cell-counting way. "I didn't come to see you again because it was too hard to look at you all messed up like that."

My turn to nod. I sort of wished I smoked.

"Hate hospitals, too, if you'll remember."

Another nod from me. I did remember. "Leza said it's my fault."

"What, you shooting yourself in the head? I'd say yeah, that's a definite." Mama Rush cackled, then puffed her cigarette nub once more before discarding it into the stand-up ashtray beside her.

I didn't cackle. For a second or two, I couldn't even breathe, and not because of the smoke. Because Mama Rush believed it. Mama Rush thought I'd been shot in the head—and she sounded pretty sure I was the one who pulled the trigger.

Mama Rush believed I shot myself.

If she believed it, then I should believe it, right? But maybe she only believed it because everyone told her that was what happened. Okay, so I didn't have a car wreck, but somebody else could have shot me, right? I tried to breathe and coughed. I wondered if I should ask her how she found out, just to be sure, but then I remembered what I was really trying to ask her.

"Not me and well—that. I mean, you." I pointed back to the building. "Being here. It's my fault, right?"

This time I got raised eyebrows. Two fuzzy white eyebrows. "Hadn't thought of it that way. Back in the day, when I first retired from the counseling center, I took care of Todd and Leza." She pulled out a pack of cigarettes and placed them on the table beside her lighter. I couldn't make out the label, but the pack was green. It matched her robes. Green. Green and gold.

I tensed a little, trying not to let my nerves make my thoughts go nuts.

"Nothing like an old social worker in a house full of young people," Mama Rush continued. "Todd, his anger bugged me, and Leza kept staying home to look after me—then, yeah, you did what you did and all in all, I thought they needed their space and I needed mine." She took out a fresh cigarette. "Besides, my boyfriend lives over here in the wing next to mine. It's easier to see each other when we don't have to drive."

"I can't drive," I said, feeling sympathetic. "Keep failing the adaptive test."

"The written part?"

"No. The therapist part. Four hours, everybody staring and taking notes." I waved my good hand. "Yuck."

"You mean, to get your license, you have to drive around with a bunch of therapists for four solid hours?" She lit her cigarette and clucked between puffs. "That's nasty. They don't even do that to us old folks. Not yet, anyways."

"Brain injury." I tapped the scar on my temple.

"Stupid-mark, that's what I see. Your big red stupid-mark."

My finger rested on the temple scar. "Stupid-mark," I agreed. If I really did shoot my own self in the head, that was yeah, a definite, like she said.

"So now, maybe since you got such a big stupid-mark so early in your life, you won't need another?"

I tapped the scar. "One." Moved my finger to the C-scar on the other side of my head. "Two." Then to my throat, to the healed tracheotomy hole. "Three."

Mama Rush let out another loud cackle. "Well, if you got three stupid-marks, I'd say you're all through with stupid for a while."

"All through." I grinned and only thought about my half-flat mouth for a second.

A minute passed, with Mama Rush doing her impression of the gold and green djinni with white fuzzy hair. "You going back to your school when the time comes?"

"Green Rangers. Yes." I grinned again. "Like your robes."

She looked down at her colors and chuckled. "Yeah, well. Listen, about school—are your parents making you go to the same school, or are you just an idiot?"

"Idiot?" I meant to say, *what?* Or, *why?* It really was

harder to think out in the world. Lots harder to talk. Pressure. "Fuzzy white."

"Boy, do you have any idea—they did assemblies about you. Three or four of them. Had doctors and suicide preventers and all kinds of folks talking to the kids. Two others tried to off themselves after you—did you know that?"

"N-No." My hands started to shake, first the bad, then the good. I thought about Kerry Brandt hanging up on me, and me hanging up on Alan's mom.

Don't waste my time.

I'd rather you didn't call here.

"I'm not sure you'll find much welcome there," Mama Rush said.

"But I've got to go back. I asked to go back. How could I go anywhere else? The answers might be there. People who knew me before I looked like . . . like this. I can do it. Up and forward."

"Oh, I see. You want me to give you platitudes."

"Platitudes." I was feeling like a parrot, wondering what she wanted me to say. The stupid-mark in my right temple tingled. I pressed against the jagged dent, thinking for the hundredth time, too bad it wasn't a magic mark like I'd read about in books. At least that would be worth something. If it kept me from being stupid for a while, though, maybe it was a little magic at least.

Mama Rush just sat waiting and smoking, a dark djinni of knowledge who wasn't about to share a bit of wisdom with me.

"Smoking isn't bad for you. Is that a platitude?"

"No, boy." Her huge eyes reflected disappointment. "That would be a flat lie. I'm an ancient overweight black woman with hypertension. These things'll kill me, probably sooner than later."

She took a drag and let out a slow plume of smoke. I watched it curl through the air, inching toward me until a breeze blew it to nothing. Smoke. Plume. Nothing. These things'll kill me. I wished she wouldn't smoke them.

"Let's try this again, Jersey. I could tell you that going back to your old school takes lots of courage, that the other kids might have some trouble, but sooner or later they'll come around. I could tell you that you're better off than you were, that shooting yourself in the head made you stronger." She paused, drew on the cigarette, and stared at me.

"Lies," I said. My scars itched, but I kept still. Smoke.

"Lies. Of a sort, yes. Designed to make you feel better. I could give you truths instead, but truths hurt a lot."

"That's okay. Truths from you, please."

"You were a big-time athlete—and a big-time player." She talked in a hurry, like she intended to finish no matter what. "You had a future in sports or at least in college, just like my grandson. Then, God knows why, you went home, put your father's pistol to the side of your thick head, and you pulled the trigger."

"How do you know that? For sure, I mean. Thick head. Trigger—me, pulling it. How do you know I shot myself?" I realized I was talking fast, too, almost imitating her. I was about to ask again because I couldn't slow down, but she knocked me quiet with a glare that would have dropped a charging rhinoceros.

"What did you ask me?"

That didn't come out fast at all. That question came out slow, trickling, each word overpronounced, and her lips barely moved. Even with brain damage, I knew better than to open my mouth. Putting on a suit of armor might have been smart, but I didn't have one.

She didn't take a puff or twitch or anything. "I can't believe . . ."

Socks. Socks. Socks. Socks. Thick head. Trigger. Armor. I wanted to scream. By the time Mama Rush spoke again, I felt like I'd been sent to hell and dragged back out.

"You listen to me like you've never listened before. If you ever want to get better, if you ever want to fix anything in your life, you own up to your choices. *You* did this to yourself. You shot yourself in the head, boy. Now look me in the eye and say it."

My mouth fell open. My brain shouted for me to do it that second. But I couldn't. How could I own up to something I didn't really believe?

The djinni looked ready to curse me. "What, you're chicken-shit enough to cop out on life, and you're too chicken-shit to admit it?"

"I'm not chicken-shit!"

"You're something." Mama Rush flicked her ashes on the ground near my feet. "Just lucky you aren't black. Whole family would have thrown you out. Church, too. Everybody who knew you wouldn't even talk to you—black folks don't commit suicide." She took a drag, blew out the smoke. "Pat Parker, she wrote a poem about that after Jonestown. Black folks don't commit suicide."

My eyes dropped automatically to the whiter than white skin on my arms. Maybe I was secretly black, since nobody but Leza and Mama Rush was speaking to me, unless you wanted to count my replaced-by-aliens parents.

57

"They do, of course. Black folks kill themselves, I mean—but nobody talks about it." She glowered at me. "You've got to talk about it. Before I saw you, I was thinking I'd have to tell you not to be so serious like you used to be, not to try so hard to be perfect. Now I'm thinking I need to say the opposite. You'd better be serious about this. Now."

And she went right on glaring. Glaring and waiting.

I sighed. Felt like I was prying out the words with a crowbar. Still, I said them. "I shot myself."

There. That wasn't so hard. I still wasn't sure I believed it, but Mama Rush did, and I said it.

"Okay. There's a start. You were an athlete, and before you got all crabby your sophomore year, you were popular. Then you shot yourself. Now . . ."

She trailed off, waiting again. She wanted me to tell her how I had changed. I knew that, but I was mad, and I really didn't want to answer her. Like I had a choice.

"Now I've got stupid-marks. I look like somebody took a hammer to my head. The left side of my body doesn't work. I can't see out of my right eye. No more sports."

Mama Rush nodded slowly. I could tell by the way she drew on the cigarette that I was on target, but not hitting the mark yet. "Leaving something out, aren't you, boy? Something more important than how you look?"

My left hand cramped. My fingers pulled into a fist because I didn't think about keeping them relaxed. "I'm good at forgetting."

"That's an excuse." She flicked the cigarette into the stand-up ashtray. "Your right-now memory isn't that bad if you slow down and concentrate on what you need to remember—and you told me you still had some smarts."

This time, my right hand made a fist. The anger came so fast my face burned, but I bit back a bunch of ugly comments. *Going off*. That's what they'd call it back at Carter. Brain-injured patients don't get mad. They *go off*.

After a few seconds of breathing, I calmed down enough to say, "The other kids might be mad at me, treat me weird and stuff, like Todd. A lot of them might not want to be around me."

Mama Rush nodded. "Like Todd, and maybe Leza, too. She went through a lot over what you did, but that's hers to tell you. And those boys you knew from football and golf and R.O.T.C., back before you got your ill temper and ran most of them off—they may have things to say. And the ones who talk to you, they're eventually going to ask the question."

My breath came in a short jerk. "Don't know. I really, really don't know why."

She gestured toward my memory book. "Leza said you keep your remembering in there, like some of the folks around here at The Palace. In notes and lists."

She read things. Leza read what she'd picked up. Heat trickled across my face again, this time because of embarrassment. Snot, snot, snot! Go off.

But I didn't. I couldn't, no matter what, not at Mama Rush. I shoved the memory book over to her.

Raised fuzzy eyebrows. Another slow lighting of a cigarette.

She flipped open the book and glanced at things. After a few minutes, she pulled out one folded sheet from the pocket and laid it to the side. She even weighted it down with her lighter and pack of cigarettes. Then she handed the book back to me.

"Tell you what, boy. We're gonna start right here. While I open my presents and lay them out on this table, you take that pen on a string attached to that white book, and you make me another list. A list of *why*. You understand?"

"Possibilities." I made myself breathe slowly, try to think slowly. "Not pragmatics. Not platitudes. Not credit cards or djinnis."

"Right." She tapped the piece of paper she had taken and weighted down. "This is your To-Do List from the hospital. It's good, but I think you have to make a better start. So, I'm going to keep it for now, and go over it with you later when the time is right. In the meantime, you'll make me a Why List and work on that."

"Pragmatics." I tried to smile, but my throat and lips felt tight.

"Good enough. Now you get busy, and so will I."

I got busy. All the while, in the background, I heard the rustle of plastic, the clink and crunch of pottery, and Mama Rush mumbling to herself. No way would I look up, though. She might have smacked me right in my stupid-mark.

In between chewing on my pen and trying not to look up, I wrote a new list.

1. *Secretly gay.*
2. *Did something awful I felt guilty.*
3. *My life sucked.*
4. *Heard voices telling me to off myself.*
5. *Parents really brother and sister/aliens/abusive.*

When I was finished, I dared to raise my eyes.

Mama Rush was between cigarettes. She had covered the left side of the table with pieces and lumps of what had been seven or eight things I had made for her in recreation. I recognized part of an ashtray, pieces of the trivet and ceramic flowerpot, bits of a toothbrush cup, even halves of a really funny-looking pig that I had intended to be a bank— I think I made it way back at the first or second hospital.

"Broken," I said, miserable and not miserable at the same time.

Mama Rush gave me the fuzzy eyebrow treatment and said, "You first."

I passed her the list. My heart started to beat really hard. Maybe she knew something I didn't. She was smart, and she'd known me for a long time.

She read, her eyes moving line to line, back and forth. I think she even read the Why List twice. After a few seconds, she grunted. "Is that the best you can do?" She shoved the list across the little round table, crashing it into my bad left hand. I felt the paper crumple against my stiff fingers. Her dark, wrinkled skin pulled tight with her gigantic frown.

I winced. I'd grown up hating to make her frown like that. It usually meant a call to my parents, being banned from her yard for a few days, or a lecture that made me wish for a beating instead.

"You put a gun to your head, shoot your fool self right in the brain, and all you can come up with is incest-alien parents?" She grunted again, like an exclamation point.

"There's other stuff." I squirmed in the metal chair.

"What about gay? Or guilty? Credit cards! Thick head."

"If you're gay, I'm big black Santa Claus flown down from the North Pole. Think. When did you ever want to pinch a boy's butt?"

"I don't remember almost a whole year." I shrugged. "Maybe things changed. Everything changed After. Maybe Before, too?"

"Well, nothing changes that much." Mama Rush snatched out a cigarette and lit it with one motion. "You were acting funny, but not that kind of funny. More mad and snappy. Didn't eat much, didn't sleep much, looked all tired and grungy. Stayed to yourself, too. Todd wouldn't tell me why he quit hanging around with you, but I knew you were depressed. Figured it might be drugs or something. You sure were trying to do a lot, and some kids take stuff to speed up or slow down, or get stronger—you know."

I uncrumpled the list, picked up the pen on a string, and revised the first item to read, ~~Secretly gay~~ *Maybe on drugs.* What kind of drugs, though? Pot, steroids, heroine, meth— lots of choices. I wondered if I should make an entry for each one.

"Course, it could have been a woman. Well, at your age, a girl."

Moving down, I dropped one more line and wrote, *6. Elana Arroyo.*

Mama Rush glanced over to my list. She saw what I had written, went very still, then nodded. "That's the girl you and Todd fought about. Now we're getting somewhere."

"Why did we fight over her? Do you know?"

"No. Wish I did, but Todd kept the girls and dating part of his life private. You'll have to ask him."

I started to ask her how, when he wanted to break my jaw, but she had already turned her attention to all the broken stuff from my bag.

"These gifts—thank you for trying, Jersey. You come back here this weekend on Saturday—every Saturday for a few hours—and we'll see what's what." She lowered her cigarette, letting the smoke make a haze all around us. "I suspect we'll find some things can be fixed, but some things are just too broken."

I thought about Elana and Todd and Leza, and Dad and Mom, and school and assemblies and the credit card woman in the red dress, and I really thought about my stupid-mark.

Some things can be fixed. Some things are just too broken.

"Credit card blue," I mumbled.

Mama Rush took a deep puff and gave me a slow, solemn nod.

chapter 6

I have this dream where both legs work and both arms work and I don't have any scars on the outside. I'm sitting on the edge of my bed in dress blues holding a pistol. Sunlight brightens the dust and sand in my room and darkens all the places where I've nicked the walls and doors. The football rug, the one Mama Rush gave me when I made the team my freshman year, is folded neatly on my dresser so it won't get messy. I give it one last look before I turn back to what I'm doing. My fingers tingle as I lift the gun to my mouth. It tastes oily and dusty all at once as I close my lips on cold gunmetal—but I can't. Not in the mouth. I'm shaking, but I lift the barrel to the side of my head. The tip digs into my skin. I'm thinking about drugs and girls and how the tip feels, and my hand's shaking, and I feel guilty for a lot of stuff and my life sucks, and that my room has so much dust and sand in places I didn't even know. Then I'm squeezing the trigger and looking at the dust and sand and feeling my hand shake and thinking guilty thoughts and there's noise and fire and pain and I'm falling, falling, my broken head smashing into my pillow . . .

Why do you stay in this room?

J.B.'s whisper woke me from my constant dream of killing myself. My head throbbed hard enough to make me think about throwing up, and my bad hand was curled up so tight I had to pry the fingers open. With a sigh, I glanced at my closet, where my hand and foot braces lived.

Why do you stay in this room? J.B. sounded more demanding this time, like he might get mad. In the three days since I had seen Mama Rush, he had talked more and more and more, hardly shutting up when I was in my room—especially when I was on the bed, trying to sleep. Especially when I had a headache.

I sat up slowly, blinked, and wished it was a rainy morning instead of being so bright. The sunlight felt like ice picks in my eye.

Or bullets.

"Shut up, J.B." I put my hand over my ear, but that didn't work. When he talked again, I heard him inside my brain.

The bullet felt like a sword in the head. Like somebody stuck a knife right in front of—

I stood up too fast, overbalanced, and fell back on the bed with my head near the bottom. "Shut up!"

This time when I blinked, I thought I saw a silvery outline standing in the sunlight. The outline looked like a tall, shimmering boy. The boy looked strong and healthy, like an athlete.

No way. Couldn't be. It was only sunlight, brightening

65

the dust. Darkening all the places where I had nicked the walls and doors—

The image vanished.

Biting my lip hard enough to block the pain in my head, I sat back up and flexed my bad hand. Then I stretched my weak leg to be sure I didn't fall again.

"I don't know why I stay in this room," I admitted as I slowly eased to my feet. "Maybe the answers are here, at least some of them."

It's a bad idea. You hurt yourself in here.

"No, I didn't. You did."

Maybe if you didn't have this room, you wouldn't have shot yourself. J.B.'s voice was distant, floaty. He sounded like he was talking through a pipe or a vent, with the hollow way the words drifted through the room.

"Pipe." I looked around, but I didn't see any pipes. My vent was on the floor, and nothing was coming out of it. "Vent."

You should move to the guest room, J.B. insisted. *Things would be easier there.*

"Pipe-vent platitudes." Ignoring him was hard, but I needed to do it. He was like some sort of demon, poking and poking all the time. Between him and my headache and my bum arm and hand, it took forever to get my pants and shirt on right.

Why won't you move to the guest room? J.B. asked as I pulled on my left sock.

"The same reason I won't go to a different school." I was imagining him now as that silvery athletic boy, twinkling dust in the sunlight of my room. "Platitudes. I need truths, and things—well, things don't need to be easy."

This shut him up long enough for me to pull on my right sock and get the Velcro fasteners on my tennis shoes opened. His next question was calmer, with lots less whine.

Why can't things be easy? Do you feel guilty?

"No. Well, yes, maybe a little? I don't know. Easy." I rammed first one foot and then the other into my shoes and worked on fastening the Velcro. "I don't remember doing anything, and I don't know why I did it. Easy. I shouldn't feel guilty if I don't remember anything, right? I mean, it's not like I'm a criminal pretending stuff to get out of jail. Guilty. Easy."

J.B. stayed quiet the rest of the time as I combed my hair, straightened my clothes, double-checked to be sure I had remembered my deodorant, and checked three times to be sure I had cab fare to The Palace for later in the day. Mama Rush had said we should meet around three p.m., and I planned to be early. I had gone over and over the first item on the Why List, even talked Dad into giving me my old emergency room records to read my lab tests. I was almost 100 percent sure I hadn't taken drugs, at least not on the day I killed myself. I mean, tried to kill myself. Just a few more things to check out, and I'd be ready for Mama Rush's grilling.

"Pipe-vents. Grilling. I'm ready for questions." I nodded to myself in the mirror and ignored the mental image of glitterboy drifting in front of my window. J.B. wasn't real. He couldn't be real, so he was just like the pipe-vents—something my brain got stuck on and couldn't turn loose.

I hope you're right, he whispered as I picked up my memory book and left the room. I didn't know whether he meant about being ready for Mama Rush or the other thing—that J.B. wasn't any more real than my pipe-vents.

Downstairs, I found my stiff, cardboard, smiley parents sitting at the breakfast table.

"You don't have to make breakfast for me every morning," I said as nicely as I could. "Glitter. Pipe-vents. I mean, we didn't eat together a lot Before, right?"

Dad shrugged. Mom didn't respond.

I held back a sigh and sat down, resting my memory book on the table beside me. The pen string was getting dirtier and dirtier. I figured I'd need a new one, but I didn't know if I could tie the knots, and I didn't want to ask the paper doll parents to help.

"Glitter," I mumbled as I stared into the bowl in front of me.

"Where did you get 'glitter' from?" Mom asked, keeping her eyes on her bowl.

I was so surprised to hear her talk that I dropped the spoon I had started to pick up. It clattered against the bowl, then bounced off the floor. "Dang! I'm sorry. I'll get it."

"No!" My parents called out at the same time, but I leaned over to grab the spoon.

"Whoa!" My head swam. Up-down. Down-up. The room shifted. My body moved, fast and heavy. Down. My good side crunched against the floor. My cheek smacked cool linoleum. Bang-ouch, down in my joints, up in my teeth.

My ears rang, but they stopped fast. Cool. I didn't even turn the chair over.

"Oh, God." Dad scrambled down to the floor to help me.

I tried to wave him off. "It's okay. I know how to—"

Dad picked me straight up off the floor like I was six or seven years old and cradled me for a second. Then he settled me back in my chair, even handed me my spoon. I wondered if he'd go find a bib before he was done, but he didn't, thank God.

For a few seconds we all just sat there, Mom and Dad staring at the table and me mentally counting the number of new bruises I would have. Spoons. I had lots of bruises already, and I wanted to try to talk to Leza, needed to ask her a question before I went to see Mama Rush. Between having snot on my face last time I saw her and bruises this time, Leza was really going to think I was a freak.

Finally, I remembered Mom had asked me a question, but I couldn't remember what it was no matter how hard I tried. When I asked her, she just shook her head.

I counted to ten, picked up my pen, and held it poised over my memory book. "Did I ever take drugs?"

Both of my parents stared at me, spoonfuls of Dad's nutritious oatmeal frozen in midbite. Dad had added a slice of whole wheat toast to this meal, with sugar-free grape jelly that looked like glue mixed with Kool-Aid.

Mom actually spoke first. "Excuse me?"

Dad stopped chewing his oatmeal and Kool-Aid glue, but he didn't seem to be able to talk.

"Pot, meth, speed, alcohol, steroids, crack, crank—"

"I know what drugs are, Jersey," Mom cut in, speaking precisely, like a banker. "And of course not. Why would you ask that?"

The pen tapped the table when I shrugged. "I need to know if I was a junkie. If I was, you can tell me. I read through all my hospital records and none of my labs showed Kool-Aid. I mean, positive results. Glue."

Dad put his bite down. "Is that why you wanted to read through all that junk? I thought you were trying to—of course you didn't use drugs. You were a good student, a great athlete. You were a good boy."

In my mind, the Mama Rush djinni landed right behind Dad, carrying Kool-Aid in one hand and glue in the other. *You* were *a good boy,* she whispered. *Were. Were. As in not are, right?*

Mom stared at me, frowning.

I started to tell the djinni to shut up and go away, that I didn't need a smartass djinni downstairs when I already had homicidal ghost-boy upstairs, but I kept my mouth shut. Pragmatics, Hatch. Kool-Aid glue. Mom was staring. And frowning. Dad still wasn't eating.

Okay, maybe I wasn't a freak, at least not the drug kind. Still, I couldn't cross it off the list just because my parents said so and the records said so. I needed to talk to one other person or Mama Rush would never be satisfied. I wouldn't be, either. Kool-Aid. That's why I needed to talk to Leza. She was just in middle school back then, but Leza—she was smart and she knew stuff. She always knew stuff.

Of course, it was Saturday, like last week, so Todd would probably be there and he would probably crush my skull. For the moment, my skull was safe enough, even though my sanity wasn't. I blinked really fast and kept blinking until slowly, slowly, the djinni image behind Dad faded away.

Acting braver than I felt, I took a big bite of Kool-Aid glue toast. It tasted even worse than it looked, like Dad had added shredded paper into the mix. Blech. It was the first time I remembered being glad my sense of taste was less than what it used to be.

"The therapists told you you'd have to work harder on focusing outside the hospital," Mom said. Her voice shook a little bit. "I'd appreciate it if you'd try concentrating on normal conversation rather than coming up with off-the-wall questions."

She still hadn't started eating again, unlike Dad, who was wolfing down his oatmeal until he stopped and said, "Sonya. He can't help that. It's worse when he's tired or nervous. Adjustment time, remember?"

Mom stiffened in her chair, but she didn't back down. "He wasn't so bad at Carter even when he did get nervous. I think he can help asking crazy questions."

"Brain cells." I put down my spoon, careful not to drop it. "Crazy questions? About what?"

"About drugs—and Elana Arroyo." Mom looked at me a little like Mama Rush did, when I thought she might be counting my brain cells. "And the way you've been talking to yourself. Is it real, or are you just . . . just . . . needling us, or something?"

"Sonya!" Dad covered Mom's hand with his. "The therapists all told us . . ."

He was trying hard to get her to look at him, but she wouldn't.

"We need to call Carter," she said. "See if they can get hold of that outpatient therapist and move up our counseling sessions. Jersey needs more help."

"Help. Carter. Needling. Brain cells." I wanted to figure out what she meant, what she needed, but all my stupid mouth did was fire back what she said. "Arroyo. Talking. Outpatient."

"Stop it." Mom jerked her hand out of Dad's and stood up so fast the table bucked. My oatmeal sloshed on the Kool-Aid glue toast. "Focus and try, and just stop it!"

Stop. Stop it. Stop what? Or was it Dad—the way he was holding her hand? Harder to think in the real world. Harder to think under pressure. Lots of pressure.

"I'm sorry," I said, just in case it was me that made her mad.

Pragmatics.

Wrong pragmatics.

Mom froze into that ice statue with moving lips. I sucked at pragmatics. Dad's toast sucked. His oatmeal sucked, too.

"Sucky ice statues." I couldn't hold my mouth tight enough to keep the words inside. When was I going to re-member that sock? I really, really needed a sock.

"Why don't we go talk?" Dad said as he stood up and put his arm around Mom's shoulder. She shrugged him off, then got up and walked away, saying something about banks or hospitals or both. I couldn't make it out.

Dad gave me a silly look. "She's—ah—she's a woman. You know?"

"Um, yeah." I nodded, but I didn't know. I didn't know at all. Something was wrong with Mom. At least I thought something was wrong, but I had no idea what, and no idea what to do.

Something was wrong with Dad, too. He looked torn in half, like he wanted to stay with me and go after Mom at the same time.

"I have a list to do," I blurted. My tongue felt heavy and all sticky with Kool-Aid glue. "I've got to go, so you should take care of the ice. I mean, Mom. I so need a sock."

"Okay, Jersey." Dad backed away from me. He couldn't smile right. As he left the kitchen, he said, "Stay away from the Rush house. I don't think they want . . . well, they still

72

aren't very comfortable with—with what happened, okay?"

Not okay. I clenched my jaw.

I wasn't comfortable, either. I needed to get some answers, didn't I? Before J.B. found a way to get far enough into my head to kill me again. Before I went off on my mom for being totally weird. Before Mama Rush poked a finger into my stupid-mark because I wasn't getting the list done fast enough.

Whatever.

Breathing hard, I stood up and lurched over to the sink to run water into my oatmeal bowl. Then I hitched back to the table, got Mom's bowl and did the same. Dad's bowl came last. Oatmeal really did turn into glue if it didn't soak. That much I learned for sure at Carter.

"Oatmeal Kool-Aid glue."

The toast, I just threw away. It seemed the kindest thing to do.

In the background, I picked out bits and pieces of my parents yelling at each other.

". . . On purpose . . . he never thinks about anybody's feelings but his own. . . ." This from Mom.

"Carter . . . brain injury . . . tolerate . . . support. . . ." This from Dad.

Mom: ". . . Do any good at all."

Dad: "Don't think like . . ."

Wiping the table took the longest because I couldn't really wipe with one hand and catch crumbs with the other. I ended up using my shirt as a catch-all, like I did when I was cleaning up in the hospital.

Dad: "Do things new . . . hope."

Mom: "Go to hell."

Or maybe she said, "Go to work." I wasn't sure.

After I got the crumbs dumped, I had to wash grease spots off my shirt with hot water, but overall, it wasn't so bad. At least my parents finally got quiet. I didn't understand the big deal, like I didn't understand a lot of big deals.

That's an excuse, insisted the Mama Rush voice in my head. *You told me you still had your smarts.*

"Sorry, sorry, glue," I whispered like a little song as I ignored her. "Sorry, sorry, glue. Sorry, sorry, glue." Moving as quietly as I could, I picked up my memory book and headed straight to where Dad told me not to go.

chapter 7

"Do I want to know why you're all wet?" Leza leaned against
the doorframe with her arms folded. She was wearing warm-
ups again, very silky, this time, gold and green. School colors.

I glanced down at the front of my blue shirt and jeans.
There was a big wet spot covering my stomach and the
front of my pants, like I'd forgotten to unzip before taking
a whiz. Great. I covered up the dark area as best I could with
the memory book. "Whiz. I mean, pee. No, no, no. Wait. I
don't know—wait. I do know. I did the dishes. Crumbs and
glue. And . . . and stuff."

She was so pretty. I was never going to be able to think
straight around Leza, much less talk. Harder to talk outside the hospital. Harder to think. But I probably wouldn't
have talked that well around Leza even if I didn't have
stress and word problems and a hole in my brain. She didn't
seem to mind, though. If I ignored the whole totally-stacked
thing, Leza was starting to remind me of Mama Rush, not
making a big deal over much.

"Todd's at the lake," she said. "And my parents have gone over to the university for a charity telethon. I just got back from the track."

"Are you going to be a social worker?" I asked too fast, still thinking about Mama Rush.

Leza's face twisted up, then she laughed. "You're weird, you know that? But funny weird. Good weird, I think. What do you want, Jersey?"

"Drugs," I said all happylike, then clamped my hand over my mouth. That absolutely sealed it. I *had* to start carrying a sock. There was no way I dared to open my mouth again. Who knew what would come out?

Thankfully, Leza didn't just slam the door. Instead, she squeezed her eyes shut and shook her head. "This has got something to do with that list you and Mama Rush made, doesn't it?"

When she looked at me, I nodded.

"I know you're supposed to take it to her this afternoon. Want to take a hike to your backyard? I've got a little while before I'm supposed to be at the mall, so I could help you with it."

"Yes! I mean, thank you. That's great."

This earned me a grin and an arm to help me heaven-hell down the porch steps and make it through our back gate without falling on my already-mashed-up head. I kept my memory book tucked under my bad arm, and I got annoyed with the pen bouncing against my wet shirt. Leza didn't seem to mind this, either.

Maybe with her, I didn't need a sock that badly.

We headed for the wooden picnic table at the edge of our patio, the one with a full view of our living room through the big back picture window. If I turned my head some, I could see my bedroom window, too, but I didn't want to look up because I was afraid I'd see J.B. standing there, glaring at us. If he kept hanging around, I'd need to hire an exorcist. But I didn't want to think about ghosts and exorcists, not with Leza sitting at the picnic table in her green and gold and looking so pretty and planning to help me and all.

"I don't need a sock," I blurted as she sat down. My bad hand curled until I winced.

"Okay, now you have to explain that sock thing." She reached across the table and pulled the memory book out from under my arm. With a few graceful movements, she flicked to the last few pages, and put it down on the table with the list showing right side up to me. The pen she placed on the paper, right where I needed to pick it up.

For some reason, Leza being nice to me and the pain in my hand made me want to cry. No. No! I *didn't* want to cry. Crying was for babies and girls and I was a guy with a beautiful girl, out at a picnic table on a beautiful day. No crying. No tears. Absolutely not.

"You okay?" Leza patted my fingers. "If you don't want to tell me about the sock, you don't have to."

"No. I—the sock." A tear slipped down my cheek and I tried to wipe it away real fast before she saw it. She didn't react, so I got to hoping she didn't see it, but I worried she did. "Just a second."

I counted to ten, used my good hand to uncurl my cramping fingers, and paid attention to the table, the oak leaves moving gently on branches above Leza's head, and an ant creeping down one of the cracks in the peeling wood. Breathing. Breathing. The tears stayed in my head. When I was sure I could say something not totally bizarre, I gave it a try.

"The idiot things I say. I thought if I had a sock, I'd stuff it in my mouth."

Leza propped her elbows on the table and rested her head on her fists. "What, you mean just chew on it in front of people?"

My cheeks got a little hot. "Yeah. Chew on it."

"Might work." She shrugged one shoulder. "But you might get fuzz in your mouth, too."

"Chew fuzz." I put my hand on my memory book. "That's better than some of the stuff I say. Thieves and murderers and blue credit cards and stuff. Oh, and sand and snot, too." I closed my eyes, took a breath, counted to five. Then I touched the cover of the book. "You read this before, right?"

It was Leza's turn to look a little embarrassed. She did this mostly with her eyes, which suddenly seemed like they belonged to a puppy instead of a girl. "A little. I'm sorry. When I picked it up—"

"No, no sorry." I slid the book toward her. "I mean, don't be sorry. It's okay. You already know I'm stupid."

Leza took the book, but she cut her eyes up sharp like Mama Rush did right before she used her tongue as a whip. I leaned back out of reflex.

"Yeah, you'd better get out of my way. Boy, I'm not going to waste my time with you if you say bad stuff about yourself. Talking trash about yourself makes you—"

"Trash." The word popped out of my mouth automatically. Mama Rush had told us that a million times. *Talking trash about yourself makes you trash. If you don't think good things about yourself, nobody else will.*

Leza was still glaring.

"Okay," I added in a hurry. *Okay* was the only thing to say to a mad Rush. Or *yes*, or *sorry*. I still had that much pragmatics, or maybe I just wanted to finish this conversation without a black eye.

"I'll be nice to you, and I'll help and be your friend and stuff—but don't go thinking I'm willing to feel sorry for you, Jersey." Leza was talking fast, her tone rising and falling like a preacher thumping on a Bible. "That bird won't fly. Got me?"

"Got you. I mean, yes."

Don't smile. She'll hit you with your own memory book. You know she'll hit you. I covered my mouth but tried not to look like I was covering my mouth. Under my hand, my lips moved upward no matter how hard I tried to keep them still. Leza said she would be my friend. Todd was gone because he hated me and everything changes, but Leza changed, and she got older and beautiful and nice, and she was going to be my friend.

Something inside me relaxed, and before I knew it, the tears came back.

"Maybe you do need a sock," Leza said, tapping on the white cover of my memory book. "If you're going to blow snot all over the book and stuff." Her face changed a little, like she was thinking too hard. "Listen—um, how—how's your mom?"

I shrugged, fighting with the tears. "Fine, I guess. Sock. She doesn't talk much."

"So she's okay." Leza blew out a breath. "I was wondering. Hoping she was." She opened my memory book. "Okay.

Here's the list."

I wiped my eyes and scratched all three of my scars as she read it to herself, then read it out loud.

1. *Maybe on drugs.*
2. *Did something awful I felt guilty.*
3. *My life sucked.*
4. *Heard voices telling me to off myself.*
5. *Parents really brother and sister/aliens/abusive.*
6. *Elana Arroyo.*

"This first one about drugs, I think that's out." Leza picked up the pen and scratched it off, but I couldn't let it go that easily.

"Are you sure? There's, you know, pot and meth and stuff. Maybe I did." I massaged my curling fingers, trying to pretend the sunlight wasn't making my head start to hurt.

"We can't be totally sure of anything since you can't re-member, but I don't think drugs were a problem. You were in R.O.T.C. and on two sports teams at the same time, and all of the coaches did random testing." Leza made some notes on the page opposite the list. "Plus, Todd never said anything, and I never heard any rumors. Believe me, I al-ways hear the rumors."

"My parents said no to that one, too, but I figured they might not know. Rumor pens. Random testing. I hadn't thought about random testing." Marking off drugs seemed more reasonable after that. No pot, no meth. Well, maybe some—who knows. But drugs weren't the problem. Drugs weren't the reason I pulled the trigger. I smiled at Leza but had to stop because my hand was hurting so bad and my head was getting worse, too.

She didn't smile back. She was looking at the list, all business. "Parents don't know stuff lots of times. Because nobody tells them and they don't know how to look, I guess."

"Yours, too?" I felt like somebody was slowly working a screwdriver into my skull, just above my right eye. Never mind the vise squeezing my weak fingers into a tighter and tighter fist.

"My parents work a lot, but my mom, she's like Mama Rush, always asking questions and trying to be involved."

"My mother goes to the bank."

Leza looked all funny again, almost like she wanted to cry. "Yeah. She does that a lot now."

"She didn't used to so much. At least I don't think she did. It was Dad who always went to work, but now he makes oatmeal and toast with Kool-Aid glue."

"Your mom's probably not over—you know—what happened. What she saw." Leza's gaze shifted back to the pen. "All that blood, and you . . ."

I let go of my cramping hand and tried massaging my right temple instead. The headache split my thinking in two, leaving Leza on one side and her words drifting around and making pictures on the other. Pools of blood, tons of it, like red paint flowing all over the table, the patio, the yard.

"But I wasn't dead," I forced out, trying to ignore the paint-blood. "I lived, and I went to hospitals and did therapy, and we had to see shrinks together and stuff."

"You really think that makes it all better?" Leza asked this like she didn't know for sure, not like Mama Rush asked things. Mama Rush usually knew the answers to all of her questions.

"I—I don't know. I thought it did. That it should have. Paint-blood. Better." I stopped rubbing my head and covered my mouth to shut myself up.

Leza was still looking at the pen. "Have you talked to her about it?"

The question was simple enough, but it made me tighten up all over. We had tried to talk about it, my mom and me, a bunch of times in therapy. It usually ended with me mad and upset because she was trying to blame me for stuff I didn't remember. Paint-blood. At first she cried. Later, she stormed out. By the time I went to Carter, she had stopped doing anything at all—including trying to ask me about shooting myself. We just sort of let it drop, since I'd never really be able to tell her what made me pull the trigger.

"All that blood." I echoed what Leza had said a few minutes ago, blinking to make the paint-blood disappear. It was fading, but my head was hurting worse. "Paint-blood."

Leza cleared her throat. "Is it okay if we talk about something else?" She sounded funny, and when I looked at her, I thought she might have tears in her head, trying to get out.

"Did you care about it? I—I—more than just, *that was gross* or *that was stupid*, or *hey, I knew that kid who shot himself*?"

"Why would you ask me that?" Leza straightened up and got that Mama-Rush-about-to-slap look again. "Dang, boy. You can really—yeah. Okay? I cared. I freaked out for a while. Lots of folks did. Like her."

She pointed to my list, to the last item. Elana Arroyo.

"That number has been disconnected," I muttered.

"You tried to call her?" Leza's mouth opened, then

closed. She looked part-shocked, part-mad. "She moved away about six months ago, to get a new start and all. If you want to know stuff about her, you'll have to ask Todd—and if I were you, I wouldn't. Not now, at least."

Her eyes drifted away from me to the windows of my house. Nervous. Ready to go. One thousand questions jammed into my head. Leza might get up and leave any second now, and I might not get more chances to talk to her. What if she started shutting the door on me? She probably should start shutting the door. Ready to go. If I cried, I'd get snot on my face, and she'd definitely shut the door next time I knocked, and I really, really didn't want her to shut the door.

"Don't shut the door. Please." I reached for her with my good hand, and she let me touch her wrist. Her skin was so soft the sensation tied up my tongue worse than ever.

"Whatever." She took a deep breath and let it out. "I know you don't mean to be a jerk, right?"

"Right," I repeated. I could usually repeat last words without disasters. "No jerks. No doors."

Leza nodded as she slid her wrist out from under my fingers. "You know, I bet you can cross off the fourth and fifth thing on this list. I don't think you heard any voices. Do you?"

I shook my head and watched her scratch through that line.

"And if your folks are aliens, then mine are from their same planet. The brother and sister thing is just gross, and my family has known you since you were little." Leza was talking really fast like I did sometimes when I was trying to get away from the tears in my head. "I guarantee you if

83

your parents were abusing you, Mama Rush would have just killed them and buried them in the backyard. She didn't trust Child Protective because she worked for them before she went private. Can you really imagine her leaving a kid in a situation like that?"

"No." Did she even take a breath when she said all that? I thought about asking, but figured I'd say idiot things. At least the paint-blood had faded almost away, even though my head and hand were still killing me.

Leza tapped the pen on the memory book. "So that leaves you doing something awful, your life sucking, and your ex-girlfriend."

I didn't know what else to say but "Yes." Her words were starting to run together.

"Okay." Leza stood up. "Progress. Now you can take this to Mama Rush and work on these three. I've got to go to the mall."

She left the yard so fast I barely had time to yell "Thank you!" before she was out of the gate and gone.

chapter 8

Three o'clock, and all's well.

I've always wanted to yell something weird like that, but I knew I shouldn't yell. Yelling would be bad. I'd probably get thrown out or something. Besides, I was sitting with Mama Rush on the patio at The Palace, and if I yelled, Mama Rush would probably bop me with an ashtray.

Don't yell.

Only, she had mended one of my presents—the ashtray, of course—so she didn't need the stand-up ashtrays anymore, unless she wanted to bop me if I yelled. She had plopped the mended clay ashtray on the table between us and started using it as she read over my notes and the list. She flicked ashes into the ashtray every few seconds, but afternoon sunlight still brightened the web of clear glue holding everything together.

Don't yell about glue.

I liked seeing her use the ashtray. I had shaped that clay and put prints of my fingers into the sides and bottom and top. I had even painted the brown clay green so it would be more colorful. That was probably a mistake. The ashes were burning little black spots into the green. It didn't smell very good. And the black spots made the green bowl look like some kind of weird upside-down turtle shell.

Don't yell about turtles.

It definitely looked like an ashtray made by a brain-damaged guy. A brain-damaged ashtray.

Don't yell, don't yell, don't yell.

"Your handwriting's pretty bad now," Mama Rush grumbled as she shoved up the sleeve of her oversized purple shirt. It was the same shade as her scooter. "Next time you write, slow down a little bit."

"Brain-damaged ashtrays," I yelled. Then I covered my mouth, took a breath, and said, lots quieter, "A turtle, but it's upside down."

She groaned without taking her eyes off the notebook. "Loosen up a little, at least with me. Quit trying to be perfect when you don't have to be. If you need to talk nonsense, then do it. Or try . . . try counting to ten over and over again, or saying the alphabet."

I counted to ten while she read. When I'd done that three times, I said the alphabet. The urge to yell it kept popping up my throat, but I wouldn't let it past my lips.

Meanwhile, the automatic porch door swung open and out came a great big guy riding a silver scooter with orange racing flames. His legs covered the small part of the flames, so it looked like the fire was flaring out of his calves. Gas gone bad.

Oh, God. Don't yell about gas. Harder to think in the real world. One, two, three, four, five—anything but gas.

Six, seven, eight, nine, ten, A, B, C, D, E—brain-damaged turtles were better than gas.

I fidgeted with the pen on the string tied to my memory book, which Mama Rush was still reading. She smacked my arm with her cigarette hand until I let the pen go, but she didn't drop the cigarette. "Be still. Just give me one more minute."

X, Y, Z. One, two, three, don't yell about gas. Four, five, six. No gas. No brain-damaged turtles. No yelling. Seven, eight, nine, ten.

The guy on the silver scooter with the gas-flames zoomed around the tables. And around again. He didn't seem to be going anywhere. No pack of cigarettes poking out of his shirt pocket, either. No smoking. Just looping around. Each loop got faster and he came a little closer to the tables. I squinted at him. The silver was bright in the sun. My headache was gone, but my scars felt sore. The bright silver made them hurt. My bad hand clenched.

"That's Big Larry," Mama Rush said absently, turning a page in my book. Flick, flick, flick went her cigarette into the brain-damaged turtle ashtray with the glue lines. "Don't mind him. He had a stroke and lost his words."

Big Larry. Huge Larry. Linebacker Larry. Don't yell about Larry. Larry looked like Frankenstein with a blank stare and his mouth hanging open. His right arm hung in a sling pulled tight against his chest. I could see his swollen, curled Frankenstein fingers poking over the sling's white edge. The right side of his lips drooped, just like his right eye.

Big Larry the Frankenstein Linebacker on his silver-flame scooter couldn't talk. He lost his words. He lost the strength on his right side just like I'd lost the strength on my left side, but Big Larry could drive, at least on his scooter. He whizzed past us again. Every time he got closer.

"Can't talk." I watched him wind up for another loop. "One, two, three, four. Larry the Frankenstein Linebacker can't talk. Five, six, seven. He's not doing so good. Eight, nine, ten. Frankenstein nutcase. Don't yell about nutcases."

Mama Rush glanced up from the book. "He can't talk, but he *can* hear. Quit pissing him off or he'll run over your toes."

She went back to reading.

I shut my mouth, tried to wiggle my toes down into my tennis shoes and scoot my feet all the way under the table. When would I remember that stupid sock? It was a good idea even if Leza thought it would taste fuzzy.

Big Larry motored by, no sign of brakes. Did that scooter have brakes? I mean, it had to have brakes or people would snap their legs and arms and heads when they slammed into stuff to stop. They'd all be brain-damaged turtles. And Mama Rush would have used a few people as slamming targets on purpose by now and been arrested. So Big Larry the Linebacker's brakes had to be broken.

"A-B-C-D-E-F-G—"

"Just another minute." Mama Rush tapped her fingers on my memory book. The pen on the string kept rhythm. "I'm trying to think."

Be quiet, be quiet, be quiet, be quiet, don't yell, I had to be quiet. A-B-C-one-two-three. Be quiet. Why wasn't Mama Rush worrying about Big Larry and the silver scooter? Could she see him? Big Larry had lost his words. Maybe Mama Rush had lost her eyesight? Be quiet.

"Did you have a stroke?" I blurted.

She didn't even look at me.

Lost words. Lost eyesight. Lost pragmatics. I had stupid-marks on my head. I was scared Big Larry would find a way to get my toes and leave a few stupid-marks on my feet, too. What if he hit Mama Rush on her scooter and hurt her?

My stomach twisted.

I couldn't stand it if she got hurt. And she was old so she would probably break really easy. Ashtray glue wouldn't fix her. Brain-damaged turtles. If Big Larry hit Mama Rush, I might have to punch him. At least he only had one good side like me. I might have a chance.

"You ruled out drugs," Mama Rush finally announced.

Trying to stop the turtle–Big Larry chatter in my head, I met her gaze. In the background, Big Larry clipped a wire-mesh chair with his scooter. The chair fell over. He was only a few tables away. Then next time he looped, he'd probably hit us.

"Bad Frankenstein driving," I muttered. "Turtles." Then, "We ruled out drugs. We, Leza and me. Leza helped. The notes—she had a point about testing. And another point about rumors she didn't hear."

Mama Rush nodded. "I read her notes on the list a few times, and I agree. I'm glad, too, even if it's a shame. Drugs would have been an easy answer to the 'why' you're look-ing to find. But I got a feeling nothing about this is easy. This whole list thing might be too simple, but at least it's a starting point."

She pushed the memory book back to me. "You hearing voices and all that silly stuff about your parents, those were useless from the get-go."

Big Larry get-go'ed around the far side of the patio.

The click of a lighter told me Mama Rush still wasn't concerned.

"Two, three, six," I said, calling out the numbers on the list as I looked down at the book. "B-C-F."

1. ~~Maybe on drugs.~~
2. *Did something awful I felt guilty.*
3. *My life sucked.*
4. ~~Heard voices telling me to off myself.~~
5. ~~Parents really brother and sister/aliens/abusive.~~
6. *Elana Arroyo—ask Todd.*

"B-C-F. Hmmm." Mama Rush tapped the ashtray three times with her cigarette. "Two, three, six. Did you work that out before you said it?"

I shrugged and closed the book. "I still have some smarts."

That got me a laugh.

She took a deep drag off her cigarette as Big Larry rumbled by, inches from her scooter. His face was all red now, and he looked like he was crying. I squirmed in my chair. My brain filled up with things I could yell at him. My head was starting to hurt again, maybe because I was clenching my fist and my teeth so tight.

Frankenstein, go home!

You're bothering me!

Don't you hit Mama Rush!

The voice inside my brain sounded like J.B. and me, too.

"Whether or not you were happy, that might be the next thing we want to consider." Mama Rush seemed far away, and a little quiet against the sudden thunder of blood in my ears. "Any thoughts on what might have made your life suck?"

Get away from us!

Frankenstein idiot—who let you drive, anyway?

Brain-damaged turtles aren't allowed to drive.

Go inside!

My eyes wouldn't leave Big Larry and his silver scooter and his shaking shoulders. I could only see his face from the side.

"Boy, you're supposed to be considering what made your life suck."

I jumped. Oh, yeah. It was my turn to talk. "What sucked my consider?"

Mama Rush tapped her cigarette in the brain-damaged turtle. "Number Three, isn't it? Or C. Whatever you want to call it. 'My life sucked.'"

The roar in my ears cut down a little. I managed to drag my eyes back to Mama Rush. She was sitting in a thin veil of smoke, sunlight reflecting off her glasses and her purple shirt.

"My life sucked," I echoed, wishing Big Larry would stop, just shut it all down right now.

He barreled straight at Mama Rush.

She didn't look at him.

My tongue tangled up with my teeth and I couldn't even yell.

Mama Rush still didn't look at Big Larry, but she stuck out her cigarette hand and waved it up and down.

Big Larry grunted. The silver-flame scooter geared down all of a sudden. He stopped right in front of her outstretched hand. My mouth was hanging open just like his now. As I sat there like a stupid Frankenstein, Big Larry's big shoulders shook even harder and he sobbed really loud. His face went so red it almost turned purple like Mama Rush's shirt.

"Just a minute," she said to me. She stamped out her cigarette in the brain-damaged turtle and turned to the crying man. "What is it? Did Attila the Red talk ugly to you again?"

Big Larry's face puffed up.

Was he going to yell? Probably he would yell. And then I would want to yell.

He opened his mouth wider and squeaked a word. More like half a word. Half of a very bad word.

Mama Rush eased off her scooter, took a stiff step, then wrapped her purple-shirt arms around his purple head and hugged him.

Big Larry reached up and touched one of her elbows. His sobs got loud, then quiet. After a while, he just shook without making any sound at all. Watching him cry made me feel like I had a hot clamp around my throat.

How long would this last?

My headache picked up enough to make me wince.

Go away, Frankenstein!

Go inside!

I tick-tacked the pen against the table, then poked at the brain-damaged turtle. Ashes shifted inside.

If I didn't get home before Dad got back from his "short" Saturday makeup day, he'd be worried. I think Mom knew where I was because she left me money, just enough for a cab ride. It was on my dresser when I got back inside from talking to Leza. Dad could have left it, but Dad told me to stay away from the Rush house. That didn't mean Mama Rush, did it? Because she lived in The Palace with the credit card blue rug, not the Rush house. Besides, I'd never stay away from her unless she told me to.

God, my head was throbbing. Stay away. Go away. Go inside. Go. Just go. Away, away, away. The pen bounced off my memory book. The sound was really loud. It took me a few seconds to realize I was the one moving the pen and making all the noise. So I stopped.

Were they *ever* going to quit hugging?

Boyfriends and girlfriends hug all the time, and—oh, jeez. Was Big Larry the boyfriend Mama Rush had been talking about? I'd never asked the guy's name, probably because I didn't want her to brain-damage my turtle head any worse than it already was. Please, please don't let Mama Rush be dating Frankenstein.

"You done?" Mama Rush asked. I jumped, then realized she wasn't talking to me.

Big Larry on his silver-flame scooter sniffed in response. He leaned away from her and mopped his wet eyes on one of her sleeves. She didn't even make a face like I did.

Without another sound, Big Larry slowly backed up his scooter, edged around Mama Rush, and left the patio. The automatic door into The Palace whooshed open, then closed firmly behind him. By that time, Mama Rush was back on her own scooter and already digging out a new cigarette.

I tapped the pen again and she slapped my hand. The edge of her lighter caught the back of my knuckle.

"Ouch!" I dropped the pen and got my hand out of her way. The sudden movement made the pain in my head flare up even worse.

"You can be rude, did you know that?" She glared at me as she lifted the yellow hammer-lighter and flicked it until a flame shot out.

Was she going to throw it at me when she was done? I tried to stay alert just in case. "Don't throw it! I mean, I'm sorry."

"No, you're not." She pointed her now-lit cigarette at the patio door. "That man can't talk. He can think, he has all his smarts, he knows what he wants to say, but he can't force out a single thing except words his mama would smack him for saying. Do you have any idea how that rips at the man's insides?"

Like an idiot, I started to open my mouth, then pressed my lips closed when she continued.

"Of course you don't. Well you didn't until you did all that to yourself." She gestured to my scars. "Spoiled and selfish. You, Todd, Leza—none of you faced much real hardship in life until you went and pulled that trigger."

My scars tightened as I ground my teeth. The throb in my head felt like knives jabbing, jabbing, jabbing. I wanted to grab for the pen so much that my good hand, the one with the tiny lighter-mark on one knuckle, actually shook.

Selfish. Did she think I shot myself in the head because I was selfish?

Mama Rush leaned toward me, bringing her cloud of smoke with her. She still looked like a djinni, but a really mad djinni in a purple shirt, about to turn me into a brain-damaged turtle and send me off to the Sahara with no water.

"Your life didn't suck, but you found reasons to think it did." She was snarling more than talking. And looking

94

at the patio door like Big Larry might pop back out again. "Stacked up things to make yourself nervous, then blamed everybody but yourself for making the stack."

I counted to ten and said the alphabet and closed my eyes so I couldn't see the stupid pen I wanted to grab. When I got enough courage up to open them again, Mama Rush's fire had turned into little sparks. No thrown lighters. No ashtrays bashing my head. She was calming down.

I watched as she settled back on her purple scooter. Her lips were moving. I got a weird feeling she was counting to ten and saying the alphabet. Wondered if she wanted to yell it.

"Sorry," I whispered through my still-crammed-together teeth. I didn't really know what I was sorry for, except I didn't want her to be mad. And I didn't want her to think I was selfish.

I wasn't selfish, was I? Selfish people were mean. Selfish people never thought about how other people might feel.

You're so self-centered I bet you think I'm mad at you.

My pounding head shook "no." But that voice I just heard shouting . . . what the hell? Was it a girl? If it was, it definitely wasn't Mom or Mama Rush. It sounded a little like Leza.

"Selfish," I said out loud, then rubbed the stupid-mark on my temple. "Self-centered."

Mama Rush took a slow breath, then focused on her cigarette for a whole minute, maybe more. Somehow, I managed not to repeat "selfish," "self-centered," the alphabet, or any of the numbers between one and one hundred.

When Mama Rush spoke, her voice was normal again, and I stopped worrying she might start throwing things.

"That was . . . harsh, what I said." She shifted on her scooter, then nodded toward the patio door. "But you should know in case it happens again—a man can only stand his own silence so long. Big Larry gets frustrated, then he breaks down. A little listening and a little kindness sets him right, and he goes on his way."

That made sense to me. Selfish. Self-centered. I could still get the basics. Big Larry took all he could take, then blew off steam. An image of my mom popped into my head. I imagined her throwing a fit at the bank, tearing up a bunch of money and screaming and hurling complementary ball-point pens at the customers and employees. Maybe a woman could only stand her own silence so long, too.

Why was I thinking about my mother?

I had to stop. If I smiled at the freaky pictures of Mom having a bank tantrum, Mama Rush might do something drastic. Selfish, selfish, selfish. I said the words to myself, keeping time with the throb of my headache.

"He bothered you, didn't he, Jersey?"

Unable to stop myself, I looked at the patio door, hoping Big Larry wouldn't come sailing back out. "Yes."

"Did he scare you?"

"A little."

"Because you didn't understand him."

"I guess." The shrug was automatic, and her glare made me regret it. I needed a sock *and* weights to tie down my good shoulder if I was going to survive my Palace chats with Mama Rush. At least she didn't climb all over me for twitching my shoulder.

"Fear's natural when you don't understand something." She tapped her cigarette ashes into the ashtray I made her.

"And silence like Big Larry's—I think it might bother folks more than your nonsense chatter."

Before I could answer, her words rattled through my broken head.

Big Larry. Me.

Him quiet, me running my mouth.

Two brain-damaged turtles, making people uncomfortable.

My stomach rolled over inside.

Did I really come across like Big Larry, all Frankenstein and scary and . . . and . . . ?

Biting my lip hard, I looked down at the ashtray, at the glued cracks, at the burned spots and scarred paint.

"See what you can find out about this 'my life sucked' thing. You got real stuck on doing everything better than everybody else—and you were doing way too much for any sane person. Poke around there." Mama Rush smiled at me through her smoky djinni veil. Her image got all blurry as I tried really hard not to cry. She just kept smiling at me, and I wondered if she was counting to ten again. Maybe twenty. Maybe thirty.

When I got up, I knocked over one of the stand-up ashtrays. Frankenstein scary. But she didn't say anything, just patted my back when I kissed her cheek.

chapter 9

For a long, long time, until my headache stopped enough for me to move without wanting to hurl, I hung around the front of The Palace. Just sat on one of the benches and held my memory book and thought. Big Larry went by once and I managed to smile at him even if I wanted to throw up all over again. He didn't seem to notice. I wondered if Big Larry needed a memory book, but I didn't want to ask him.

It was nearly dark before I called the cab. I only did it then because Meki Shansu Residential Director handed me her personal phone and made me do it.

I bothered her, just like Big Larry bothered me. That much I understood now. I just didn't like it.

The cabdriver stared at me when I got in.

I bothered him, too.

Big Larry and I, we probably bothered everybody.

All the way home, I kept hearing pieces of my conversation with Mama Rush and having that weird hallucination of somebody yelling at me. I was pretty sure it was a girl.

You're so self-centered I bet you think I'm mad at you.

It wouldn't stop, even when I wrote the sentence down in my book. I wrote it down five times. Then I filled up a whole page. If I was self-centered before I shot myself, people would have been mad at me and they would have yelled like that.

Mama Rush said I got stuck on doing too much, and doing it better than everybody else. So maybe my life sucked because I was selfish and nobody liked me? Todd had stopped talking to me, so maybe other people had stopped talking to me, too. Maybe I was totally selfish and all stuck on doing too much and being better than everyone. Maybe that's why Mom didn't seem to like me much anymore, either. I hurt her feelings a lot, being selfish. And the way she looked at me now—

The tightness in my throat just wouldn't go away, and my headache blasted along big-time.

The way Mom looked at me now, it was a lot like I looked at Big Larry.

Frankenstein.

Frankenstein scary.

I slammed my book closed and tried to hold the words inside.

When the cabdriver let me out, I handed him all the rest of my money. And I tried not to care if he stared at me or if he thought I was a Big Larry if I paid him too much. I didn't want to be selfish.

And sock or no sock, I was going to try to do what the therapists taught me and try harder to focus—and shut up.

As I walked up the driveway and stumbled up the porch steps rubbing my aching head, I felt more determined than ever. Somehow, I was going to keep my mouth closed. Focus. Focus.

The front door bounced off the doorstop when I opened it, and I frowned. Selfish. I didn't focus. I pushed it too hard. I should have thought about what kind of noise that would make. If Mom and Dad were home and reading or talking or something, that noise might have scared them.

"Jersey!" Mom came running out of the kitchen.

She grabbed me and hugged me, then pushed me back and shook me. That made my brain hurt. I dropped my book, and my eyes got squinty from the pain.

"Where have you been?" Mom gave me another shake. "It's dark! You should have been back hours ago."

Dad came up beside her and the two of them stood there staring at me. Mom's eyes were red and teary. Dad's face was stony and way too calm.

I realized I was opening and closing my mouth. Nothing came out. Concrete. My headache doubled, tripled, got so bad so fast I couldn't really see straight. I barely could keep my eyes open. I wanted to apologize for not trying harder since I got out of Carter. I wanted to apologize for the door noise. That was selfish. Staying gone too long to think was selfish, too, but I wasn't sure how. What could I say that wouldn't be stupid? How could I say anything without saying too much?

Selfish, selfish, selfish.

"Jersey." Mom squeezed my shoulders. "Are you going to answer me?"

I'm sorry, I'm sorry, I'm sorry. My fist clenched. My scars ached. Stupid, selfish, stupid, selfish.

Mom let me go.

I kept trying to speak as she backed away like I had wanted to back away from Big Larry.

"Sonya." Dad's warning voice punched through my headache, but it didn't break up the concrete.

"Damn it, I'm just trying to help!" Mom's sharp tone drove more nails into my brain. "What am I supposed to do?"

"Give him a little space. Let him get his bearings."

It got quiet and cold all of a sudden, like an ice-wind blew through the house.

When I focused my eyes and squinted up at Dad, I realized Mom was gone. She left with the ice-wind.

Before I said or did anything else stupid or selfish, I picked up my book and headed for the stairs. Ice-wind. I shivered. My feet felt like weights as I moved them up, up, one at a time, good boy, bad boy, one two three, stop talking nonsense, *you're so self-centered I bet you think I'm mad at you.*

Ice-wind. The hall seemed long, but I made it to my bedroom door, made it inside.

You're back! J.B.'s voice smacked me cold in the face, like a whole new ice-wind.

Frowning, I covered my ears to shut him out, but that was no use. He got even louder. *Selfish-sailfish-selfish. You look upset, Frankenstein. Why don't you call somebody and talk about how upset you are? Oh, wait.*

He laughed and it sounded—it felt—like acid. *You can't call anybody. There isn't anybody to call.*

I closed the door and managed not to slam it.

Can't call anybody. Not even a counselor. Not for six months.

My bed sagged under me as I sat down hard. Not a

single person to call. There was Leza, but she was always busy and I didn't want to bug her and make her stop talking to me. Mama Rush was probably in bed. And none of my old friends had come to see me in the hospital. None of my old friends wanted to talk to me. The friends at Carter were gone or busy with Carter stuff. Maybe I didn't have any old friends. Maybe they had all left before the big bang, just like Todd. Maybe I didn't have any new friends left at Carter, either.

Because you were selfish. Selfish Before. Selfish After.

If I could have found J.B. in my brain and wrapped my hands around his neck, I would have. I would have choked him and shook him as hard as I bet Mom wanted to shake me. What was wrong with me? I couldn't shut up when I needed to be quiet and I couldn't talk when I had something to say. Just a brain-damaged turtle. Just a broken, glued-together ashtray with holes burned in the sides. And my head hurt way, way bad.

I put my book beside me on the bed, then put my face in my hands.

You're so self-centered I bet you think I'm mad at you.

Someone was touching me, hugging me, holding me, asking me if I was okay.

It was all I could do to pay attention.

Dad.

In my room.

He was stroking my head. His hand was all shaky.

". . . Don't want you to put yourself under too much pressure, get too upset."

He switched on the bedside table lamp, and I yelped as

the light pierced my eyes.

"I'm sorry. Is your head hurting? Should I get you some aspirin?"

Dad was gone before I could answer.

Time didn't seem to be moving. At least J.B. wasn't talking anymore. He'd said enough, hadn't he?

When Dad came back with aspirin, water, and a really nervous expression, I asked him to get my hand brace and my foot brace out of the closet. He helped me put them on, and he kept looking all jumpy and twitchy. As my fingers tried to curl against the hard plastic and my ankle throbbed from being straight, my broken brain flashed back to Big Larry making his loops around and around the patio.

He bothered you, didn't he, Jersey?

Only, I wasn't really bothered. Mama Rush had been right about that. I was scared of Big Larry. Scared of what he would do, like Dad was scared of me getting too upset.

Frankenstein scary.

"You—you think—" My voice cracked.

"Ssshhh." Dad sat down beside me and kept an arm around my shoulders as I took a drink of the water he had brought me. He offered me the aspirin, and I took them, too. Another drink, and my throat unlocked a little.

"You think I'm Big Larry," I said.

Dad stared at me.

I sighed. "No, wait. Not Big Larry. Frankenstein. Not Frankenstein. But you think—"

"It's okay. You don't have to try to talk." Dad hugged me a little closer. "I just want to be sure you're okay."

"You think—you want to be sure that I won't break down like Big Larry. That I won't break down, I mean."

Break down *again*, I wanted to say. Go off and do something stupid, or turn purple and explode with tears. Or worse.

Dad's stunned expression and fast blinking gave him away.

He thought if I got too upset, I'd crack. Only, he wasn't afraid I'd drive my scooter too fast and blubber a lot. He was scared I'd hurt myself like I did before.

I needed to tell him I understood that, or ask him if that's what he thought for sure, or ask him if he thought I was selfish. All I could do was drink the rest of the water, put the glass down, and say, "I won't."

I said that over and over.

Dad just hugged me and blinked even faster.

Mom never came to my room.

chapter 10

I have this dream where both legs work and both arms work and I don't have any scars on the outside. I'm sitting on the edge of my bed in dress blues holding a pistol. Sunlight brightens the dust and ashes in my room and darkens all the places where I've nicked the walls and doors. The football rug, the one Mama Rush gave me when I made the team my freshman year, is folded neatly on my dresser so it won't get messy. I give it one last look before I turn back to what I'm doing. My fingers tingle as I lift the gun to my mouth. It tastes oily and dusty all at once as I close my lips on cold gunmetal—but I can't. Not in the mouth. I'm shaking, but I lift the barrel to the side of my head. The tip digs into my skin. I'm thinking about how selfish I've been, how everyone's sick of me and mad at me. I'm thinking I don't have friends, I'm ashamed. I hate myself, and I hate my room and all the dust and ashes in places I didn't even know. Then I'm squeezing the trigger and looking at the dust and ashes and feeling my hand shake and there's noise and fire and pain and I'm falling, falling, my broken head smashing into my pillow . . .

You shouldn't go to school. J.B. hadn't shut up since I woke up two hours ago. The quieter I got, the noisier he got. *You're talking really bad now. You can't do it. You'll run your stupid mouth or turn to stone when you're supposed to talk.*

I didn't have time to fight, so I ignored him.

My hand and ankle felt all stiff from wearing the braces for the first time since I left Carter, my hair still felt damp from the shower, and my jeans felt too heavy and too tight. Were jeans okay? I mean, I'd been locked up in brain injury hospitals for a year and the only place I'd been since discharge was The Palace. I wasn't really sure what to wear. A solid green shirt and jeans seemed safe enough for now, but the snap and zipper on the pants would be hard. Pragmatics. Even brain-damaged turtles knew better than to show up at school dressed like a geek.

Geeks bit the heads off live chickens at carnivals. I read that somewhere, about the word "geek." Chicken heads. Just the thought was gross.

"Chicken heads."

Oh, great. Load up on stupid things to say. Why did you think it would be a good idea to go back to your old school?

"Answers." I fought with my left sock, trying to pull it over my weak foot. The ankle wouldn't bend. Putting socks on one-handed was a real bitch. I was glad I wasn't a girl. I'd never be able to put on a bra. "Bra," I muttered. "Chicken heads. Harder in the real world, but I can do it. Get some answers. Bra."

See? That's what you'll do. J.B. actually sounded nervous. *March into the main hall at Central and yell, "Bra! Chicken heads!" It'll go over real well.*

"No yelling about bras or chicken heads or geeks." I finally finished with the sock and started on the shoes. Then I wondered why I was comforting the ghost who had tried to kill me. "Go to hell," I added, just to keep things straight between us. "Bras. Socks. Hell."

I needed to quit listening to him, but that was hard. He was so loud in my room I couldn't ignore him.

Stay home. Even Mama Rush thinks you shouldn't go back to that place.

"Going." Both shoes were on. Dad would tie them. I refused to do Velcro for school. Stupid-marks or not, I knew Velcro was just . . . out.

Don't talk about bras. Don't talk about anything. This is a bad idea, I'm warning you. School will be a disaster like you can't imagine.

"Bras," I echoed even though I didn't want to. "Imagine bras." The urge to shout "chicken heads" nearly overpowered me.

The digital clock on my bedside table made a whispery noise as the numbers changed.

I picked up my memory book.

Hatch, Jersey.

Time to go. But I would do something about the bra-chicken-head problem, for sure.

"Oh, no, you do *not* have a nasty old sock sticking out of your mouth." Leza made a noise somewhere between a

107

laugh and a scream as she hurried down Central High's front steps.

She was dressed in nice jeans and a Green Rangers cheer-leading shirt.

I looked down at my own jeans. At least those were probably okay.

She was right about the sock, too. It tasted pretty fuzzy, but it reminded me to be quiet. Dad had finally agreed just to drop me off. Per the instructions of the principal, I was arriving one hour late at nine a.m., and I was supposed to meet my guidance counselor and go to class. As soon as Dad pulled away, I had fished the sock out of my backpack and shoved it where it would do the most good.

But Leza had yelled about the sock. Her hair was straightened, with little flipped-up curls at the bottom. I thought it was cute. I thought she was beautiful. I didn't expect her to be waiting, since I was there one hour late at nine a.m.

She reached me and snatched the now-wet sock out of my mouth. Before I could say anything, she hurled it into the bushes and turned back around to point her finger in my face. "No more socks."

"No more socks," I repeated. "I'm not going to be self-ish anymore, and I don't wear a bra."

I clamped my teeth on my tongue. It was coated with fuzz.

Leza only shook her head. "I'm really glad about you not wearing women's underwear, but be quiet about bras and come on. Ms. Wenchel's waiting in the office."

As we climbed the school's front stairs, she walked on my bad side and steadied my elbow. My memory book felt heavy in my right hand. I needed a new backpack or something. The book might be as bad as the sock, especially if somebody read it.

Hatch, Jersey.

I winced with each step, then winced as I realized I used to run up the front steps to Central, even skipped a few sometimes. Sweat beaded on my forehead just from the bad-boy, good-boy march I had to do now.

"There's a wheelchair entrance around the side by the gym," Leza said as we finally made it to the top. "It might be easier."

"Like Velcro," I answered as I glanced at my shoes.

Leza looked down, too. Her head cocked to one side like she was thinking. "Oh, I get it." She took my arm and steered me toward the main school doors. "You thought people would laugh at the Velcro shoes."

"Yeah."

She shrugged as we walked. "Maybe they would have. I've got some Easi-laces at home. I'll bring them over after school since I don't have practice today."

"Easi-laces?" I tried to open the door for her, but it was heavy.

Leza waited while I yanked at it. "Yeah. They're cool. Laces you don't have to tie. Kind of a compromise."

I finally got the door open. She smiled at me as we walked inside, and my heart did a goofy-dance because smiling made her even prettier, and she was going to bring me shoelaces.

Shoelaces.

She made me open my book and write down where

the wheelchair entrance was. Then she made me write *shoelaces*. Like I'd forget that.

When I grinned, Leza said, "Close up that notebook and come on. We're going to be late."

The air inside was barely cooler than the air outside, and I caught a whiff of sour locker and bleach. The halls were empty, and I figured everyone was in class. Leza and I walked past the main auditorium toward the office. A short redheaded woman wearing a black dress was standing outside the office door. She looked all bunched up and nervous and dark, like she was going to a funeral. Shoelaces. I hoped that wasn't Ms. Wenchel.

Jeez, I didn't need to think about funerals or shoelaces or bras or geeks or chicken heads. Leza threw away my sock. Shoelaces. My backpack hurt my bad shoulder. I was still sweating and my jeans were definitely too tight and some funeral-woman might be waiting for me. If Leza hadn't been there, I would have wanted to go home even if J.B. laughed at me and made me tell him he was right after all.

When we got to the office, the weird woman in the mourning dress stuck out her hand. "Hello, Jersey. I'm Alice Wenchel, your helper for the day."

Helper for the day? *Helper?* Funeral shoelaces. What the hell? I opened my mouth to say, "Oh, no way. No way!"

What came out was, "Chicken head bras."

Alice Wenchel stared at me.

Leza wrinkled up her nose. "You're a little worse in public, aren't you?"

I wanted to bang my broken head on the concrete wall. Focus. Focus! Why didn't I remember to focus? After Big

Larry, I swore I wouldn't forget. Focus. No forgetting. Not again.

At that moment, the auditorium doors banged open.

A roar of voices washed through the halls. Half the school was suddenly right there beside us, all around us.

Did I have sweat on my lip? I wiped my face on my good arm really fast, just in case.

Ms. Wenchel glanced at the crowd, then gave me a huge smile that reminded me of my dad when he was being all weird.

"Sorry," she said. "The junior-senior group ran a little over."

Teachers filed by.

All of them looked at me as they passed, then tried to act like they didn't.

A lot of the students stared without bothering to hide it. I saw guys I recognized from the football team and the golf team. They were the ones in Green Rangers T-shirts, not looking at me. It was like they didn't want to see me. They were pretending me away like I pretended J.B. away. They didn't want me back in school with them.

Did I used to walk like that, all fast and confident?

I knew I did, but that didn't seem real.

I shut my eyes and turned to the side so I wouldn't see anything, either. Well, not as much.

When I opened my eyes again, Todd went by with a very pretty dark-haired girl. Her head was down and he had his arm around her shoulders.

Who was she?

I leaned toward them and squinted. Took a step. Todd

shot me a glare of pure fire and hate. I stepped back. Todd directed a wicked frown at Leza, then he and the girl moved on down the hall, kind of in a hurry.

You're so self-centered I bet you think I'm mad at you.

The hallucination sentence ran through my head four times, really fast, with the last word the sharpest. My book jerked in my hand like it wanted to pop open to the page where I wrote that down over and over again.

Was Todd walking with the girl who said that to me?

Was that girl Elana Arroyo? She looked like the picture. Did Elana really move away? Leza said Elana moved away.

"Leza?" I called her name before I had time to be scared of what else I might say trying to ask what was happening.

"It was an assembly." Leza sounded embarrassed and annoyed. "You know, to, um, get people ready for you being here. Remind them not to ask you questions and stuff."

I turned to face her. "What?"

She pointed to the auditorium. "The principal thought the crisis specialists should talk to everyone one more time today, before you got here."

"An assembly . . . crisis . . . about me?"

All the teachers staring. All the people in the hall gaping. It made a lot more sense now. I might as well have been on-stage next to the specialists. They could have pointed and sighed and looked all serious and therapeutic like the doctors at the brain injury center.

The geek is back. Will he bite the heads off live chickens?

Ms. Wenchel was talking, but I couldn't hear her through the noise in my brain. The skin around all my stupid-marks tightened. My teeth clenched. The hallway image blurred a little, but if it was the last thing I ever did, I wasn't going to cry.

Leza's hand brushed my good arm. "It'll be okay, Jersey. I'll see you between classes and at lunch."

"Are you my helper, too?" The question fell out of my mouth, but it didn't sound mean. At least I hoped it didn't.

"Sort of, I guess." Leza's smile was a lot more real than anyone else's. "Just a friend. Gotta go."

She took off into the crowd and left me with Ms. Wenchel.

I looked at the woman's bright red hair and dark black funeral dress, and I really, really, really wanted to go outside, dig through the bushes, and find my sock.

As it turned out, the sock didn't matter. I was so busy trying to take notes and keep up with stuff in class that I didn't talk to Ms. Wenchel much. In between taking notes, I made lists of stuff I needed.

1. *Get a better backpack. Bigger.*
2. *Get pencils that don't break so easy.*
3. *Maybe get pens.*
4. *Get a tape recorder.*

And I made lists of stuff I didn't need to say out loud.

1. *I need a math tutor.*
2. *Do I even have to take math?*
3. *Did math suck this bad before? Ask Dad.*

4. *I think the Earth Science teacher hates me.*
5. *Ms. Wenchel has a pimple on her nose.*
6. *Ms. Wenchel shouldn't have nose pimples.*

Ms. Wenchel kept trying to look at what I was writing, so I covered it up with my bad arm. Then I made lists of stuff I kept saying out loud so maybe I'd stop saying them out loud.

1. *Wenchel pimple*
2. *Funeral*
3. *Funeral pimple*
4. *Geek*
5. *Chicken*
6. *Bra*
7. *Chicken bra*
8. *Helper*
9. *You're so self-centered I bet you think I'm mad at you.*

Focus. I had to focus. But it was hard. Wenchel pimple.

The next time I saw Leza was at lunch. She was waiting for me at the side of the salad bar, where everybody lined up for hot plates or the grill.

When Ms. Wenchel stopped and stood beside us, Leza gave her a Mama Rush look. Sort of down the nose and out from under the eyebrows. "Do you have to stay for lunch, too?"

"I—well, yes, I'm supposed—but, well." Ms. Wenchel clasped her hands together. "I suppose I can sit over there with the teachers, as long as I can see Jersey."

Leza's *you do that* went unspoken, but it shouted out of her eyes. She pulled my memory book out of my hands, looped the dirty pen-string around it, and tucked the pen into the binder before handing it to Ms. Wenchel. "Keep this so it doesn't get food on it, okay?"

Ms. Wenchel looked upset, but she took the book, tucked it under her tray, turned back to the salad bar, and started piling up her plate with lettuce and fruit Jell-O squares.

"You'd think you were some escaped convict," Leza grumbled, tugging my elbow and urging me into the grill line. "Hamburgers okay?"

"Sure. Why is she supposed to watch me?"

Leza shrugged. "Who knows. Maybe they think you'll fall down some steps and break your head and they'll get sued."

"My head's already broken. Do you think she'll read my book?"

"What do you want on your hamburger, Jersey? And no, she won't read your book. Your handwriting's really bad, anyway. Trust me. She wouldn't get much if she did read it."

"Handwriting. Do you think I'll need my book? Hamburger."

"No."

"But what if I—"

"Don't talk about the book anymore, Jersey."

"Okay."

So, we talked about hamburgers and nothing much and lots of stuff except the book until Leza put my plate beside hers on her tray and we left the grill line. As we rounded the salad bar, we came face to face with Todd, who was carrying a tray with two plates on it—hot lunches, barbecue on top of something that looked like cornbread but probably wasn't.

Todd scowled at me, then Leza. "What are you doing with him?"

Leza puffed up like she used to when she was little. Her fists clenched. "Helping. Like you should be."

I wondered if I should grab my hamburger before it ended up in Todd's face.

"Don't tell me what I should be doing." Todd's voice came out in a low growl. "You know how I feel about this."

Should I ask him why he hated me? Or about Elana Arroyo? He was standing right here. I could ask. But Todd could throw food just as well as Leza, and that barbecue looked hot and messy.

"Get on with yourself, then." Leza gestured with her head, and when I looked over her shoulder, I saw tables full of Green Rangers shirts alternating with the pinks and yellows and whites of girl-clothes. Pretty-girl-clothes.

The jock tables.

Some of the jock table jocks looked up. One of them stared at me and cringed.

Did I know him?

Oh, yeah. I used to sit there.

Before.

How could my life have sucked if I didn't take drugs, my parents weren't brother and sister, I didn't hear voices, and I sat at the jock tables with barbecue and pretty girls? I stared at the jocks, and stared. And stared a little more. Neat hair. Neat clothes. No stupid-marks.

I used to look like that. I used to be like that. I used to sit at those tables. Golf, football, R.O.T.C. I used to sit there like them, talk like them, laugh like them. Didn't I? Mama Rush and Leza said I did my freshman year, but I got different my sophomore year. Neat. Clothes. Hair. Before. Maybe I didn't sit there my sophomore year. Maybe I was too busy. Hair. Maybe I made everybody mad. Golf and football. Maybe I wasn't perfect enough anymore, or too perfect, or something.

Loosen up a little.

Mama Rush's djinni-voice ran through my head once, twice, while Todd and Leza snarled at each other a couple more times. Finally, Todd stalked off. The girl he sat beside ran her fingers through her dark hair as he handed her the extra plate on his tray.

Elana. It looked like Elana. In the picture. In my head. Elana from when I was perfect and busy and sat at the jock tables with a life that didn't suck. Elana moved away.

Did she move away?

I ground my teeth.

Loosen up a little.

How could I loosen up? I needed to tighten up. At least my mouth. Something. I had to tighten up to get better.

"Quit staring," Leza whispered.

"I need to know some stuff from Todd," I whispered back. "Can you get him to talk to me for five minutes?"

"No." She took hold of my elbow again and led me across the cafeteria, past a clump of teachers including Ms. Wenchel and her funeral dress and her tray on top of my memory book. We walked straight to a long table full of gorgeous girls and one or two guys.

The cheerleaders.

Oh, God.

Loosen up a little.

If I had been carrying my own tray, which of course I couldn't, I would have dropped it. This was a bad idea.

"Come on," Leza instructed, all but dragging me. "It's only the junior varsity, and they're all my friends. Just keep eating and don't say anything. You'll be fine."

The sheer number of horrible things that could pop out of my mouth—even full of food—made my heart thump hard on my ribs.

Loosen . . . loosen . . . loosen . . .

She almost had me to the table when I broke away. "I—um—need to go. You know. Go."

I nodded toward the restroom.

Leza gave one of her shrugs and nodded. She set her tray down between two girls with blond hair and told one of them to scoot over. The girl did. Most of the table gazed up at me like they had been expecting this, like maybe they had all agreed to it beforehand.

The geek can sit at our table if he doesn't bite off any chicken heads.

Are his scars gross up close?

How can we make him say stupid stuff we can repeat all over school?

The cheerleaders were blurring.

Leza was biting into her hamburger.

I took off for the bathroom and stayed there the rest of our short lunch period. I stayed there until Ms. Wenchel knocked and made me come out. We barely made it to the next class on time, and I didn't see Leza anywhere.

. . .

Sixth period, last class, last desk, in the corner. Why did she keep staring at me? The teacher was staring at me, just like the Civics teacher and the Algebra teacher. Staring at the freak. The freak with the scars and no pragmatics. I had no pragmatics. I wanted to hop up and down and make monkey noises. Yeah. Stare at this, why don't you? If it hadn't been for Ms. Wenchel, I probably would have made monkey noises. Pragmatic monkey noises.

"Monkey," I said quietly. "Pragmatic monkey."

The teacher glared. She had white hair and big glasses, and she missed her mouth with her lipstick really bad, so her top lip looked like it was coming out of her nose, but she was staring at me.

"Pragmatic monkey."

"Jersey," Ms. Wenchel whispered. "Ssshhh."

I opened my memory book and wrote *pragmatic monkey* five times as fast as I could.

Some of the other kids glanced at us, but they turned back around. Nose-lip started talking about charity organizations. I tried to listen, and I opened my notebook on top of my memory book. I tried to take class notes in between writing *pragmatic monkey* every time I wanted to say it. My hand was cramping. My head felt heavy, heavy. Pragmatic monkey naps. If I could just close my eyes.

Ms. Wenchel nudged my shoulder. "Stay awake," she murmured. "Write notes in your class notebook, not that journal."

My stomach growled. Kids looked around. Nose-lip

stared another few seconds, then started talking again. I blinked. Closed my eyes.

Ms. Wenchel poked me.

If I poked her back, I'd probably get suspended. Pragmatic monkey naps.

I didn't poke her back.

I didn't.

But I wanted to. Her and all the rest of the class. Monkey. Monkey naps.

I had tried to talk to my old R.O.T.C. commander before this class, but he sort of dismissed me.

Nothing much to say, Hatch. All his buttons shining. His false teeth shining. The sun shining as the drill team worked out behind him and he told me I couldn't pass the physical to get back in uniform. *But keep that chin up. You'll find another niche.*

The football coach was worse.

How ya doin', Hatch? He had slapped my back so hard I almost fell over. *Come see me if you want to do towels and water.*

Monkey naps.

Towels and water.

Towels and water.

Niche.

I used to catch passes, but it was towels and water now. The golf coach had been gone over a year, or so the Wench told me. Even if he'd been there, I don't think I would have tried to talk to him. Towels and water. I saw a few teachers I remembered from freshman year, and they were nice, I guess. But they had stuff to do. I had stuff to do. Not towels and water, though. Monkey naps. I did need a monkey nap.

Everything hurt. I felt like I'd walked twenty laps around the track instead of sitting in a desk for hours. How could sitting at a desk make me so tired? At Carter, I was used to half-hour therapy sessions separated by a lot of nothing, a lot of free time, I guess. Not six straight hours of books, teacher-talk, towels and water, notes, Nose-lip, Ms. Wenchel the funeral lady poking me, and worrying about how mad Leza might be.

1. *Nose-lip*
2. *Nose-lip*
3. *Nose-lip*
4. *Nose-lip*
5. *Nose-lip*

When the last bell rang, I wanted to yell with relief, but I didn't have the energy. My stomach growled. Ms. Wenchel sighed, shook her head at me, and took off. Nose-lip followed her. Monkey naps. Thank God.

With help from the notes in my memory book, I found the wheelchair exit, limped outside, and dragged myself around the side of the school, toward where Mom was supposed to pick me up.

The car was already there.

"Thank you, thank you, thank you," I mumbled as I crammed my memory book under my bad arm and rested for a second. My stomach made freaky noises. Somebody giggled.

I looked up. Leza was standing right beside me.

"Chicken," she said. She chicken-clucked as she made

sure my memory book was tucked tight under my bad arm.

Her smile made me feel a lot better, like I had enough juice to get to the car after all. She dug around in her purse, then took out something wrapped in napkins and handed it to me. My hamburger. Cold now, but man did it taste good when I took a huge bite.

Leza laughed again. "Don't you choke. Your parents would kill me."

I tried to answer, but my mouth was full. I swallowed instead.

"You're sitting with me tomorrow. If not tomorrow, the next day, or the day after. I won't give up. Got that?"

Between bites and chewing, I studied her face and nodded. The entire Rush family had problems with the word *no,* so I didn't bother trying to use it.

Leza walked me to the car and opened the front door for me. I climbed in awkwardly beside Mom, unwilling to surrender my hamburger. Leza looked inside, saw Mom, and backed up in a hurry. Then she just sort of looked down, closed the door, and took off.

Mom watched her go, but she didn't say anything. When Leza disappeared into a crowd of people, Mom grimaced at the cold hamburger, but she still didn't say anything. She even held it while she helped me fasten my seat belt and put my memory book in my lap.

The minute I got the hamburger back, I took another huge bite.

"Slow down," Mom said automatically as she pulled out of her parking spot. "Focus, remember? The speech therapist said—"

"Small bites," I mumbled around hamburger, bun, and

pickles. I'd heard "small bites" over and over again since I'd woken up and started eating for myself. Small bites. The speech therapist had never been this hungry, and I could eat without choking now, no problem. But I didn't want to be a Big Larry, so I focused and took small bites, small bites, small bites. Why did Mom have to be so uptight? Small bites. Don't ask that. Focus. Small bites.

Soon, small bites after small bites, the hamburger was gone and my stomach quit sounding so weird.

"Did your day go okay?" Mom asked, keeping her eyes on the road.

"Yeah. I guess."

There was a long pause.

Mom kept her gaze straight ahead. "I'm—I'm proud of you for having the courage to go. Really proud of you, Jersey. Any problems with your classes?"

"No." I stretched and yawned. "But they had a funeral woman and an assembly about me. Not fun."

Mom nodded. "The principal told us they were going to bring in the counselors one more time. What did you say about a funeral woman?"

I looked at her. Her face was still and blank and her fingers went tap-tap-tap against the padded steering wheel cover.

"The assembly—you knew?" My voice was louder than I intended. Selfish. Self-centered. I would make her look at me like I was Big Larry again.

Mom said nothing. Her fingers stopped tapping.

Doing my best to focus and turn down the volume, I asked, "Why didn't you tell me?"

"We didn't—I guess we just didn't think about it, Jersey." Her expression never changed. Her fingers didn't start moving again.

My face got hot. I knew my cheeks were turning red. My teeth clenched, but I refused to go off. No Big Larry. Not me. I was going to wear my braces and keep my mouth shut and do what I learned at Carter. And since I left Carter. So I made myself relax by singing the alphabet in my head over and over again. Then I opened my memory book and started writing the alphabet. It was all I could think of to keep my mouth shut.

Focus. Small bites.

Mom and I rode the rest of the way home without talking.

chapter 11

Three weeks. I'd survived three weeks.

But the lunchroom was really, really loud, and hot, too. Even though I was sitting with Leza and the cheerleaders, I was bugged about a bunch of stuff. Hot didn't help at all. Hot made everything worse. For the first time since school started, I forgot my memory book. That made everything worse, too. The book was at home on my dresser, so I thought about it every time I needed to write something down. At least I had good shoelaces. Leza had given me three packs of Easi-laces, in lots of colors. Today I had on dark green. White shoes. Green laces. I thought about green laces, and how it would have looked if I'd picked blue, and my memory book. Mostly, though, I was thinking about the Wench.

If I had to look at Ms. Wenchel one more day, I might go off. One, two, three, four, five, six, seven, eight, nine, ten, do it again, One, two . . . Red hair. Dark dresses. Nervous smiles. Three, four, five . . . Every time I even thought about her, my scars hurt. Shoelaces. Counting didn't help much.

Pragmatics. Behave myself. I didn't want to be a Big Larry, and I knew the teachers at school were still all squint-eyed and jumpy like my dad about me hurting myself again, but I really, really wanted to ditch the Wench.

"It's only been three weeks." Leza had to yell so we could hear her over all the other yelling in the lunchroom. Something smelled like seriously bad armpit stink. I thought it was the onions on Leza's hot dog. "Maybe she'll just be your shadow for the first month."

Nobody else seemed to care about the body odor onions, so I tried not to scrunch up my nose. Shoelaces. Green shoelaces.

One of Leza's friends gulped down a big bite of salad, then wiped her mouth. "Wench is a total headcase. Maybe you should complain and make them give you some other babysitter."

She wiped her mouth again, and I looked down at the nuts on my plate. I was eating peanuts because that was something I could eat in front of cheerleaders without accidentally sneezing and dribbling all down my shirt or something. Small bites. At least I didn't need a babysitter when I ate peanuts.

"Peanut wench," I muttered even though I had my teeth clenched to keep from saying it. "Body odor. Small bites. Shoelaces. Nuts and onions."

Leza giggled. So did her friends. I did my usual—swallowed a lot, tried to focus like I was supposed to, turned red, put my hand over my mouth and hoped it didn't look like I was putting my hand over my mouth.

Leza wasn't trying to torture me, making me eat with cheerleaders. Her friends were nice, and it was cool to have a place to sit—especially a Wench-free zone—but still. Eating with cheerleaders wasn't easy, even though they were just junior varsity. They were all so pretty, and they didn't have stupid-marks, and none of them were eating peanuts, either.

Salad, salad, salad.

"Lettuce," I muttered, even though I had my fist nearly crammed in my mouth. "Wench. Stinky onion peanuts."

"Frog farts," said Leza.

"Toad turds," one of her friends agreed.

"Horseflies," a third girl said way too loud.

"Hoochie-mamas." Leza again. "Frog farts *and* hoochie-mamas."

"Knock it off!" I smacked her shoulder with my good hand. "Frog fart."

Everyone laughed, even me.

Leza got out of my way, kept giggling, and still managed to take the last bite of her hot dog and stink-onions. She didn't eat healthy salads very much. She crammed down lots of junk food and worked it off during practice. She said that all the time, along with frog farts and hoochie-mamas and lots of other headcase stuff. It was her new strategy. Hers and Mama Rush's.

You can't stop it, boy, and you can't prance around school with a sock stuffed in your mouth. So why not let all that silly talk be a trademark?

Frog farts.

My new "trademark."

Yay.

Pragmatics.

At least Leza liked me anyway. I liked her a lot, too.

I looked at my green shoelaces and chewed a few more peanuts and didn't say anything even though hoochie-mama-trademark-farts flashed through my brain a lot. Laughing about my big mouth seemed to make it smaller, at least for a little while.

I had stuff to figure out even though I didn't have my book to write everything down.

One glued trivet and one patched-up little flowerpot later, Mama Rush and I had crossed *my life sucked* off the list.

Okay, so, the toothbrush cup wouldn't hold water. The flowerpot had a big chunk out of the rim, and the trivet only had three straight sides. The fourth side looked like a clay-eating mouse had chewed it up.

Some of these presents can't be fixed all the way, but it's the best we can do.

Like shoelaces that didn't really tie. Like peanuts. Not really lunch, but lunch enough to count. Good thing the salad bar always had a lot of peanuts.

I knew my life probably didn't suck after Mama Rush got so mad about it, but I had to check things out anyway, and I wrote everything down for her to read. It was at home on my dresser. In the book. *My life sucked* had its own page.

Dad's opinion: *Of course your life didn't suck, son. At least I hope it didn't. Do you think your life sucked? If you need to talk about it, I'm here for you. Want some toast and jelly?*

Mom's opinion: *I wish you'd stop asking ridiculous*

questions. Have you done your homework? Good.
Good. I'm proud of you, Jersey. It's going to be hard
enough for you to keep up. Try not to get distracted
by nonsense.

Todd's opinion: *Get out of my face, freak.*

Leza's opinion: *Everybody's life sucks sometimes.*
You might have had a few sucky days, but noth-
ing to blow your head off over.

Mama Rush's opinion: *I know you don't want to ask*
me that question.

My opinion: *I don't remember. But I remember stuff*
way back before I shot myself, and that stuff
doesn't suck. Leza's probably right. And Mom.

So, now I was trying to figure out if I'd done something
awful. Awful enough to feel guilty. Awful enough to put the
gun to my head and pull the trigger.

Leza thumped the stupid-mark on my temple. "What are
you thinking about, Jersey?"

"Frog farts." I flicked a peanut at her. She flicked it
back. The other girls laughed and kept on girl-chattering.

I looked at the oldest one. She wouldn't have been at
this school when I shot myself. None of them would have
been here. Leza was the only one who knew me Before, but
she was lots younger then.

That was kind of weird. I was eating with younger
kids, I guess. Like a baby. Leza didn't know about anything rotten I had done, but she said I was a "total
butthead" sometimes, even though she liked me.

I didn't think I was ever a butthead. But I didn't think I
was selfish, either, until the whole Big Larry thing. So maybe

I was a butthead. Was being a butthead enough to make me pull the trigger?

"Butthead," I muttered. "Trigger."

The girls were laughing too hard to hear me. That was probably good. I wasn't up for another round of hoochie-mamas.

I went to the bathroom when lunch was over. Thank God the Wench didn't follow me to the urinals like she tried to do the first few days. I'm not sure I could have squeezed out a drop with her nearby. But I shouldn't think about squeezing out drops, because then I'd probably talk about them.

No drops. No drops.

About the time I finally fumbled with my zipper, got it down, and got busy, the door banged open.

For the worst second, everything tried to dry up because I just knew it was Ms. Wenchel. But when I took a quick look, it wasn't.

It was worse.

Three guys—Kerry and Zero, seniors from the golf team, and Todd.

Don't waste my time. I could still hear Kerry saying that before he hung up on me. *Don't waste my time.*

And I hadn't tried to pee in front of any of my old friends before. I'd been sort of avoiding the bathrooms they went to, but now, here they were.

Don't waste my time.

I looked down at my zipper.

Please don't let me pee on myself, or accidentally get a drop on one of them. No drops, no drops.

Todd glanced at me and went to use the urinals on the far wall. Zero and Kerry nudged each other, then came over to take a whiz beside me. I tried to finish real fast, but stuff just wouldn't cooperate.

Don't waste my time.

"You do pretty good with one hand," Zero said. He was wearing jeans and a Green Rangers shirt. I nodded and looked at the wall. "Must be hard to button and zip."

"Button. No. I have a snap. No button. And green shoelaces."

Zero laughed.

Was he being nice or making fun of me?

Hurry, hurry, no drops. No buttons. Buttons. No buttons.

Why was I so nervous? Being nervous was stupid. I knew these guys. They used to be my friends. Didn't they? They hadn't talked to me, but I didn't think they hated me or anything.

Kerry had on khakis and a white shirt. No wrinkles or drops. He always looked neat and clean. I remembered that much.

"Those scars are pretty gross, Hatch." He sighed really weird and long, like he had a huge problem. "Did you have to break your whole head open? Why'd you do it, anyway?"

Something twisted way down inside. I could almost hear J.B. yelling from way over at my house.

Get out! You used to do stuff like this, remember? He isn't being nice. Get out!

But I wasn't finished.

Still, things were drying up for sure.

"Hey, Kerry," Zero said. "You heard all the quack-shrinks at the assembly. We aren't supposed to ask him why he did it. Might upset the poor itty-bitty wittle boy." He finished up and took care of his fly really, really fast and easy. "You used to kick my ass off the tee, Hatch." He shook his head. "Mr. All-That. Mr. Better-Than-You. Look at you now. I bet you pinch when you zip. Need help? Wouldn't want anything important to get scarred up."

"No help, thanks." I didn't mean to say anything. It just popped out. My face got hot. "No scars."

Get out!

Kerry snickered.

I was trying to cram things where they belonged. Frog farts. Nothing would go. At least I got my underwear adjusted. Drops, drops, drops. The bathroom felt a lot smaller than it had when I came in. I wanted to leave. But I didn't want any stains. And I had to wash my hands. But first I had to zip my fly. And it wasn't zipping. Why wouldn't it go up?

Snap, snap, snap first. Then zip. Snap and zip. I grabbed at the snap and tried to push the metal parts together.

"Oh, man, call the babysitter, Todd," Kerry called over his shoulder. "Poor wittle Jersey can't do his zip-zip."

Todd didn't answer. He wasn't making much noise at all.

Zero banged into my good side. I lurched sideways, couldn't keep my balance, and fell against Kerry.

"What the hell?" Kerry said way too loud. He shoved me upright with his shoulder, turned toward me, and I felt something warm seep onto my knees.

Pee. From him.

Pee from Kerry. On me.

"Oh." He laughed as he turned back to the urinal to finish up. "Sorry."

He didn't sound sorry.

I stared down at my leg. My face was so, so hot. I let go of my snap and clenched my good hand into a fist. I could see myself hitting Kerry in the mouth. Or maybe Zero, because he was laughing, too. Or Todd. Yeah. Todd. Because he wasn't saying anything at all.

My pants.

My pants were wet.

Zero stopped laughing long enough to say, "Good shot, Ker. Want a Mulligan?"

That was golf-talk for do-over.

"We've heard Leza and her little friends talking to you," Kerry said. "If we say stupid stuff, you'll repeat it, won't you?"

If I hit Zero, I might knock him into a urinal and he'd shut up. If I hit Kerry, he'd probably pee on me again. My fist was going back, going back, and Zero just laughed harder.

"Do it," Kerry urged. "Think you can, Hatch? You total loser. Loser, loser. Can you say looo-ser?"

"Loser." I started to swing.

Somebody grabbed my arm.

Spun me around.

That fast, I was face to face with Todd. My fist kept trying to move, but it wasn't going anywhere. Todd's lips were all tight and his eyes were squinty. Mad. Really, really mad.

"He peed!" I yelled. "Why? Loser. He peed, not me!"

Todd turned me toward the bathroom door and shoved me. I had to hitch and run not to fall on the gross floor. The sinks—I grabbed one to steady me, then got to the door. Loser.

Zero and Kerry were laughing, laughing, laughing.

Nothing from Todd. Nothing.

Loser.

Get out!

I didn't wash.

I got out.

Falling more than walking. Out the door. Straight into Ms. Wenchel. Her eyes got really big. She opened her mouth. I turned around so I wouldn't have to look at her.

Turned around and there was Leza. And a girl with Leza. A girl with dark hair and eyes black enough they made me stare.

You're so self-centered I bet you think I'm mad at you.

The voice yelled so loud in my head that I jumped. "Self-centered," I blurted. "Selfish. Drops. Frog farts—frog—frog—"

Leza closed her eyes and shook her head really fast.

I wanted to cram my hand in my mouth, but I hadn't washed it.

Elana Arroyo was standing in front of me wearing jeans and a yellow shirt. Right here. Where I could see her. Not moved away. Here. Right here.

"F-f-f-frog." I took a deep breath. "Frog-selfish. Sorry."

The girl—Elana? Was it Elana? It had to be.

She just stared at me and looked totally uncomfortable.

Leza was still shaking her head.

I couldn't help shaking my head. Then I tried to get a grip. "I—I'm not a Big Larry. Elana?"

"Stop, Jersey." Leza sounded as sharp as Mama Rush. "She's not Elana."

When Ms. Wenchel came toward us, Leza froze her with a full-on Mama Rush glare.

Elana-not-Elana took a step back.

What did I say?

If I'd washed my hands, I would have reached for her. "I'm sorry," I said, just for good measure. Was I being selfish?

Elana.

Not Elana.

The bathroom door opened.

Someone pushed past me. Blocked my view of Elana-not-Elana in the yellow shirt.

Todd.

"What did I do to her?" I asked really fast, before he could walk away. "Why did we fight over Elana? Is she? Elana, I mean. Fight."

He swung around and glared at me. "What did you say?"

"Nothing, Todd," Leza answered like I couldn't talk for myself. "Get out of here and take your girlfriend with you."

"I didn't ask you—," Todd started, but Elana—no, no, no. I squinted my good eye at her. Not all the way Elana. A little different from the picture. Rounder face. Bigger nose. Todd's girlfriend who looked like Elana said something too quiet for me to hear.

Todd turned back to her. His shoulders got looser. I saw him breathe once, really deep. Then he nodded and took the girl's hand, and they walked away without looking back.

"Frog farts." I was about to ask them to wait, to answer me about Elana and what happened, when Leza popped my head. No little girl-pop, either. My ears rang.

The Wench started toward us again. "Leza!"

"I swear, Jersey!" She popped me again before I could get my arm up to block her. "What the hell's wrong with you? Calling her Elana. And Todd—you come off with frog farts and Big Larry and bringing up the past. I ought to hit you till you're cross-eyed. And for God's sake, zip your fly."

That stopped the Wench cold.

Me, too.

I looked down at my jeans. They still weren't fastened. When I turned my head a little, I could see my underwear around the wads of my shirt.

The bathroom door opened again. Out came Kerry and Zero. They bumped me on purpose as they went by, still laughing. The Wench called after them, but they didn't stop.

All I could do was look at my pants and think about Todd and his girlfriend and drops and frogs and Leza seeing me look so stupid and all kinds of selfish stuff.

"Did you pee on yourself? Did you?" Leza snorted. "Sometimes . . ."

Whatever else she said, I didn't hear it, because I turned around and went back into the bathroom.

This time I went into a stall and locked the door behind me.

It smelled really bad in there, but I stayed a long time, way into the next class.

The Wench never came after me.

Neither did Leza.

chapter 12

"Alicia went home yesterday." One of the nursing techs from Carter—I didn't know which one—had on her best perky voice as she answered my questions. "No, no forwarding number for her, and Hank's gone to the movies with the gang."

The gang. I used to be part of the gang.

I told the tech that, but she only sighed. "I think it's time to move on, Jersey. Get on with your real life. But I'll tell Hank you called. Bye, now."

The phone gave a loud noise in my ear a few seconds later, reminding me to hang it up. I put it on my bedside table.

Then I went back to Algebra. Algebra and more Algebra, until my eyes crossed. It didn't take long.

$2x + 6 = 12$

"2x." I sighed and rocked backward on my bed. X, y, x, y. When I closed my eyes, I saw x's and y's.

"X, x, x."

It's eight, J.B. said. *That's the answer.*

I leaned down and scribbled 8. Probably wrong, but I had no idea. Resource Algebra sucked, but not as bad as regular Algebra. I'd been switched into Resource after two days. It was better, but yeah, it still sucked. English sucked, too, but in English, x's and y's were just letters, not pretend numbers. In between trying to call Hank and Alicia-who-went-home and the gang I wasn't part of anymore, I'd been working on pretend-numbers since I got home.

At least I hadn't peed on myself or gotten peed on at school. A whole four days with no pee. And Leza was talking to me, which was good, because I couldn't stand it when she didn't. And the cheerleaders were talking to me, too. No peanut-choking. No hoochie-mamas. But Todd's girlfriend took off every time she saw me coming.

Couldn't blame her.

I was Big Larry + 2x = 12 to her. Big Larry with his fly unzipped and his underwear hanging out and pee on his jeans. Big Larry with Todd's fist in his face. I got a sixty-five on a Civics quiz and a forty-eight on the Earth Science test we got back.

"X." I sighed. "Big Larry."

Dumbass, said J.B.

"Dumbass. X. Big Larry." I didn't want to be talking to him, but it was Friday night and Leza was out on a date. Mama Rush was out on a date. My parents were watching a pro football game on tape, so I came upstairs a while ago. I didn't like football games anymore. Watching them made me sad.

Saturday, I was supposed to tell Mama Rush if I did something awful and felt guilty. Tomorrow. I was pretty sure I did bad stuff, but I didn't know what.

J.B. laughed. *You probably did lots of awful stuff.*

"Not me. You. Big Larry."

You should feel guilty. I bet you broke Elana Arroyo's heart.

"Did not. Don't even know if I went out with her much, or how long." I looked back at my math paper. $2x + 6 = 12$. $X = 8$. Eight didn't look right. Dumbass.

You probably went out with her a long time. Maybe you made her do bad stuff. Maybe you stole her from Todd and got her pregnant and that's why Todd—

"Shut up."

You made her cry. You make everybody cry. Eight's right. Leave eight.

"Eight."

The sound of raised voices made me look at the door. Was it the television?

No.

Mom and Dad, arguing again.

"Big Larry." I closed my Algebra book. Did I do home-work on the weekends before I got my stupid-marks? Prob-ably not.

J.B. laughed again. *Definitely not. You weren't home on the weekends. You had hearts to break.*

"X! I didn't break any hearts." I shoved the Algebra book off the bed. It landed on the football rug next to Earth Science and English and my hand and foot braces and my memory book. *Hatch, Jersey,* on the floor. "Dumbass."

My parents—or one of them, Dad—was stomping up the steps, still yelling a lot. I couldn't tell what the words were, but they were mad words. Mom was still yelling, too, but she was downstairs, so she didn't sound so loud.

"Football games. Too many tackles."

They hate each other now. That's why Mom stays gone most of the time. It's your fault. They liked each other before you pulled the trigger.

Couldn't help looking toward the sound of J.B.'s not-yet voice. "You pulled the trigger."

He didn't answer.

He wasn't there. J.B. wasn't ever there, not when I really looked. X, y. Dumbass multiplied. I squinted at the darkest corner, down into the shadows. Maybe he'd be there if I looked harder.

The bedroom door opened.

I jumped. "Dumbass! Oh, jeez. Sorry, Dad."

"Um, right." Dad shrugged. He looked all white and sad in the double light of my room and the hallway. "I just— sorry about all the noise." He rubbed his hands together. "Don't let it bother you, okay? We'll work it out."

Weird. He was looking at J.B.'s dark corner, too.

Don't say dumbass again.

"Sure," I said. Dumbass. Frog farts. Hoochie-mamas. If I'd called Mom a dumbass, she would have killed me. Or slapped me. Something.

Dad's eyes slid from J.B.'s hiding place to the books on my floor. "You're studying on a Friday night?"

"Yeah. I need to keep up. Focus. Try harder, you know?"

This made him look a little happier. Then the back door slammed, a car started, and he looked sad all over again.

"Sorry!" Dumbass. "I mean, the fight. You fighting. It's my fault. I'm such a Big Larry. Sorry."

Dad rubbed his hands together again, but this time, he

didn't stop. "I don't know what you're talking about, son. Your mother and I disagree over a lot of things. Tonight, it was the television. It wasn't you."

It was hard to make my mouth work. Harder to swallow. I wanted him to leave so I could talk to J.B. because J.B. was way easier to talk to than Dad. $2x + 6 = $ J.B. Besides, Dad was lying.

"It's always me. I did something awful."

"Are you still on that? Honest to God, Jersey. You need to leave the past alone." Rub, rub, rub went his hands. "You used to get so stuck on things, so obsessed with doing them your way. Don't be like that now. Don't be like—you know. Before."

"Before I pulled the trigger?" Dumbass! Dumbass!

Dad's hands froze.

My brain didn't.

I pulled the trigger. I shot myself. Shot myself with his gun.

What was wrong with me?

Pragmatics.

His gun.

A weird taste in my mouth—oil and dust. I could feel cold gunmetal on my lips, then again, at the stupid-mark on the side of my head. Digging. Digging in. I clenched my teeth hard. Frog farts, frog farts, frog farts, one, two, three, four, five, six, seven . . . his gun, his gun. Not fair. Not his fault. Big Larry. Selfish. Be quiet. Focus. Try harder. Be quiet.

Dad looked at the football rug instead of me. "Yeah. Before you pulled the trigger. You probably made some people mad, got stressed out—but I don't think you ever did anything awful. Let it be. And the fight tonight wasn't

141

your fault."

He sniffed and shut the door before I could say anything else. The floor creaked as he walked away toward his bedroom.

For a long time I just sat there. My hands made fists. My brain made me open my fingers. Fist, fingers. Fist, fingers. J.B wasn't talking. Dumbass. He only talked when I didn't want to hear him. X, x, x, y. Fist, fingers. Had I been selfish with Dad, asking him my question? Making him talk to me? I had probably been selfish. Frog farts.

One fist, two fists. $2x + 6 =$ fists.

"Should apologize for being stupid."

My words sounded flat in the room.

J.B. Still didn't answer.

"Just go down the hall and say, 'I'm sorry for being weird.' I'm good at sorry." Fist, fingers. Frog farts.

After a minute or two of breathing, I got up. Tripped on my books and braces. Sat back down.

Graceful. J.B. sounded mean . . . and a little sad.

"Now you start talking." I kicked my Algebra book on top of my Earth Science book. Dumbass. This time when I stood up, I stayed up. "Graceful."

This is a bad idea. You should leave him alone. He doesn't want to talk to you.

"I'm going to say sorry. Then I'll leave him alone."

Just put your braces on and go to bed. J.B. sounded even sadder. It creeped me out.

"In a second. Graceful. X and y." I headed for my bedroom door before he could talk me out of it. He didn't call after me as I stumbled into the hall and made the floor creak.

Then the house sounded so quiet I stopped moving. Like I shouldn't make any more noise or something. Like I'd bother Mom, but Mom was on her way to work or wherever Mom went when she got mad. Graceful. I wasn't bothering anybody. Not yet. X, y, 2x.

I started walking again, toward Mom and Dad's room. When I got closer, I heard crunching and clunking and rustling, kind of like a mouse. A big mouse. Dad-mouse, maybe. When I got to his door, it was open. The bedside lamp was on, and in the bathroom, a little light. I figured Dad was in the big walk-in closet Mom called "the storage shed." Except it wasn't really a shed. It had lots of Mom clothes and Dad clothes and lots of shoes and bags and suitcases and boxes. Around the top, it had more shelves with more boxes. Tax boxes, picture boxes, keepsake boxes. Something Mom called "what-not boxes." Some had labels. Lots didn't. $2x + boxes = junk$. Graceful.

Dad was in the storage shed, in the junk. X. Y.

When I walked up, he had a shoebox open, looking at something. I couldn't see it. Whatever was in that brown box, he was touching it over and over, like it was a kitten or something alive.

"Um, Dad?"

He slammed down the box lid.

"Sorry." I rubbed my hands together like he'd been doing in my room. My bad hand felt numb and cold and clumsy. "I mean—about scaring you, yes, but, sorry for before."

As I got closer. Dad moved the shoebox away from me. "You don't have anything to apologize for. I told you, the fight wasn't your fault."

That again.

143

Did he think I was stupid? Graceful. Dumbass. I quit rubbing and made fists by accident. Let them go. Fist, fingers, breathe. One, two, three . . . fist, fingers, breathe.

Coughing and blinking, Dad stuffed the brown box back on a shelf over his head. When he turned around again, I was ready.

"I'm sorry about my questions," I said really fast before I could get stuck on Algebra problems or call him a name. "I'm . . . sorry . . . for getting stuck. On questions. And stupid stuff."

"You can't help that. I understand." Dad rubbed the top of his legs like he was drying off his palms. Then he patted my arm.

"No." Fist, fingers, breathe. Fist, fingers, breathe. "I could . . . do better. I can do better . . . when I'm slow. I mean, when I slow down. When I focus." Fist, fingers . . . "And pay attention like I learned at Carter."

"Fair enough." He stepped forward and steered me out of the junk box storage shed closet.

"So, I'm sorry." Fist, fingers, breathe. I was doing it! Focusing. Trying harder. Making sense when it mattered. Why wasn't Mom here for this? She might get un-mad, at least a little. "Okay?"

Dad stopped, put his hands on my shoulders, and turned me to face him. His eyes were red. "Yes and no. I don't want you to have to worry about how you act around here. I want you to be able to relax at home. Do you understand?"

"I—uh, yeah?" I blinked. I didn't understand. Not really, but sort of. Kind of.

Dad squeezed my shoulders. "Talk however it comes out. Just—talk to me more. Tell me what's going on. This is where you live. It should be a supportive place. A peaceful, no-stress place."

Here?

I almost laughed, but fist-fingers-breathed and thought about hoochie-mamas and frog farts and $2x + 6 = 12 = 8$, but 8 still didn't look right, even in my head.

Here with J.B. and Mom and the wrong-color bedspread and the football rug I had folded up and all the downstairs pictures of ghosts, here, me, relax? Fist, fingers. 2x, 2x, 2x.

"Relax" popped out of my mouth.

Dad smiled. "Yeah. So don't worry so much. Say what you want. Ask what you want."

"But Mom doesn't. Relax." I bit my lip, took a breath, slowed down. "I mean, she doesn't like it when I ask. When I stupid-talk. Big Larry."

"She'll come around. Just give her a little more time, Jersey."

Another squeeze to my shoulders. Another smile. Dad looked like he really believed that.

I couldn't get mad at him when he really believed it, could I? Mama Rush would have gotten mad at me. Graceful. But, I wasn't Mama Rush. No robes. No cigarettes. So I didn't get mad.

"A guy peed on me at school. Dumbass." I bit my lip again. Stopped the next five or six stupid words. "I have to eat peanuts with cheerleaders and I don't want a babysitter anymore. No funeral Wench. Please."

Dad let go of my shoulders. Looked like he was trying to sew up a rip in his brain. A couple of times, he opened his mouth, but shut it again and scratched his head where he would have gotten a stupid-mark if he'd shot himself like I did. But Dad wouldn't shoot himself. He'd never pull the trigger. Graceful dumbass.

All of a sudden, his face got all shiny. "Wenchel. Wenchel in the black dresses. You don't want her to escort you anymore?"

"No!" I let out a great big breath. "I mean, yes. No Wench. No more."

"Even though some guy peed on you?" He got hold of my shoulder again, but only one hand this time.

"Yes. Even with pee. No Wench." I smiled. Half my mouth, anyway. Good enough.

Dad smiled back. "I'll call the school and see what I can do. Now I'm hungry all over again. Come on downstairs and let's heat up a pizza."

I nodded. "Pizza Wench." My stomach actually growled, never mind pot roast only a couple of hours ago.

With a wider grin, Dad put his arm around my shoulders. As we half-walked, half-lurched down the hall together, he said, "So you're eating lunch with Leza Rush and the cheerleaders? I'd eat peanuts, too. Can't dribble those on your shirt."

chapter 13

I have this dream where both legs work and both arms work and I don't have any scars on the outside. I'm sitting on the edge of my bed in dress blues holding a pistol in one hand and a brown box in the other. Sunlight brightens the dust and ashes in my room and darkens all the places where I've nicked the walls and doors. The football rug, the one Mama Rush gave me when I made the team my freshman year, is folded neatly on my dresser so it won't get messy. I give it one last look before I turn back to what I'm doing. My fingers tingle as I touch the box. Inside, there's proof. Inside, there's a reason. Everyone will understand when they see what's in the box. I lift the gun to my mouth. It tastes oily and dusty all at once as I close my lips on cold gunmetal—but I can't. Not in the mouth. I'm shaking, but I lift the barrel to the side of my head. The tip digs into my skin. I'm thinking about what's inside the box, and all the dust and ashes in places I didn't even know. Then I'm squeezing the trigger and looking at the box and the dust and ashes and feeling my hand shake and there's noise and fire and pain and I'm falling, falling, my broken head smashing into my pillow . . .

The box. The box in Dad's closet.

I wrote about it in my memory book. I fell asleep thinking about it. I woke up thumping my stupid-mark with my hand brace and thinking about it, and I got dressed thinking about it.

You need to check out that box, J.B. whispered while I pulled on my tennis shoes. The green laces were still springy.

"Box, fox, rocks. It's Dad's box. Dad's got problems right now. Later, maybe." When I pulled the laces, they snapped back in place. "Rocks. Knocks."

What if there's something important in the box?

"I'm not looking in the box. Knock, knock."

I know there's something important in that box. You need to find out.

I made my shoelaces spring again, then stood up. "No box," I said, just in case J.B. decided to listen. "No rocks, no fox."

Could be some kind of doctor's papers. Or maybe a picture. What if it's a letter you wrote? Do you think you really left a letter and your dad's hiding it?

"Dad's not hiding stuff. Rocks. He's getting dressed."

Maybe it's a tape. You could have left a tape . . .

I hummed so I couldn't hear him.

But it might be a suicide note. You might have said something about him in the note, so he hid it. Or maybe he found out about something really awful you did, and he's hiding the proof.

I hummed louder as I picked up my memory book and headed for the door. No more forgetting the memory book. I'd written that down.

A note. That's probably it. Or something that'll get you arrested.

Even though I got to the hall and shut the door, I could still hear J.B. talking about the note. But I didn't want to think about notes. I hadn't left a note. If I'd left a note, that would explain everything, and Dad would never hide that from me.

Would he?

A note. In the box.

I squeezed the cover of my memory book and stumbled down the steps. Maybe if I thought about shoelaces, I wouldn't think about notes. Shoelaces were better than notes. If I said shoelaces, it wouldn't bother Dad. But if I said notes like a note in that box, he might understand and get mad. Or worse, sad.

No note. Don't say note. Say shoelaces. Say frog farts. Say anything else.

When I got to the kitchen, Dad was pouring healthy oatmeal into a bowl for me. I didn't know if Mom was still asleep, since it was Saturday, and she slept late now, even though she never used to do that Before. Note. Box. Shoelaces. Shoelaces!

Dad had a conference to go to all day, for the next two days. Continuing education. CEUs. I wondered if I got CEUs, if I'd be able to do Algebra and Civics and Earth Science.

Civics, maybe. But probably not Algebra. Probably not Earth Science, either.

There probably wasn't anything in that box. Especially not a note.

"Note—I mean, Civics," I said as I sat down. "CEUs."

No note!

When I stirred my healthy oatmeal. It stuck to my spoon. No, no, no, no note.

Dad grunted and ate a bite of his oatmeal, followed by a bite of not-so-healthy leftover pizza. Don't know how he swallowed oatmeal-pizza, but he managed. With milk. Gross.

"Make you a deal, Jersey. If you go to my conference, I'll do your homework." Dad wiggled his eyebrows.

"Earth Science and Algebra, too? CEUs. Milk-pizza."

"Ugh. No on the Algebra. Deal's off." He smiled. That made the circles under his eyes look bigger. He really needed to shave.

Shave. Shave. Shave.

I passed on the leftover pepperoni pizza when he offered me some, counted a lot in my head, and let him burn some Kool-Aid glue toast for me because it made him happy. Then I used it to scoop up the oatmeal. The oatmeal made the toast taste a lot less like Kool-Aid glue. Nothing like milk-pizza. At least I didn't think it was. I managed to chew up and swallow a bite. Milk might help a lot with the glue, only it wouldn't taste so good with the Kool-Aid part.

"Is, um, Mom—is she still asleep?"

Dad sniffed and put down his pizza. "She pulled an all-nighter at the bank. They're being audited next week, I think. Just a normal audit, but still. It's a lot of work."

The circles under his eyes got bigger whenever he talked.

There was a fairy tale about that once. Every time some kid told a lie, the circles under his eyes grew. No, wait. It was his nose. His nose got bigger.

"Nose," I said, only it came out "Naw" because of the glue toast and sticky oatmeal. *Naw* sounded less like *note* than *nose*. Good. Naw, naw, naw, naw.

"Are you seeing Mama Rush today, Jersey?"

"Naw. Wait! Yes. Glue."

"Okay." Dad grinned and went after his last bite of pepperoni pizza. "Finish up and I'll drop you off on my way to the conference."

"I told you already, you're tense, boy." Mama Rush's voice sounded like a dog growling. She stared at my memory book. "Loosen up."

I took a deep breath. Tried to make my face look relaxed. How did a relaxed face look? Hands on the table. Slow breathing. Look relaxed. Look relaxed.

The sun was bright.

I could see heat rising around our patio table at The Palace, but at least I couldn't see Big Larry. For now, anyway. My eyes kept jumping from the glued ceramic piggy bank to the patio door, like the door might pop open any second. I was tense, boy. And I had sweat behind my ears. Gross. Wet ears. Worse than pizza and milk. But not worse than the glued piggy bank.

Loosen up. Loosen up. I was tense, boy. Boy was I tense. Wet ears. The pig looked like a pink alien with a great big butt-face. Its nose was all smashed. One of the ears squiggled

151

sideways. It didn't have a tail, half of a back leg was missing, one front leg looked like my springy shoelaces, and the rest of it was all lumpy. Wet ears. It was hot. I think Mama Rush glued some of its smashed nose to its sides. Or maybe she glued pieces of something else all over it. I couldn't tell. Those sides looked like pink butts, too. It was a really bad piggy bank.

Yeah, but it holds the money. Can't have everything.

That's what Mama Rush said when she put it on the table. It holds the money. She turned my memory book around a little, squinting at my scribbles. Wet ears. Her lounging dress was red, and she had a red ribbon around her hair bun.

"You need a little computer." Her gaze flicked toward the patio door, then back to the memory book. "Maybe there's money in that box you're worrying about. If there is, your dad should buy you a computer so I can read what you write."

"Shoelaces. I think there's a note in the box. Maybe. Money." I glanced at the patio door and rubbed behind my wet ears. "Or a tape. Secret papers about me. Maybe I wrote a note."

Mama Rush blew smoke out of her nose. "I can't believe your father would keep something like that from you. Y'all had all that therapy—and he knows you're hunting for answers."

She was looking at the patio door, not at me. So I looked at the patio door, too. The table felt so hot under my fingers, from the sun. No wind. Nothing moving. The air smelled like wet and smoke and glue, with a little bit of flowers and perfume. The patio door wasn't opening.

"Therapy. Shoelaces. Answers—what if he thinks the note's too bad?" I couldn't quit staring at the door. I wished Mama Rush would stop so I could stop, too. "He might think I don't need to know. Or that it'll make me upset again."

She thought about this for half a cigarette. Both of us stared at the door. Smoke floated around the butt-faced pig like flat pieces of fog. From the corner of my eye, I kept seeing red from her lounge dress and ribbon. A red djinni today, looking at the patio door even more than me. Her eyes seemed kind of wet.

Was she waiting for Big Larry, too? Was he her boyfriend? He couldn't be her boyfriend. Did she miss him? No way. How could anybody miss Big Larry?

Mama Rush sighed and closed the memory book. "What do you think about Number Two on your list, Jersey? Do you think it's possible you did something to feel awful about—so awful you'd want to hurt yourself?"

"Yes, I did. I had to." Finally, finally, I quit looking at the door, but only because Mama Rush stopped. I pointed at the memory book. "Almost out of reasons. Butt-pig. Alien."

"You've still got one more on that list. Number Six, that Arroyo girl."

"Awful guilt. It's got to be guilt. I wouldn't blow my head off over a girl. I like my head."

The next thing I heard was a big cackle. "Boy, you used to dress up in your mother's yoga tights, stick a Viking helmet on your head, and bash into the furniture—and that was just a prelude to football. You never treated your head very well."

"Viking? Tights. No way."

Mama Rush was belly-laughing now. "They were pink as

this piggy bank, and yes, you did." She waved her hand and chopped up one of the smoke-fog-pieces. The butt-face alien pig rattled when she stamped out her cigarette in the glued ashtray. She used the ashtray I made her every time we talked. It had lots of burned spots, but she didn't act like she cared.

"Not fair!" I grabbed my memory book and dragged it across the table to me. "I didn't know you when you were little. If I did, I'd have stories on you. Butt-alien-pig. Tights? Tights."

My face was hurting from smiling so big. And I was laughing in little chokes. Pink tights. Viking helmet.

Not possible.

Frog farts.

"Catherine," said a deep voice.

"Farts!" My bad hand clenched tight. My teeth clamped together.

Mama Rush quit laughing fast. Her face went flat. Her eyes got squinty and her lips tightened up.

Both my hands made fists as I looked up at the man standing between us. Farts. Tights. He scared me. Sneaking up and talking. He was tall. Looked like he might have had muscles a long time ago. Talk. Talking! He must have come through the door while we were laughing. Sneak. And he called Mama Rush by her first name. I didn't know a single person who did that. Except the tall sneak. Whoever he was. Not Big Larry. At least Big Larry didn't make Mama Rush look like she'd eaten Dad's toast and oatmeal.

"Kool-Aid glue." I tried to relax my fingers. My bad hand throbbed. And my jaw. And my head was starting to hurt, like a toothache behind my brain.

The man stared at me. Mama Rush stared at him. She tapped her fingers on the table, sighed, and said, "Carl, this is Jersey. Jersey, Carl."

Carl wasn't anything like Big Larry. He didn't act like Big Larry, either. No red face, no crying, no bad arm in a sling, no scooter. Carl had on jeans and a black shirt, and he would have looked lots younger except his hair and beard were silver white. He was frowning like my dad used to Before, right before he grounded me or took my computer or did something else creepy "for my own good."

"I'm sorry to interrupt you," he said in that deep voice, "but Catherine, can we please talk for a moment?"

Mama Rush still had that flat, narrow-eyed, tight-lipped look. Carl might not have been Big Larry, but he wasn't any smarter. If Mama Rush looked at me that way, I'd duck. Or run. Probably both. But I'd known her since Viking helmets and pink yoga tights, and maybe Carl hadn't.

She didn't hit him, though. She just said, "We have nothing to discuss."

Whoa.

My pragmatics might have sucked, but even I heard the ice falling off those words.

Carl—who must have been stupider than me and Big Larry put together—folded his hands and tried again. "Please. If you'd just hear me out, you might understand. It was a bad moment. A weak moment. I—"

"You what?" Mama Rush got loud in a hurry. On instinct, I scooted the alien butt-face pig and the glued ashtray closer to me before she could throw one of them. "You don't have any better sense than God gave a box turtle! You got one mashed-up brain cell that can't tell

155

right from wrong? Don't make me get off this scooter, Carl. And don't make me keep talking. You won't like anything I have to say."

This time, Carl got the message. People on the street in front of The Palace probably got the message. Part of my brain got the message, too. For a second, I saw faces. Girls. Not Leza, not Elana. Girls I didn't know. Faces. Three or four at least. Some laughing. Some crying. Then Elana, or maybe it was Todd's girlfriend, looking at me like Mama Rush was looking at Carl. Bad look. Faces. Faces. Bad. I shook my head to make the faces stop.

You're so self-centered . . .

No. Not that. Not that now. Need to be quiet.

Carl—really, really, stupid Carl—he wasn't quiet. He tried to talk again. I blinked. Faces. The faces stayed and went, came back and went. Self-centered, self-centered. You're so self-centered.

Mama Rush started to yell. She didn't take a breath, and she used lots of words I was never supposed to say again because I shot myself and brain-injured people don't know when to use words like that and when to shut up.

If I were Carl, I definitely would have shut up. Even if I couldn't see faces. But Carl needed stupid-marks like me, great big shiny ones on both sides of his head, because he kept going, "I—I—but, I—"

Mama Rush talked so fast and loud I only got pieces in between the faces.

"Floozy" and "faithless" and "far-fetched." F-words to go with faces. Lots of f-words, and another one I can't say. She used that one a few times, in different ways.

Girl faces. I shook my head again. Too many faces.

You're so self-centered I bet you think I'm mad at you.

Faces. Attila the Face. No. Attila the Red, who was still wearing red, appeared at the patio door, hit the auto-open button, and hurried over to where we were sitting. She had her hand on her credit card headset and she was breathing hard like she ran all the way from wherever Attilas come from.

"Is there a problem here?" Her eyes automatically went to me.

"Faces. Tights and Vikings." This time, I did duck. Just put my head down, hugging the alien pig and the ashtray. Too many faces. Too much yelling.

You're so self-centered . . .

You're so self-centered . . .

"Young man, do you need to go home?" Attila asked.

Mama Rush came off her scooter. "How many times do I have to tell you people? This boy's with me. He's my visitor. And I say when I'm finished with my visitors, not you! Jersey, sit up straight."

I sat up fast.

"See what I've been telling you, boy? See? You don't loosen up, you'll end up like *her*." Mama Rush glared at Attila, then back at me. "Do you want to go home or not?"

Butt-face. Pigs. Faces. Tights. No matter what I said, I was so dead. Aliens! What should I say? No? Yes?

You're so self-centered—no. No. Shut up.

My lips started working. I tried to swallow, but that part of my throat didn't work. Nothing came out but an idiot-sounding "Aaah, uuuhh . . ."

Carl folded his arms. Attila kept tapping her headset.

Mama Rush's expression softened a little. "Listen. I don't

want to let you down, Jersey, but today's probably not the best day for me to help you. Maybe you should go on home, and let's do this tomorrow or next weekend. Do you have money for a cab?"

"Tights." I croaked, scrubbing my pocket with my hand. "Pigs. Aliens. Faces."

"Okay, then." She patted my shoulder. Her eyes were starting to look a little wider and more watery. "Go up front and call a ride."

When I stood, she reminded me to take my memory book, and she asked me to put the pig and the ashtray back in her room. She said all that calm and sweetlike.

Without looking at Carl, she said, "Why don't you catch a cab, too, Romeo man?"

She didn't say that sweetlike at all.

I wondered where she wanted the taxi to take Carl, but I didn't stick around to find out. As fast as I could, I tucked my memory book under my bad arm, picked up the mended presents, lurched over to the auto-open button, elbowed it, and got the hell off that patio.

Without looking behind me, I headed toward Mama Rush's room with the alien pig and the ashtray full of ashes. Would she hit Romeo man with her scooter and turn him into ashes? If she did, Attila might throw her out. Ashes. Where was I? This hall didn't look familiar. My bad hand burned. I looked left and right. The numbers on the doors blurred. This place did look lots like all the hospitals I'd been to. Smelled bad, too. Like raw stink here and there. Did Romeo man ever stink like this?

Carl had to be Mama Rush's boyfriend, not Big Larry.

Carl, the Romeo man. Nice. But, also, sort of gross if I thought about it too much. This Juliet was way unhappy with her Romeo man. Tights. If I'd stayed on the patio, she might have gotten unhappy with me. Pink tights. Pink pigs. Butt-face aliens. I had no idea where I was going. I couldn't remember Mama Rush's room number.

"Frog farts," I said out loud. "Hoochie-mama. Frog farts. Frog farts." I kept saying it, made myself walk slower, made myself breathe slower. "Frog farts." Little by little, I stopped walking. Didn't even drop my memory book, or the ashtray, or the alien pig.

"Frog farts." More deep breaths. Look around. Look around. Tights and frog farts. Okay, the next hallway looked right. A few steps later, I found it. The door was cracked, so I just pushed it open.

Mama Rush's room was about the same size as mine, except it had a kitchen on one wall. She had a bedroom and a bathroom, too, but those were so little only one person fit inside them. Just her. Not Romeo man. Good. Because that was the gross part.

I put the pig and the ashtray on her bedroom dresser where I knew she kept them, and for a minute, I stared at the pile of clay and ceramic that hadn't been fixed. It was right there, beside the mended presents and her glue.

Probably no way to save that mess. I couldn't even tell what those presents used to be. They were just broken pieces of nothing now, but Mama Rush hadn't told me she couldn't fix them, so I figured she hadn't given up yet. Or maybe she didn't want to hurt my feelings because she was scared I'd cry like Big Larry. Romeo man would have been smarter if he'd just cried. She might not have told him to call a taxi if he'd cried, even though she was mad.

Only, halfway home, in the back of the stinky-sock-smelling cab, I remembered what was waiting at home. No Dad, no Mom. No friends. No girlfriends, no tights, no Viking helmets. Just J.B.

J.B. and the box in Dad's closet.

By the time I got to my house, I was sick of the faces.

Sick of the pictures and words in my head.

You're so self-centered I bet you think I'm mad at you.

God. My head hurt so bad I wanted to throw up.

Who were those faces?

You're so self-centered . . . so self-centered . . . you're so . . .

Head, head, head. I wanted to beat my head against the front door. It hurt. Hurt bad. It wasn't even lunchtime yet, so Dad wouldn't be home for hours. I'd be alone with the faces. And the box. If I stayed downstairs, maybe J.B. would stay quiet. But the box was upstairs, and the box felt like a big magnet even though I was still standing outside the front door.

I kept squeezing my memory book as I squinted at the Rush house, hating the bright sunlight. No cars. Leza was probably at the track, so I couldn't call her yet. Maybe soon, though. If I could last long enough. I unlocked the front door and stuffed the keys back in my pocket. It would be okay. I'd just stay downstairs and rub the sides of my head until I could move without my brain exploding. I wouldn't go upstairs, so J.B. and the box wouldn't bother me.

No box, no note, no bother. No being selfish, no being a Big Larry, and definitely no being a Romeo man, even if I had taken a cab. Faces. Faces, faces, faces.

Don't drop the memory book, turn the doorknob, close the door behind me. No air-conditioning the neighborhood. See, Mom? I remembered. My pragmatics were better. I didn't look up at all the ghost pictures, just put my memory book on the steps and stood still. Little by little, the faces faded away. No faces. Thank you. No faces. Thank you.

No faces now.

Just the box.

The box was up those stairs, in my parents' room, in their closet. Just sitting there waiting. Maybe waiting for me. J.B. was up there, too, in my room. He got on my nerves, but at least he talked to me, even if he was a ghost.

The box. Closet. Ghost.

My fingers curled hard, making me grind my teeth. My throat ached. There was no way I left a suicide note. Did I? Ghost.

But if I did . . .

No, no, no. Ghost. Tights. Viking helmets. I needed to talk to Mama Rush again before I looked in the box. Or Leza. Somebody. If I found a note, my dad . . .

"Note," I whispered. My voice sounded awful. I needed a glass of water, or maybe Dad didn't drink all the milk with his pizza. Viking helmets.

I started for the kitchen and heard a noise.

Stopped. Listened.

Nothing.

Was I hearing things?

Shoelaces. Tights.

Had J.B. come down from my room and gotten in the kitchen? Tights! My heart started beating, beating. I didn't know whether to go to the kitchen, go upstairs, or go back outside.

Another noise.

"Tights!"

And then, "Jersey?"

Mom's voice.

My knees almost bent and made me fall. Mom came out of the kitchen. She was wearing jeans and a T-shirt instead of bank clothes, and she was smiling. Then her eyebrows jumped together over her nose. "Are you all right, honey? You're pale and shaking."

"S-Scared me," I managed. "Thought—bank—tights. Aliens." Get a grip! If I go Big Larry, she'll just get mad and leave.

But she didn't get mad. She came up and gave me a short Mom-hug. "I'm so sorry. I came home because I knew your father had a conference, and I thought you might be . . . um, that you might want to do something together today. Like, have a big lunch and go to the movies?"

She smiled and looked all hopeful and kind of nervous.

I was too surprised to say anything, but I thought about butt-face alien pigs in tights and Viking helmets and pragmatics and a whole bunch of other stuff I needed to keep inside my mouth. My hand hurt. My head hurt. I didn't even care. My mom wanted to go to the movies. This was my mom. Mine. The mom I used to know.

Refusing to scream anything about Big Larry or frog farts, I made myself smile at her and say, "Sure."

The word came out right! Just one word, but it made her look bright and shiny. My mom. The mom I knew. Pragmatics. I wanted to fall down again, I was so happy.

"It's a date, then." Mom ruffled my hair. "I'm—I'm so proud of you for trying so hard. Now come to the kitchen. I promise not to make oatmeal or toast."

chapter 14

Sunday felt new and happy, even though it was raining.

I woke up early and smelled eggs. Eggs and biscuits and unhealthy bacon. Probably gravy, too.

Mom was cooking!

No oatmeal. No toast. No Kool-Aid glue. Hallelujah. This might be the best day since I came home. Yesterday was pretty cool, too. The movie was fun, and I ate lots of popcorn to keep from saying idiot things and upsetting Mom. It worked. She stayed calm and shiny all through eating dinner out and coming home. She even said nice stuff to Dad about how he was dressed and about the brochures he brought from the conference.

Now I was about to get a real breakfast.

I couldn't get my arm and leg braces off fast enough.

J.B. didn't even open his loud mouth until I was tugging up my shorts. Of course, when he did, he tried to ruin my morning.

You haven't looked in the box yet. You need to look in

the box.

"I went to the movies with Mom. Box. Note. I mean, I don't want to look in the box. If there's a note, I don't want to read it."

Yes, you do.

"Do not. Frog farts. These laces aren't so springy now." Maybe Dad would change them for me. Or Mom. She might not get weird about springy shoelaces since she was cooking breakfast. If she was cooking breakfast, she had to be happier. "Blue laces. Maybe yellow this time. New laces. Shoelaces."

That sort of rhymes. You're a genius.

"I'm a five-year-old genius. But I'm trying harder, and sometimes I focus. Sometimes I slow down and get it right like they taught me at Carter. And I'm eating with cheerleaders and doing my homework and wearing my braces every night, so maybe I'm six now, or seven. I think I'm a little older, at least. Shoelaces. Not so Big Larry. Not so selfish."

J.B. laughed while I did my best to tighten my shoelaces even though they weren't so springy.

You're still selfish. His voice changed a little, got higher pitched. *You're so self-centered I bet you think I'm mad at you . . . Remember that, genius?*

"Not listening to you."

That was a lie. For a second, I saw faces again. Girl faces. Yelling in girl voices. Self-centered. So self-centered.

Humming to make J.B. shut up and keep the faces away, I grabbed my memory book but didn't open it. Inside was the list with two numbers still not crossed off. If I opened the cover and flipped a few pages, I knew exactly what I'd see.

1. ~~Maybe on drugs.~~
2. *Did something awful I felt guilty.*
3. ~~My life sucked.~~
4. ~~Heard voices telling me to off myself.~~
5. ~~Parents really brother and sister/aliens/abusive.~~
6. *Elana Arroyo—ask Todd.*

I did something awful and felt guilty, and Elana Arroyo. Sooner or later, I had to get Todd to talk to me.

Maybe you did something awful to Elana Arroyo. Maybe that's why you keep remembering her yelling at you. Maybe you did something really awful. Ask Todd. He'll stuff your teeth down your throat.

The cover of my memory book was dirty. I needed to wash it. I needed a new string and a new pen. Maybe I should use one of the not-so-springy green shoelaces so they wouldn't go to waste.

You're so self-centered . . .

Did J.B. say that, or did I think it?

I looked toward the corner of the bedroom, into the dusty shadow where J.B. lived. Rain blew against the windowpane. I blinked, but I didn't see any sign of him, not even sparkles. Had I ever seen sparkles, or did I imagine those, too?

"Shoelaces."

"Jerrrr-seeeeey!" Mom called. "Breakfast!"

"Breakfast," I muttered. "Shoelaces."

Okay. Okay. Mom sounded happy and she made real food and she and Dad weren't yelling at each other, so no freaking out. No going Big Larry. No talking about stupid stuff.

No talking about the note in the box? No talking about

"Boxes. Elana. Todd. Faces. Shut up."

He didn't shut up, and I slammed the door behind me. Then I worried Mom would get mad about that, but she didn't. Neither did Dad. He just ate a lot of biscuits and got crumbs all over his suit. I couldn't say anything, because I got crumbs everywhere, too. Bacon crumbs, egg crumbs, biscuit crumbs. We talked about school but not about grades or getting peed on. We talked about Dad's job and Mom's job but not about fighting or spending nights away from home.

Whenever I wanted to say stupid stuff, I just took another bite of something. Definitely better than oatmeal and Kool-Aid glue toast. Way better than peanuts. Even better than cheerleaders. Sort of. Outside, it thundered and rained, but inside, we ate breakfast. It really was the best day since I left the hospital, until Dad had to go to his weekend conference, and Mom had to go to the bank to finish getting ready for the audit. They both cleaned up the kitchen, and they both kissed me, made sure I had their phone numbers, told me they'd call—then they were gone, and I was alone.

Alone in the house. Full, smiling, but alone.

With the box.

But I wasn't going to look in the box. If I did, and I found something bad or something that upset me, I might ruin everything, and I didn't want to ruin anything.

"Big Larry. Romeo man. J.B." I wasn't going to be a ruiner like them.

The kitchen table was so clean I could see my reflection in the dark brown wood. I could see reflections of the rain on the kitchen windows, too. If I just stayed at the table staring at myself and the raindrops, I'd never go upstairs, and I'd never open the box, and I wouldn't ruin anything.

I tapped my fingers on the reflections.

Was Leza home? I could call her. Or Mama Rush. That's what I'd do. I'd call them. After I sat for a while. If I was careful, I could stretch things out and only go upstairs with enough time to do Algebra and Civics for tomorrow. Then I wouldn't be tempted to look in the box and Dad would come home and probably Mom since she was so happy, and everything would be fine.

But it was hard to sit and do nothing.

I yawned.

Then I stared at the raindrops.

It took a few seconds more before I thought about the box. So I looked up Leza's number and dialed it.

Somebody answered on the first ring.

"Hello?" Todd. Just my luck.

Don't say Elana, whatever you do, don't say Elana Arroyo.

"Hello?" Todd said again, sounding a little annoyed.

Focus. Focus. Go slow. "Is . . . Leza . . . there?"

I yawned. I couldn't help myself, but I hoped Todd hadn't heard that. He might have, because he wasn't saying anything. Did I forget something?

"Please?" I said just in case, and, "Sorry."

Todd made a bull-snort. "Yeah, just a minute."

Freak.

He didn't say it, but I sort of heard it along with the rain, which was still tapping away outside. Todd calling me a freak didn't bother me like it did when I first got home. I knew I wasn't a total Big Larry. Not yet, anyway. I was trying harder and harder not to be.

Leza came on with, "Jersey? Is something wrong?"

"No." I stared at my still-sleepy face in the kitchen table. Her voice sounded so soft on the phone, like music. "Just calling."

"I don't believe you. Mama Rush told me about that box."

Should have figured that. I couldn't get mad at either one of them, though. Especially not Leza. "Romeo man. They had a fight."

"Yeah, I know. Carl really pissed in his Wheaties." Someone grumbled in the background and Leza said, "What? But Mom, he did! Oh, okay. Jersey, Carl really, um, messed in his nest. Anyway, I think you should stay away from that box. It's none of your business."

"Me, too. No box." Romeo man. I couldn't be anyone's Romeo man, not with all my stupid-marks. But Leza was nice to me. It was almost like she didn't care how I looked. "My parents are gone right now."

"You could ask your dad about the box when he gets back," she said. "But nosing through his things, that would be wrong."

I couldn't smell breakfast anymore, and my stomach rumbled, and it was still raining. All gray and dark outside. How long had I been asleep on the table?

"No box. You want . . . to talk? Over here?"

She sighed. "I can't. It's Sunday family time. Ever since you—well, you know—my parents have been doing this. We have to eat lunch together, and we all play stupid board games, then go to Lake Raven for dinner." Grumbling kicked up in the background. Leza groaned. "Okay, whatever. The games aren't stupid, but I can't come over. Just a second."

She put her hand over the phone. I could hear a little

bit, but not much. She was asking something. Mumbled voices answering, and one loud one—Todd, I figured. Then Leza got louder with, "Why not?" And, "My choice if I want to talk to him, the doctors and Mama Rush said . . ." And, quieter, "God . . . forgive . . . ashamed."

More mumbling. More loud stuff from Todd.

Then Leza came back. "I'm sorry, I've got to go, but I want you to promise me—stay out of your dad's stuff."

It was my turn to sigh. "Okay. Frog farts." The rain was getting louder.

"Promise me, Jersey."

"I promise."

"No opening that box."

"I promise. Frog farts."

"Do all of your homework, clean up your room, and do something nice for your parents. That should keep you busy."

"Homework. Major frog farts."

"I'll talk to you tomorrow." She laughed. "Hoochie-mama."

She hung up without saying good-bye, and the last thing I heard was her starting to yell at Todd again. I was grinning. It was nice to talk to her. I never wanted to stop, but I knew she had to play stupid board games that weren't really stupid. Wouldn't want her to mess in her nest or piss in her Wheaties.

"Wheaties." I turned the phone off and looked up the number for the Palace. Then I turned the phone back on and dialed. No answer. I pushed the off button and put the phone down, pulled all of my money out of my pocket, and counted it. Not enough for a cab ride to The Palace and back.

I could check in with Mom and Dad. That would waste a little more time. I turned the phone back on, and the low-battery warning chirped.

Great.

The only other cordless phones were upstairs, one in my bedroom and one in my parents' bedroom. Guess it was time to do homework after all.

My body felt heavy when I stood up. I'd been at the table so long it was hard to move, but I stretched and went to the downstairs bathroom. Peed without peeing on myself. When I was finished, I washed my hands, washed my face, washed my hands again. Stared at myself in the mirror for a while and made some faces.

The left side of my smile still didn't work right. All of my stupid-marks were still where I left them. I needed a haircut, and I needed to borrow Dad's electric razor.

After a while, I got tired of standing there.

"Don't be stupid. You can go upstairs without looking in the box." When I talked, my mouth looked funny. Half-a-mouth. Frog farts. Did Leza really not care what I looked like? I told her I'd do my homework and clean my room and do something nice for my parents. I promised I wouldn't look in the box. So, I'd go upstairs and do all that other stuff. Then one of my parents might come home, and everything would be okay.

. . .

I just needed a phone. Really. That's the only reason I went into my parents' bedroom. The phone downstairs was dead, and I hadn't put my phone on the charger so it was dead, and I'd finished my homework. Cleaned my room, too, but I couldn't think of anything nice to do for my parents, and I was sick of listening to J.B., so I wanted to call Mama Rush. Only, I didn't have a phone, so while the rain tap-tapped on the roof, I went to get one off Dad's dresser, right across from the closet.

Now I was standing there with the phone in my hand, staring at the closet. If I went into the closet, I'd see the box. So I just wouldn't walk into the closet. I'd take the phone and go back to my room. Frog farts. Simple. Take the phone, leave. Take the phone, leave.

I threw the phone on the bed and cursed instead.

Enough with this crap. I was sick of thinking about the box. Really sick of trying not to look in it. I'd just go in the closet, look once, and leave. Then I'd know. Then it would be off my mind, and nothing would be ruined.

But I'd promised Leza.

Leza wouldn't have to know, would she?

God, I sounded just like J.B. I'd been listening to him too long, which was another reason to get this box thing over with. Just a fast look. In and out.

Went fast enough getting in, too. I had to climb onto the bottom shelf of a closet organizer to reach the box. Hold on with the bad hand, reach with the good. Good boys go to heaven. Good, good. The box moved—ah, crap! Boxes! Boxes! Crashing. Going thud. Something hit my head. A shoe. An old checkbook bounced off my shoulder. Old paper-smell. Dust. I sneezed. More thuds. Boxes. Boxes everywhere. Shoes everywhere, and tax records, check stubs, pictures, and old jewelry. I got down off the organizer with the brown box I came for, but frog farts. In and out. In and out? I was such a total Big Larry, with lots and lots of work to do.

Box, box, box. I took the special box to my room and put it on the bed, where I could concentrate on it later. Then I went back to my parents' closet.

At first I tried to get stuff in the right boxes. After a while, I stuck stuff in whatever box was still open. I put boxes on the shelves. Other boxes fell off. Stupid!

By the time I finished, I was sniffing like a Big Larry baby. How would I ever get the brown box back on the shelf without knocking stuff off? But I had to try. Otherwise, my parents would know and get upset and I'd ruin everything all over again.

When I got to my room and sat down on the bed next to the box, my head was hurting. My hand was hurting. My scars felt like somebody was throwing darts into them.

About time, J.B. said. *You're slow.*

"Be quiet." I rubbed my nose with my shirt. "I'm tired."

Better hurry up and look and take it back. You'll be in big trouble.

"I promised Leza I wouldn't look. What if—"

Look in the box, Jersey.

Sweat broke out on the back of my neck. I shivered. My fingers drew up into a fist. "I'll just take it back. Bad idea. I didn't mean to do it."

You didn't mean to come upstairs, go to your parents' room, go into their closet, destroy stuff, bring this box here, look in the box—which part?

173

"Leave me alone!"

You don't want to be alone. Look in the box and go put it back.

My stomach growled. I needed some lunch. Or was it dinnertime? The rain took away all the light. I couldn't tell.

When I picked up the box, it felt sort of heavy. Why didn't I notice that before? Because of the closet disaster?

"Disaster." The lid felt rough under my fingers. "Look in the box and go put it back."

Could answers really be inside this stupid brown box?

Open it. J.B. sounded weird and different. Meaner. *Open it now.*

I closed my eyes and pulled off the lid.

When I opened my eyes, what I saw didn't make any sense.

My ears started to buzz. My scars and my bad hand hurt big-time. There were a lot of socks in the box. And around the sides, some pictures of me dressed for football and golf and R.O.T.C.—little-sized and worn out, like they came out of Dad's wallet.

And in the middle of all the socks and pictures, there was a big black thing.

I kept staring at it, trying to make my brain work. Socks, pictures. Socks, pictures. Socks, pictures, and the black thing. Socks, pictures. A green tag had my name on it, and a date, and a long number. The tag had EVIDENCE printed on it, and the police department's phone number, too. The green tag on the black thing.

My good hand shook harder than my bad hand as I picked it up. So cold. So heavy. Dad's box. Dad's box full of socks and pictures, and . . .

And? J.B. whispered. *You know what it is. Say it.*

"Socks. Pictures."

I swallowed.

"And the gun."

chapter 15

Rain.

There was never any rain in my dream.

No rain.

But it was still raining outside. It had been raining all day.

I coughed, but it sounded like a hiccup. The gun weighed so much it made my wrist droop. In the dream, it wasn't heavy. I lifted it easily, but now I couldn't. The barrel pointed toward my knee. In the dream, I had it in my mouth, then I moved it to the side of my head, but there wasn't any rain. Rain, rain, go away. No rain.

In the dream, there was only sunshine, enough to show the dust and ashes, if there were ever any ashes. In the dream, I didn't think about hot or cold, but now I was cold. I was shaking. And in the dream, I could taste the oil and metal, not smell it. Here, now, I could *smell* the gun. It might have been the socks, but all the socks looked clean and I didn't think socks smelled like metal.

"Metal," I whispered. "Socks."

I was wearing shorts. No uniform. And the rug Mama Rush made me, I hadn't picked it up and put it on the dresser. Socks. Socks. I could smell the gun. Smell it. It wasn't supposed to be like this.

"Socks. Oh, God. Socks." I had the gun in my hand. It was touching my leg. The tag on it was from the police—this had to be it. *The* gun. In my dream, it was bigger, but lighter.

Tears ran down my cheeks and across my mouth. Half of my mouth didn't work. I had scars on the outside now. One of my legs didn't work right and one of my arms didn't work right.

Socks. Metal. Smells. Heavy gun.

Did it have bullets? It was raining. Getting dark. I should have turned the light on, but the light might have made it sunny in my room and I might see all the dust and shoot myself again. Socks, socks. Breathe. I needed to breathe. Air. Bullets. Socks.

God, did the gun have bullets in it? I hadn't even looked. Didn't know if I could, one-handed. If it had bullets, I might shoot myself by accident. Back in the box. Put the gun back in the box. Pragmatics. When I left, the hospital banner said *Up and forward*. Up and forward, Hatch. The letters on the sign flashed. The letters changed colors. Did I write that in my memory book? The dirty white binder with the pen on the dirty string and *Hatch, Jersey* on the spine. Up and forward. Put the gun in the box. Don't be a Big Larry. Don't be a Romeo man. Don't be J.B. the second. No ruining. No ruiners. Pragmatics. Socks.

Put the gun in the box. Be careful. The gun might have bullets. I'd probably drop the box and shoot a hole in my foot. Or the wall. If I dropped it wrong, I might shoot my head again, only this time it would be an accident but nobody would believe me. Where was J.B.? Why wasn't he talking?

I couldn't make my body move. I sat there. Just kept sitting. Kept holding the heavy gun. I stared at it. I stared at the box and the socks. My head. It was hurting. Throbbing. Burning. I felt like my eyes would pop out. My scars ached, especially the one on my temple, I could feel the gun pressed against it. All I had to do was pick up the gun and it would be just like my dream, except I wouldn't shoot.

"Socks. Please. Socks. Pragmatics."

Who was crying? The world looked funny. My face was wet. Was I crying?

The gun had to go back in the box. I had to get it off my leg and put it up. Careful, careful, there might be bullets. No accidents. Socks. No ruining. I wasn't a ruiner.

My hand shook. The gun shook. I lifted it up, up. *Put it in the box. Just lay it in the box on top of the socks. Don't smell anything. Don't say anything. Don't think about shooting yourself. Put the gun on the socks. Put the gun in the box.*

Someone screamed so loud I screamed, too. Dropped the gun on the socks and screamed again—but the gun didn't shoot. It just fell and lay there on the socks and didn't move. I looked up at my bedroom doorway.

Mom.

Mom in her black bank skirt and black bank blouse, one hand on the doorframe, one hand on her mouth, frozen like ice. But her eyes. They moved back and forth, back and forth, and got bigger and bigger.

I thought about ponds, and walking out on bad ice, and how if it cracks, you fall in and drown before anybody can save you.

The ice statue was starting to break.

And the cracking was loud, loud, like gunshots.

First her fingers, then her hands, then her arms. She grabbed her hair and tore out big handfuls. Blond hair falling everywhere. Her mouth started to move. She said, "No! No! No!" Her eyes got huge like a cartoon. Her face went red. Tears. Spit on her mouth.

"Put it down!" she yelled. "No! Put it down!"

What? Put what down? Her hair. Oh, God. She was ripping it to bits. I tried to say something, coughed, choked a little. My teeth bounced together. My hands shook. The box and the socks and the gun shook. And then I knew. The gun. Put the box with the socks and the gun down.

Mom thought—she thought—

"No," I managed to get through my chatter-teeth. "I'm not—I just—I—"

She jumped toward me and knocked the box out of my hands. I covered my head with my good arm as the socks and the gun fell on the football rug.

The gun didn't shoot. It might not have bullets, but I couldn't think about bullets because my mom had me by the shirt and she shook me, shook me, until my teeth bounced together harder and the room moved. I tried to grab her hands, but I couldn't.

"Why?" she was screaming now. "If you don't tell me, I'll kill you! Why? Why?"

"Just—looking!" I shouted back.

She let go of my shirt and slapped me hard. My jaw popped. Fire on my face, racing from my chin to my stupid-mark. Water spilled out of my eye. The eye closed. Mom slapped me again, and I fell over on my pillow, holding

179

my face, crying. It hurt. God, it burned. My whole face throbbed. My scars felt like they were ripping open. Broken ice. Drowning before anybody could save me.

"I'll kill you!" Mom was screaming and sobbing and trying to hit me again. "I'll do it right. I won't mess it up. I'm not going through this again!" She grabbed at my arm, my shirt. Dug her nails in, trying to drag me back up to hit me better. Drowning. Drowning in broken ice. My scars would tear in half and I'd start bleeding and bleed to death, and she'd just keep hitting me, but she wasn't hitting me anymore, and she wasn't yelling.

"Stop," Dad said. "Sonya! Be still. I've got you. Jesus!"

I heard slaps and ripping sounds. Mom trying to kill Dad, too.

"Where did it come from?" she yelled. "How did he get it? You tell me that. Tell me, damn you!"

She was really hitting him.

He didn't answer her. He was trying to get his arms around her. Trying to hold her.

My face hurt. I rolled off my bed on the other side and pushed up on my good knee. My bad eye was all closed up. My good eye kept blinking. Tears splattered on my cheek and the green bedspread.

Dad wrestled with Mom until he got her sitting down on the floor. She beat on his arms and cried, but she didn't yell anything else. More like whispering between crying, "Why? How? Tell me." When she saw me hiding behind the bed, she said, "I'm not doing this again. I can't keep getting my hopes up for nothing. I can't do it anymore."

"You don't have to." Dad's voice was hoarse. He rocked her back and forth.

I looked from the socks to the box to the gun to my mom and the way she was looking at me. Flat. Tears. Dead eyes. Dead face.

"I can't do this anymore."

My dream played in my head, from the folded rug to the gun to the noise and fire and pain and falling, falling, smashing into my pillow. And Mom coming home from work early and opening my door and breaking like bad ice on a frozen pond. Blood and screaming and tearing out her hair. Mom in all the blood, touching me, grabbing me, dead eyes, dead face. Mom, dying.

I pulled the trigger and I didn't die, but Mom did.

Head pounding, I let go of the green bedspread and fell backward against the wall. Then I turned my head to the side and fought not to throw up. No mess. Not another mess. I made messes. I was a Big Larry. A ruiner who ruined everything. All my strength went away. I felt like I'd just opened my eyes in the hospital, and I still didn't remember, only this time, I knew. I knew about breaking Mom. I broke her just like that stack of clay on Mama Rush's dresser, the presents she didn't know how to glue back together.

Mom kept crying and crying, and Dad kept talking to her. After a while, I heard rustling and scraping, then Dad picked up the box and the gun and said, "Wait right there, son. I'll be back."

Outside in the dark, it rained and rained. Inside by the little light on my bedside table, I cried and held an ice bag on my cheek and eye. Mom was on medicine from the doctor and asleep. Her hair was still on my floor, and some socks, some photographs, and the lid from the box.

My stomach growled.

No eating. Don't think about food.

It took forever to clean up Mom's hair off my floor, but I managed so Dad didn't have to. I was a ruiner, but I could also be a clean-upper. Like it mattered.

When Dad came back in, he didn't notice I cleaned up. He just sat on my bed with his head down. I shifted the cold ice on my swollen face and kept staring at him.

"It won't shoot," he said again without looking up. "The gun, I mean. The police never gave back the bullets."

Pragmatics. Lots of pragmatics was just being quiet, and I had that much, so I stayed quiet with my big swollen face and my ice bag. I didn't feel like I should talk to Dad, anyway, or Mom, not after shooting myself, being a Big Larry, and messing in the boxes and upsetting Mom so bad with the gun. People like me shouldn't talk. Pragmatics.

Dad sighed. "They offered to destroy the gun, but I—it's strange, but I—couldn't let them do it. I should have, but at the time, I couldn't. We'll do that, okay? We'll take it in and let them melt it down."

No talking. Listen, don't talk. I bit my lip and pushed the ice bag harder into my cheek. Dad wouldn't look at me. He didn't want to see me. I didn't blame him. If I had a Big Larry for a son who did such awful things, I wouldn't want to look at him, either.

"I know it doesn't make much sense." Dad shrugged, then let out a shaky breath. He finally did lift his head so I could see his eyes. They were wide and watery and sad. His lips worked as he tried to make his next words, but he couldn't.

Was I supposed to say something? It would probably be better if I never talked again.

"The gun . . ." Dad rubbed his hand against his leg. "I should never have gotten it in the first place. My Dad always kept one for just in case, but . . ."

Never talk again. Never talk again. Jersey the Big Larry will now be quiet.

"If I hadn't had the gun, you couldn't have used it, son. But at least—at least it was a good gun." Dad looked straight at me.

I kept my teeth in my lip to make my mouth stay shut. The ice bag froze my face. Was I freezing like Mom?

It was a good gun. A good gun? Because it shot me? What the hell? Don't ask. Don't talk. Leave it alone. Leave him alone, and your Mom, and everyone else.

"The—ah—gun—" Dad's voice broke as he started crying hard. "It didn't kill you. You shot yourself, but . . ." He stopped looking at me and rubbed his leg. His hand was shaking. "It was a good gun. And with no bullets—well, if you ever tried again, it would be a good gun, and it wouldn't kill you again, see?"

A good gun that didn't kill me.

The gun was Dad's good luck charm against me dying.

I bit my lip harder and put down the bag of ice. My face was too cold. Ice like Mom. Outside, it kept raining.

Inside, I knew I had broken Dad, too.

My head, Mom, my dad, everybody, and everything. Trigger. Boom.

Shattered.

chapter 16

"You looked in that box, didn't you?" Leza walked beside me going up the school steps. She climbed really fast. Talked too fast, too. "I *told* you not to look in that box. You deserve that black eye."

"Sorry." I didn't want to tell her what was in the box. Not, not, not. Not telling.

She glared straight ahead as we got to the top. "Don't tell me you're sorry. You *promised* me you wouldn't do that."

"Sorry. I mean, not sorry. I mean—"

"Shut up, Jersey." She snatched open one of the glass doors and waited for me to walk inside.

I shut up and walked inside.

She let the door hit me in the butt. I almost fell. She didn't try to catch me and I had to sort of run to catch her.

"Did you call Mama Rush and tell her you snooped in your dad's stuff, Jersey?"

"No!" Just the thought made me want to cover my head.

People got out of Leza's way as she marched toward my

classroom. "I'm calling her, then."

"Don't. No calls. Please." I caught up to her.

She punched me in the arm. "Was there a note in the box?"

"No." Don't tell. Don't say gun. Especially don't say gun inside the school.

"Well? What was it?"

"Nothing." Don't say gun. Don't say gun.

"Which one of them slapped you?" She punched me in the arm again as we stopped outside my Algebra class. "I hope your dad, since it was his stuff you bothered."

"No. Sorry. It was Mom."

Leza's face twisted up. She didn't hit me again. Her hand dropped to her stomach like it might hurt.

"Are you—," I started to ask, but she cut me off.

"Shut up, Jersey. Your mom. God. Just shut up."

I shut up.

Leza's face looked like she'd gotten hit instead of me. "I can't believe you upset your mom again. You need to just leave her alone!"

Before I was stupid enough to open my mouth, Leza stormed off.

She was pretty, even when she yelled and hit me and stuff. I watched her until I couldn't see her anymore. Mad and pretty. Maybe she hit me because she likes me. She might like me. It wasn't impossible or anything. My shoulder hurt. She liked me enough to hit me. Maybe I should tell her I like her. After she isn't mad and wanting to hit me, I mean.

I went into class, sat down, and wrote in my memory book.

1. *Get earplugs before Mama Rush calls.*
2. *Get shoulder pad.*
3. *Don't break promises to Leza without shoulder pad for when she hits you.*
4. *Don't break promises to Leza at all.*
5. *Tell Leza I like her.*
6. *Don't look in boxes.*
7. *Don't say gun.*
8. *Don't talk about taking the gun to the police station.*
9. *Don't even write about guns.*
10. *Wait until Leza isn't mad to tell her I like her.*

The bell rang.

I kept writing for a minute, then stopped when the teacher talked. And talked. And he talked some more.

After a while, my brain started to melt. I thought about the gun. I wondered when we would go get the gun melted like my brain. And I thought about Dad, and Mom, and Leza. Would Mama Rush yell at me? She might hit me, too. Maybe Mom would feel better if she hit me again. My cheek hurt.

The teacher kept talking. He wrote numbers on the chalkboard and pointed at me.

I stared.

He pointed to the numbers, then back to me.

"Mr. Hatch," said Mr. Sabon. Hot and stinky already. The room, not the teacher. Resource room, little round tables, nine of us, all guys. And lots of sweat and Algebra books at the biggest round table and Mr. Sabon at the board, scratch-scratching with chalk. Did Mom wake up after I left for school?

I didn't want to be in Algebra, but Dad made me go to school. He had the gun back, the good gun that didn't have bullets and made Mom tear out her hair. He said we'd take it to the police station so they could melt it really soon. I wished I was at the police station melting the gun. Or at home checking on Mom. Anywhere but school and especially anywhere but Algebra.

"Mr. Hatch?" Mr. Sabon was losing his patience.

Math shouldn't be allowed on Mondays, especially Algebra, even if it was Resource Algebra. I didn't know the answer to $3x - 3 = 3$. All those threes made me say, "Three."

Mr. Sabon looked a lot like Santa Claus with a shorter beard. He sighed. "Try again, Mr. Hatch. Keep your mind on the variable."

Santa. Santa beard. Three. Mom. The answer should be a three. All those threes. She had to wake up some time, even with medicine from the doctor. At least I didn't have the Wench anymore. Dad called before the whole gun thing. No Wench. Mom asleep. Three. Dad said he'd stay home with her all day. They'd be two instead of three. "Three," I said. "Two. Santa."

Mr. Sabon shot a look at the empty chair beside me, where the Wench would be if Dad hadn't de-Wenched me. I think Mr. Sabon missed her. Maybe he liked her and her funeral clothes. Or maybe he just missed the freak-tamer who could tell him if I meant three or two or Santa Claus.

"Two," I said, because it wasn't three, and it might be right.

Some of the other guys snickered.

"Two," Mr. Sabon echoed. Then he scratch-scratched it onto the board and showed how the problem worked out.

$3(2) - 3 = 3. \ 6 - 3 = 3.$

I got it right? Sort of. By accident. I always figured the first number I'd get right would be six-six-six, mark of the devil, if the movies and preachers were right about that. "Devil. Santa Claus. Two."

Nobody snickered or said anything. Mr. Sabon went back to scratch-scratching, but this time he asked somebody else for the answer. Mom was probably so mad at me she never wanted to talk to me again. I'd be that mad if my son broke me, then broke me all over again before I could even get glued back together.

"Devil. Six, six, six. Santa." I tapped my pencil against my paper, which was on top of my memory book.

Mr. Sabon raised his big white eyebrows. "Do you—ah—need to go to the office, Mr. Hatch?"

Office? I raised my little black eyebrows back at him. "No office. I'm fine. Devil."

"Could you stop talking about the devil and Santa Claus, then?"

"Oh. Yeah. Sorry." I closed my eyes, took a deep breath, and tried to relax. Instead I thought about Mom.

"Frog farts," I muttered.

Santa Claus sent me and my memory book and my six-six-six to the office for the rest of class.

I made it through Civics without getting banished, but when I went into the Earth Science room for third period, Ms. Chin said, "Hold on. Where's Ms. Wenchel?"

Fired. Fired. Santa Claus! "The W—I mean, my dad called."

Called her off. Fired her. Could Mom fire me? I was sweating. This room was stinky, too, but it wasn't little like

188

Resource and it didn't have round tables. Six-six-six. Don't say devil. We had desks in Earth Science. Ms. Chin didn't look like Santa Claus, though. She was short and skinny with long black hair. Don't say Santa Claus. Don't say devil. Don't say frog farts. Did I have my homework done?

Ms. Chin folded her arms and stared at me as all the other kids sat down. I started to sit down. I had my homework. I knew I had it.

"Don't take out your book yet." Ms. Chin shook her head and frowned. "I'm not comfortable with this. With you being here without your aide. What happened to your eye, anyway? Did you get in a fight?"

"Homework," I muttered, then counted to ten in my head three times really fast and said, "No. I don't remember. The eye, I mean. I probably fell. I fall a lot. Two, three, four." If I kept counting, I wouldn't say devil or sixes or get sent to the office. My cheek hurt. If I got sent to the office again, they'd probably call Dad and bring back the Wench.

Ms. Chin beckoned me toward the door. "Come on. Let's go talk to the principal, or guidance. Somebody."

Devil. Homework. I didn't want to follow her. Why should I have to leave? I didn't need a babysitter. Wench was history. My cheek hurt. I didn't want Ms. Chin to call Dad. If Mom was awake and only a little bit glued, I didn't want her to get broken.

We went to the office. The principal talked to Ms. Chin for a few minutes. I didn't hear much because of where I was sitting, except Ms. Chin got a little loud. When she came out, she definitely didn't look like Santa Claus. Santa Claus would never frown like that.

"Come on," she said. Her voice sounded high and tight, all nervous, like she didn't have much air. "But if you cause any trouble—and I mean *any* trouble—you're coming straight back here." A little ways down the hall, she added, "And no falling down in my class. I don't want the paperwork if you black your other eye. Understood?"

She clenched her hands together.

I nodded and kept my head down so she couldn't see the tape. It was clear, but she'd probably see it if I looked up. I'd found a roll of packing tape on the table next to my chair in the office. Tape fixed things. Tape would definitely keep lips closed, better than socks, even, and it wouldn't make my tongue fuzzy. If I kept my head down, she'd never see the tape, and I'd never say devil, and I wouldn't go back to the office, and they wouldn't call Dad and upset Mom.

Ms. Chin didn't call on me in class. I didn't think she would, the way she kept giving me that nervous stare and holding her own hands. Maybe I was ticking, like some kind of bomb. "Tick," I tried to say. Then, "bomb." But she didn't hear me, because the tape kept my mouth closed and I sounded like I was grunting.

I scratched my lips. Maybe I used too much tape. But I had to, or it would just pop open every time something wanted to come out of my mouth, which usually was a lot. But Earth Science was all about convection currents and inner and outer mantles and athenospheres and stuff. I couldn't even say athenosphere right in my head, so I didn't much want to say it out loud. My eyes drooped. I had to go to the bathroom. But first I had to make it through lithospheres and start tectonics, and by then I really, really had to go. Ms. Chin started talking about volcanoes and pressures and eruptions, and that didn't help anything.

When the bell rang, I got up so fast, I knocked my book off my desk. The next class was already coming in. Devil, devil, devil. Volcano. Eruption. I tried to bend over and grab my book, but almost fell. No falling. No paperwork for Ms. Chin.

So I had to get all the way down on one knee to get the book.

Somebody bumped me. I fell hard against the desk, but I didn't hit my eye. No paperwork. Devil. I had to go to the bathroom. I got part of the way back up and somebody else bumped me. I heard snickering, then, "Sit, Hatch. Stay, Hatch. Need a water bowl? Be a good dog, now."

Zero. Great.

Kerry said, "What's wrong with his mouth? Hey, check out his eye. Somebody busted him!"

More snickering.

I tried to get my balance and use my good leg to push myself up, but one of them kneed me in the back and I fell flat all over again. This time my Earth Science book jammed into my stomach and took some of my breath. I wished I didn't have tape on my mouth. My nose felt too small to get all my air back. People were standing everywhere and talking and nobody really seemed to be paying attention except Zero and Kerry, who were both behind me.

"Arf, arf," Kerry said. "Can you bark for us, Hatch? Come on. Arf, arf."

Ignoring him, I tucked my book under my bad arm and tried to get up on my knees again. The tape bugged me. I tried to pull it off, but it just tore around the edges. I wanted to breathe. I wanted to go to the bathroom.

A foot pushed against my back. "I said bark. I'm not letting you up till you bark, loser."

Fine. Whatever. I'd bark, if I could get the tape off my mouth. If I didn't bark, he'd push me down again, and I had to go to the bathroom. I needed to breathe. Devil. Volcano. The tape wouldn't come off.

"What are you doing?" Zero's voice sounded closer, like he was bending down. The foot stayed planted on my back, pushing just a little. "What's that on your mouth?"

"Wha—hey. Cut that out." Todd's feet and legs came striding through the bunch of girl-legs in front of me. He sounded pissed. Volcanoes. He'd probably black my other eye. Paperwork for Ms. Chin. Call to Dad. Unglued Mom. I so had to go to the bathroom.

"I mean it!" Todd's snarl made me flinch.

Then, "You—" from Kerry.

Zero cut him off with a loud "Whatever, man."

The foot left my back.

Somebody grabbed my good arm and lifted me to my feet. I found myself eye to chin with Todd. He tilted his head. "Your eye—did they hit you?"

I shook my head.

He let out a breath and relaxed a little. Zero said something rude I couldn't think about or I'd start repeating it, and Todd gave him a Rush glare that shut him right up. Kerry didn't try to say anything.

Todd kept staring at me. "What *is* that? Did you put tape over your lips?"

I nodded and thought about the bathroom.

He rolled his eyes. For a second, he looked just like

Leza, and just like the Todd I knew before I broke everything. Then he glanced around the room and frowned and let my arm go.

"Can you get it off?" he asked quietly.

I shook my head.

"Here." He reached up and dug his nails under the tape on both sides. "This is gonna hurt. You ready?"

I shook my head.

"Too bad." His frown got deeper. "Hold your breath."

I closed my eyes instead.

Todd ripped the tape clean away. Some of my lips went with it. Todd threw the tape down like it had rabies. I clapped my good hand over my mouth and said words head-injured people weren't supposed to say.

Ms. Chin picked that minute to bring her clenched hands back into the room.

"Jersey Hatch!" she shouted. "You will not use that kind of language in my classroom. Come here this instant!"

I kept my hand over my mouth and looked at Todd.

He shrugged like, hey, man, you're on your own with this one. Then he turned around and walked off, all cool and madlike all over again.

Wondering if I had any lips left, I managed to stuff Earth Science in my backpack next to my memory book and make the walk to Ms. Chin. Almost everybody from the next class was sitting down now. If I didn't go to the bathroom soon, I'd die. I'd just die.

When I got to the front of the class, Ms. Chin grabbed my arm and I knew she meant to march me to the office. The bell rang. Everything went quiet. She narrowed her eyes and said, "God, did you kiss sandpaper or something? No. Don't answer that. Just . . . just . . ." She let me go. "Go to the nurse's station, okay? You're bleeding."

I went to the bathroom instead.

Volcanoes and tectonics and convection currents and all that stuff.

What a relief.

And I managed to go without dropping anything or peeing on myself, and I zipped my fly. When I washed my hands and looked in the mirror, I knew I did need to see the nurse. My top lip was split down the center, and it kept bleeding even when I held toilet paper against it for a minute. If I didn't let the nurse fix it, it'd get on my shirt, and Mom would see it, and she might unglue over that.

It was hard to get the toilet paper to stick to my lip, but it finally did, and I picked up my backpack and started out of the bathroom. I didn't have a pass to be in the hall during class, but I figured the toilet-paper-bloody-tape lip would be enough.

I opened the door and walked straight out, almost knocking into a girl coming out of the girls' bathroom.

For once, I managed to catch somebody and do the steadying.

"Jersey," the girl said, startled. "Um, thanks."

I let Todd's girlfriend go in a hurry. My heart beat really fast all of a sudden, and I opened my mouth to say something intelligent. That's when I remembered the toilet paper and blood and stuff.

But my fly was zipped.

"Sorry," I mumbled. I pulled off the toilet paper and my lip bled.

Her dark eyes got bigger. She picked at the collar of her

194

white shirt. "What happened?"

I shrugged. "Nothing. Tape. My mom."

"Did Todd do that?" She picked her shirt harder. "Because if he did, I'll—"

"No! He pulled my lips off. I mean, no. Lips. He helped me."

She eased up on her collar, then lowered her hand and rubbed the leg of her jeans. It wasn't so stinky in the hall. I could smell her perfume, and it wasn't so hot, and I didn't need to pee. She had a red hall pass in one of her hands. Her nail polish was red, too. She was really pretty. Not as pretty as Leza, but definitely nice to look at. I knew she wasn't Elana now. She wasn't. She wasn't Elana.

"Cheerleaders," I muttered. "Peanuts. Lips. Sorry. What's your name?"

The girl laughed. "Maylynn."

"Maylynn. Doesn't sound like Elana."

I started to cover my mouth, but she caught my hand. "Don't. It's okay. You need to go see the nurse."

"Going." I nodded. Then the rest erupted like one of Ms. Chin's volcanoes. "Did I do something awful? To Todd, I mean. Did he tell you? There was this girl, and she told me I'm so self-centered. You're so self-centered I bet you think I'm mad at you. She said that, and Todd and I had a fight, only I don't remember. You're so self-centered I bet you think I'm mad at you."

Maylynn-not-Elana just looked at me. "I'm sorry. I have no idea what you're talking about."

"Somebody said that. I was selfish. Self-centered," I stammered idiotically. "Somebody should have said that, right?"

She smiled and shrugged.

"It's okay," I said, not wanting to be more stupid. "Sorry. I didn't mean to be a volcano." My lip bled into my mouth. I wiped it with the back of my hand.

"You should go on to the nurse."

"Maylynn!" Ms. Chin's voice sliced through the quiet hall. "Did you lose something in that bathroom? Get in here. The quiz is starting."

To me, Ms. Chin said, "Do I need to take you to the nurse's office?"

I didn't need pragmatics to know she wasn't being nice.

"Maybe you and Todd can talk soon." Maylynn waved at me. "Good luck." Then she turned around and jogged over to Ms. Chin.

"Volcanoes," I called after her. "Eruptions."

Ms. Chin glared at me and made a shoo-motion with her hand.

I shooed.

chapter 17

I have this dream where both legs work and both arms work and I don't have any scars on the outside. My mother isn't broken and my dad isn't broken. Todd's my friend, Elana's my girlfriend except she looks like Maylynn, Mama Rush still lives next door, and Leza's a scrawny kid with big teeth and lots of braids. They're smiling and laughing in my backyard, until they see the gun. I'm standing at my window holding it. They all turn to clay. I lift the gun to my mouth, and everyone cracks down the middle. Mom's arms fall off. Dad's legs break at the knees. It tastes oily and dusty all at once as I close my lips on cold gunmetal—but I can't. Not in the mouth. I'm shaking, but I lift the barrel to the side of my head. Todd turns away and snaps into five pieces. Mama Rush puts her head on the table and it shatters. The tip digs into my skin. Leza's braids fracture. I'm thinking selfish thoughts about nothing at all. Elana-Maylynn falls apart, hands and arms and eyes and face. By the time I pull the trigger, there's nothing left of any of them. Nothing but dust.

You're losing it. J.B.'s voice reminded me of Zero or Kerry. Couldn't tell which. *Mom's never going to talk to you again if you lose it.*

I yawned. "Shut up. I want to sleep. Not losing it. And Mom's talking to me."

What? A "hello, honey" over breakfast and a kiss good-night? J.B. couldn't touch me, but I imagined him poking my head while I tried to pull the green bedspread over my eyes. *She hasn't even been home most of the week. She's leaving. She's gone. She can't do this anymore.*

"She's still busy with the bank audit. Losing it. It's almost over." I rolled over and jerked my pillow on top of my head.

That's bull. J.B. sounded just as loud.

I threw the pillow onto the floor. "You're bull. Losing it."

You and Dad should have gone to the police station by now. That gun needs to get melted. And stop saying "losing it."

"Losing it." I sat up. "Bull. Losing it, losing it. Frog farts." What time was it? I needed to get dressed.

I'd tried to call Mama Rush a few times during the week, but after she yelled at me for a half hour solid over looking in the box, she wouldn't talk much and kept telling me she'd see me Saturday. Today. A few times, she didn't even answer her telephone. I wondered if she was still that mad at me. She probably was. Or maybe she had made up with Romeo man.

Maybe she'll get married and forget about you, J.B. said as I got dressed. I ignored him.

198

You really don't have anybody left, he tried again.

"Leza's nice to me when she's not hitting. She likes me."

No. You like *her. She'll never like you back—at least not like that.*

I finally found my shoes under the edge of my bed. Dad had changed my shoelaces . . . to purple? Purple shoelaces. I picked at one of them. It had lots of spring. Purple spring.

"Shoelaces. Spring. Purple. Leza. Frog farts." I let out a breath and sat down on my bed. Had to get a grip and focus before I went downstairs. Mom might be awake. If Mom was awake, I needed to have good pragmatics. And the scab still hadn't come off my top lip, so I shouldn't use any tape because I'd probably pull off the scab and make myself bleed.

Up and forward.

At least my cheek didn't hurt anymore, and my eye wasn't so black. More like light blue with a little green. Gross, really, but nobody asked me about it anymore.

Because nobody really looks at you. You're invisible.

I shut J.B. out of my mind and picked up my memory book and wrote down a few things.

1. *Don't flip out.*
2. *Say the alphabet instead of flipping out.*
3. *Don't break Mom or Dad.*
4. *Don't be a Big Larry.*

When I got downstairs, nobody was at the breakfast table and nothing was cooked. Somebody had left money, though, right on the counter where I could see it. I put my memory book down beside it so I wouldn't forget either of them.

For a second, I looked at my shoelaces. Purple shoelaces.

Nobody was up. Was that good or bad? Was I glad or not glad? Purple shoelaces.

Stop it. Stop it. Mom might get up. Quit thinking about shoelaces. If you think about shoelaces, you'll talk about shoelaces.

Did Mom not want to see me? This would be our first chance to really talk, if she'd gotten up. But she probably didn't want to talk. Dad probably didn't want to talk, either. If we didn't talk, how would I ever say I'm sorry enough times? I'd say it as many times as they wanted. I didn't mean to break them, especially Mom. I didn't want to break her. I shouldn't have looked in that box. Maybe Mom should have punched me harder. I shouldn't have looked in that box.

Shoelaces, the kitchen was quiet.

Wait a minute. Maybe Dad and Mom were sleeping in together. For some reason, that thought didn't gross me out like it usually did. It seemed kind of nice. Shoelaces.

I went to the refrigerator and got a few slices of turkey and cheese. After I ate those, I ate a banana and some peanuts. Peanuts were always good. As I was washing my hands, Mom came into the kitchen. She was wearing one of her silk gowns and robes, with matching slippers. The robe seemed really big on her. Her hair was neat and fixed, but her face looked all runny and smudged, like she'd slept in her makeup.

She waved at me. "Hey. You're up early. I left you some money, did you see?"

"Yes, thanks. Peanuts. Oops. Sorry. Just, thanks, okay?" God, I was worse than Ms. Chin, holding my own hands. My weak hand felt like wet, cold rubber. "Sorry. I'm really sorry."

Mom crossed over to where I was standing and took my hands in hers. Her skin didn't feel like cold rubber. She picked up a kitchen towel and dried mine off as she said, "I know."

I nodded, still trying not to think about peanuts or shoelaces. For some reason, I had trouble looking at her. Eye to eye. Face to face. But I had trouble looking. That volcano feeling, the one that made me blow words all over Maylynn-not-Elana, built up in my chest. I wished I had some tape. I didn't care if it pulled my lips off.

Mom finished drying my hands, put the towel down, and took hold of my fingers again. "I know I got really mad at you, but I was wrong. I'm sorry."

No, I'm sorry. I pulled the trigger. I broke you. Trigger. I'm sorry I ruined everything. Tears tried to come out of my eyes and the volcano tried to blow up, but I made myself look at the peanut can and think about cheerleaders. Cheerleaders made me laugh. Laughing made me warm inside. Leza made me warm inside.

Mom . . . made me nervous.

Especially when she tried to be nice. It was better when she growled at me. I knew what she really wanted, then. What she really thought about me and everything else. Growling was better. No volcano. No spewing words. You'll only say the wrong thing.

"Sorry," I whispered. "Sorry, sorry, sorry."

"Jersey, look at me." Mom squeezed my fingers.

"Sorry." Peanuts, peanuts, peanuts, frog farts, cheerleaders. I blinked. Made myself do what she asked me to do. Yeah, she definitely slept in her makeup. Why was I thinking about her makeup? Shoelaces. Big fat purple springy shoelaces. Don't explode. Trigger. "Sorry. I'm sorry."

Mom sighed. I wondered if she could hear my brain. Shoelaces.

"You don't need to apologize anymore." She squeezed my fingers even tighter. I kept looking at her smeared-up face and didn't say shoelaces or peanuts or anything else out loud. "I'm the one who's sorry. So, so sorry I hit you. That won't *ever* happen again, I promise."

"It's okay," I managed. "Peanuts. Sorry."

Mom didn't seem to notice the extra word. She just went right on choking my fingers to death and talking. "It's not okay. I'm the mom. Moms don't hit their babies like I hit you."

"Not a baby," I mumbled. "Sorry."

Oh, no. She had tears. If she let her tears go, I'd flip out and sob like a little kid. Peanuts. Shoelaces!

I didn't know what to do. No idea what to say. Pragmatics, Hatch. Yeah, right. Big Larry. Ruiner.

Hoping for the best, I nodded.

Mom smiled.

I wanted to smile back, or run. Both. Peanuts. Shoelaces. I had purple shoelaces. Did she want me to say something else? She looked like she wanted me to say something else, but I didn't know what to say that wouldn't go sideways. If I tried to talk, I'd be a volcano.

Mom's smile got a little sad, but she kept it up for a few seconds. Then she let go of my hands and went to get herself a glass of juice.

I pocketed the money on the counter and picked up the phone to call a cab.

"That's okay," Mom said. She downed her orange juice. "I'll drive you, or your father will. Jersey, I'm proud of you, honey. For . . . for holding it together as well as you have. And for sticking with Mama Rush, and trying so hard with your friends."

The telephone rang in my hand. It scared me so bad I dropped it.

Mom grabbed it off the floor, looked to see who was calling, then hit the button and said, "Hello?" And, "Oh, okay. Sure, Mama Rush. I'll tell him. Yes, I'll tell him that, too." She paused and frowned. "And that. You, too. I hope you feel better."

When she hung up, the first thing out of my mouth was, "Shoelaces. Is something wrong with Mama Rush?"

My head buzzed. I almost couldn't think enough to listen to Mom's answer.

"No, not really. Well, yes. She's at The Palace, but she said she's come down with the flu and she doesn't feel like meeting with you today." Mom sounded worried for me, like I might get all upset.

I was getting all upset. "But she's okay? She's really okay, right?"

Mom frowned all over again, then made her expression turn into a smile. "Yes. Settle down. She said to tell you she's not mad at you anymore."

"Good. That's good." I tried to breathe right.

"You—ah—told her about that box, didn't you? About the gun?"

The look on Mom's face was way past weird. I blinked at her, trying not to make mistakes. Probably I'd make one no matter what I said, even though I didn't really know why.

"Yes. Box. Sorry."

"Do you tell her everything?" Mom crossed her arms. She wasn't frowning, but she didn't smile, either.

"Sorry." I swallowed and blinked. "No. Yes. Sorry."

Mom shook her head. Sad and mad flickered like candles on her face, then went out. Back to flat and blank. "I miss the Rush family. We used to do a lot of things together. But you and Todd were growing apart—then, well, what happened. Leza was so upset, and Todd. And we spent so much time at the hospitals. After that, it just didn't seem normal when we talked to them. It didn't seem normal when we talked to anybody."

Leza upset. Okay. Leza told me that before. But Todd? Todd upset? Leza *and* Todd upset? Now I really wanted to run. But Mom kept talking.

"Mama Rush said she's working on fixing some more of your presents, and that you should go to Leza's track meet. It's the last one before cross-country starts."

"Cross-country." I tried to catch my breath. "Presents." My hands made fists and I had to make my fingers relax. "Okay, okay."

"Okay you'll go to the track meet?" Mom sounded confused. "Or okay about Mama Rush?"

One, two, three, four . . .

Breathing as best I could, I said, "Okay to both, I guess."

chapter 18

Mom and Dad both drove me to the track meet. Then they decided to stay.

Shoelaces.

I hope nobody saw me come in with them. I mean, going with my parents was okay, but sort of bad pragmatics. At least I thought it was. Purple shoelaces might be bad pragmatics, too. People kept staring at them while I stood next to the row where Mom and Dad decided to sit. People looked at my shoelaces or my memory book or my scars. Then they quit looking. Mom and Dad didn't try to make me sit next to them. Shoelaces. That was good.

I saw Todd and his girlfriend, but I didn't try to sit with them, either. Good, good. No Big Larry at Leza's track meet. Shoelaces. I needed to talk to Todd, but I couldn't figure out how to do it without making him mad. Shoelaces. Maybe I'd get a chance soon. Shoelaces. Where was I going to sit?

"Frog farts!" somebody yelled from down by the front bleacher rail.

"Hoochie-mama!"

"Hey, Jersey!"

Four of the lunch cheerleaders were waving at me.

I left my memory book with Mom and Dad and walked down the concrete steps really careful, bad boy, good boy, just like I was supposed to do. Pragmatics. Up and forward. Sitting with cheerleaders wasn't so bad, even if I had purple shoelaces and no peanuts at all.

They explained that Leza had already been running. She ran early in the morning in heats and things. Now she was running in finals at 400 and 800 meters. Peanuts. The cheerleaders said Leza was getting good and she was best at going the distance, and one day, she'd probably take 1,500 meters, too.

That sounded like a lot of meters to me. It made me think of Algebra problems, but I didn't talk about Algebra problems. I talked about peanuts and frog farts and stared at the black track and its bright yellow lines and listened to the cheerleaders yell and wave at people and waited for the girls who ran short races to get finished.

What was left of my brain remembered stuff like our track was a 400-meter track, so Leza's first race would be one time around. I wondered what color shoelaces she'd have in her shoes. Probably not purple. Probably green. All the girls in our school shirts had black shoes with green laces. Not the springy kind like mine. The girls were lots springier than me in other ways, like hopping up and down and stretching.

When did the guys run?

Oh, yeah. After. First girls, then guys. The guys would run later today. I remembered that. And I remembered that seven and a half laps equaled a mile in the eighth lane, and that it took a little over eight laps to make a mile in the first lane. But our track team started using meters instead of miles when they built the new track and this concrete stadium with the metal bleacher seats. I was in eighth grade then, and I didn't have any stupid-marks.

"You all right, peanut?" one of the cheerleaders asked.

"Don't call him peanut," another one said. I never got their names straight. They all wore their hair the same way and their lipstick was the same color and their clothes were different colors but the same style.

"Why not? He says peanut all the time." The first cheerleader messed up my hair. "Besides, I think it's cute, like him. He's our little peanut. Aren't you, Jersey?"

"Little peanut," I mumbled. My cheeks got un-cold and turned red. "Shoelaces."

"There's Leza," said the cheerleader who didn't like calling me peanut. She pointed to one of the tunnels running under the stadium. Three girls in green shirts and green warm-up pants were standing at the opening. All of them were stretching. One of them was definitely Leza.

"Peanut." It came out like a sigh.

Real fast, I glanced at the cheerleaders. None of them had noticed. A starting horn sounded, and they got busy watching the race. I got busy watching Leza stretch.

Even though she was far away, I could tell how pretty she was. I loved the way the sun made her skin even darker and more perfect. She'd probably think my purple shoelaces were stupid. But maybe not, since she gave me all the different colors. Still, I thought my purple shoelaces might be stupid. Dad and I needed to throw out some of the colors Leza bought me, but I didn't want to throw any of them out because Leza gave them to me. Peanuts. Peanut.

Leza crossed the track between races and came closer. I grinned at her and waved, but she didn't see me. She sat in the grass with some other girls, and they all stretched some more.

Track meets were fun. Why hadn't I come to more track meets? Shoelaces. Did I have sweat on my face? I wiped my forehead and cheeks with my shirt.

Wet stains on white. Great. I stuffed the front of my shirt down my pants. Sweat was better than stains. Pragmatics, Hatch.

The cheerleaders got noisy again. Leza and her friends kept stretching in the grass while the girls on the track got ready. A starting horn sounded and girls started running. Leza and her friends stood up. This time when I waved, she saw me and waved back. Todd yelled something to her about being sure to be faster than a half-dead snail, and she started to do something she shouldn't have with her middle finger. After a second, she just made a fist and shook it at him. I thought I heard him laughing. Other hands waved at Leza, and I saw Mr. and Mrs. Rush sitting together a few rows away from my parents.

Before, my parents and the Rushes would have been sitting together. But I messed that up.

I fiddled with my shirt snaps.

Shoelaces.

Trigger. Boom. Everything shattered. The clay people from my dream popped back into my head.

No, no. No dream-thinking, no bad-thinking, no Big Larry-thinking. Keep it together. Say "frog farts." Frog farts helps.

"Frog farts." The back of one of my shirt snaps tore through the shirt and dropped onto the concrete under the metal seat, between my legs. "Double frog farts. Triple!"

If I tried to pick it up, I'd probably fall off the first row and out of the stadium. Or all over a screaming cheerleader. Frog farts. When I lifted my head, Leza had moved. She was coming to the starting lines with the other girls. Eight girls, four in green shirts for our school and four in red shirts for the other school.

"Christmas." I stood up with the cheerleaders. "Red and green. Dropped my snap. Frog farts." My heart beat really fast as Leza took her place in the middle lane and stretched. She had this Rush glare on her face now. Get-out-of-my-way glare. I'll-run-you-down glare. If I'd seen that glare on her face and she wasn't in a race, I would have ducked.

The starting horn blared.

Leza and the girls took off.

The cheerleaders started jumping up and down beside me.

I watched Leza and jumped up and down. She was behind, but she had to catch up. She ran so fast! Was she ever some little kid with goofy braids? No goofy braids now.

"Go! Go!" the cheerleaders shouted.

"Christmas!" I yelled. "Green! Snap! Go!"

At the turn, Leza wasn't behind anymore. She was a lot closer. Three or four back. My heart pounded so hard it hurt. "Christmas! Christmas!"

"Go, go, go!" The cheerleaders yelled like they were all one person.

Leza passed somebody else.

I jumped up and down and waved. "Snap! Snap! Go!"

Almost back now. Almost to the yellow lines. Almost to the finish. She passed another person. One of the cheerleaders grabbed my bad arm and used it to hold on to while she jumped up and down really hard. I almost fell down jumping with her.

Leza plunged across the line right next to another girl—second! She came in second!

"Her first ribbon!" the cheerleader killing my arm shrieked. "She got a red! A second!"

"Christmas!" I yelled.

Then cheerleader-screams made my ears go numb. Did I still have an arm left? Shoelaces.

The cheerleader didn't let me go. She and the others dragged me away from my seat and pushed and pulled me down the front steps of the stadium, right onto the track. Leza and the girls had moved off to the side, to the grass between the end of the stadium, the track, and the fence. Some were bouncing like the cheerleaders. Some were bent over catching their breath.

"Giiiiiirrrrllll!" shouted the cheerleader who'd murdered my arm. She finally let me go and ran over to Leza. So did the other three. For a minute, they all bounced around together and yelled about how Leza might just win her next race.

My face hurt from grinning so big. I hoped I didn't have sweat on my face. I couldn't wipe the sweat off my face because I'd stain my shirt some more. Leza won a ribbon. I watched her win her first ribbon. I was a peanut. I had purple shoelaces. Red and green were Christmas. Snap, snap, snap.

She broke away from the cheerleaders, saw me, and ran straight toward me.

I grabbed her as she hit me full-on, laughing. I barely got to enjoy having my arm around her before we both almost fell in the grass. I would have fallen headfirst if she hadn't stopped me.

"I did it! I did it, Jersey!"

"Christmas." I grinned as she helped me get steady and let me go even though I didn't want her to. "Snap. Good job!"

"Christmas, Christmas, Christmas!" She did a funny dance and the cheerleaders helped out. Then she pointed at my missing snap and my belly showing through and giggled, then danced some more.

I wanted to tell her how pretty she was, and how happy I was, and how much I liked her, but every time I opened my mouth, some other stupid word popped out. As soon as the cheerleaders left, I'd tell her. I'd tell her—I'd tell her—nothing, because Todd came around the corner of the stadium with his girlfriend and Leza's parents and some guy I'd never seen before. He had more muscles than Todd, and he was taller, too. I stared at him.

Todd and Maylynn went straight to Leza and hugged her and told her how fast she ran.

"Nothing like a half-dead snail," Todd admitted.

Maylynn punched him in the arm. "He doesn't know much. Just ignore him. You were great!"

"I knooo-oooow," Leza said dramatically, and laughed a bunch more.

Todd and Maylynn glanced at me as they walked away, but didn't say anything. The Rushes did their congratulating, hugged Leza, gave me a once-over with nervous smiles, and they left, too. Tall-muscle-guy didn't hug anybody or leave. He just smiled at Leza.

She quit bouncing. Her smile got bigger. She straightened her shorts and shirt and moved her hair around with the palms of her hands.

"Ewww-weeeee." One of the giggly cheerleaders got my arm. "Come on, peanut-man. Let's give Leza some time with her honey-honey before she has to go rest for her next race."

And we were leaving, too, all of a sudden, the cheerleaders pulling me and pushing me and talking and bouncing as the announcer was saying something about a break ending and people getting back to their seats. We left. We left Leza and her honey-honey on the grass between the end of the stadium, the track, and the fence.

When I got back to my seat, I just stood there awhile, staring at the end of the stadium. Nobody came around the corner.

Honey-honey.

Did she call him that?

He had a lot of muscles. He was taller than tall.

Why hadn't I known there was a honey-honey? I should have known a girl like Leza would have a honey-honey. I should have known he'd be tall with lots of muscles. Pragmatics, Hatch. Up and forward. Girls like Leza have tall honey-honeys with muscles and it's a good thing I kept my big mouth shut about liking her.

I stared down at my shirt where the stains were. I stared at the missing snap and how my stomach showed. I stared at the weak hand hanging against my left leg. Then I looked up at my parents, who were looking down at me.

Another race lined up. From the corner of my good eye, I could see greens and reds, only I didn't want to say Christmas anymore.

The cheerleaders tugged at me to move or sit down. I kept standing.

Mom stood, too. Her face clouded up. She punched my dad in the shoulder.

I bumped past the cheerleaders to get to the stairs, then took them one, the next, and the next. Good boy leading, bad boy following. Good boy goes up. Good boy, bad boy. Concentrate. Don't fall. Honey-honey. I didn't have a snap. My belly showed through my shirt. My shirt had stains. Good boy, bad boy, up, up, slow and careful. I didn't have a lot of muscles like I used to. Good boy, bad boy.

"Jersey?" Mom met me halfway and got hold of both of my arms. "Jersey, honey, look at me."

I did. I tried to tell her I was fine, but what came out was, "I had muscles Before. Didn't I? I had muscles Before."

Then, after a few seconds, "I want to go home."

"We were thinking about going to the lake, and—"

"I want to go home!"

Mom didn't say anything else. She just helped me up the steps, yelled to Dad, and we left.

Later, in the car, they tried to talk to me.

I didn't want to talk.

Mom fussed at me about talking to them instead of other people, then Dad fussed at Mom about fussing at me. They kept on fussing. Mom said it didn't matter what she did, it never made any difference.

I quit listening. I didn't want to listen, and I didn't want to talk. Didn't want to think about honey-honey or muscles or snaps or stains or any of it. I just wanted to go home and go upstairs and lie down on my bed with the green spread. I just wanted to be nowhere for a while, and not see anything or hear anything or feel anything at all.

chapter 19

My parents fought a lot that night, the night I found out Leza had a honey-honey that wasn't me. I couldn't hear what they said, but Mom got a lot louder than Dad.

Dinner that night and breakfast the next day weren't loud, though. They were quiet. Dad found some reason to go to his office. Mom cleaned the house and mowed. I ate lunch and dinner in my room and tried to do my homework. I didn't call Mama Rush at The Palace because she felt bad. I didn't call Leza to see if she won a ribbon in her second race because I felt stupid. I didn't call anybody else because I didn't know anyone who wanted to talk to me.

Mom sort of wanted to talk to me. She checked on me about two hundred times.

"You okay?"

"Just wanted to make sure you're doing okay."

"Are you hungry?"

"Is that homework or are you writing in your memory book?"

"Don't shut me out, Jersey, please. Give me a chance."

"Are you still upset about the track meet? If you'd just tell me what happened, maybe I could help."

"Did somebody bother you yesterday? Tease you or hurt your feelings?"

"You shouldn't let people get to you, Jersey."

"Do you want a snack?"

A couple of times I heard her crying and talking on the phone and saying she couldn't do it, but I didn't know what she was trying to do, so I finally went to sleep early just so I wouldn't have to eat anything else or worry about Mom.

But I didn't stay asleep.

I kept dreaming and waking up. Dreaming about clay people turning into dust. Especially Mom. She turned to dust so fast, no matter what I did or didn't do.

Monday morning, Mom and Dad started yelling again, this time in their bedroom where I could hear a little better.

Maybe my parents needed counseling more than I did.

But it's your fault they're yelling again, J.B. told me as I got dressed for the half day at school. *If you hadn't been such a wimp at that track meet, you wouldn't have worried Mom.*

"She's not worried." I sat on the bed and pulled on my shoes. Black shoelaces, thanks to Dad. Better than purple, except they did have bright gold sparkly stripes.

She keeps thinking you're better, then you get worse again. She's broken because of you. You break everything.

"You always say the same stuff, and it sucks." I grabbed my memory book off the nightstand and made my list for the day.

1. *Go to the school library and check out a book on getting rid of ghosts.*
2. *Say hi to Leza so she doesn't think I'm stupid.*
3. *Don't mention frog farts in Mr. Sabon's class.*
4. *Don't mention frog farts anywhere but lunch.*
5. *Don't mention honey-honey at lunch.*
6. *Don't miss the bus because it'll be early because it's a half day.*
7. *Call Mama Rush and check on her.*
8. *Find a spell or something in a library book to kill J.B.*

J.B. laughed as I finished the list. *You really think you can find a spell to kill me?*

"I can try."

Dad yelled something about being positive. Mom yelled something back about things getting better then falling apart all over again.

I decided to take a box of dry cereal and go catch the bus.

If you hadn't shot yourself, you'd be driving, J.B. said as I closed my bedroom door.

"Yeah, yeah, yeah. Positive. Falling apart. Logical. Whatever."

"Why are you being so weird to me?" Leza punched my shoulder as we headed back out to the early buses. I'd forgotten my memory book after last bell, and I had to go back to third period to get it. That's when I ran into Leza and honey-honey. His name was Nicholas. Nick for short. Nick sounded like a tall honey-honey with muscles.

217

"Boy, you better answer me." Leza punched me again. Honey-honey Nick walked behind us and didn't say anything. I guess he'd already figured out some stuff about how to deal with the Rushes.

I stopped by the front doors. A few buses pulled away. "Ghost book on the list. Forgot it. Can't kill the ghost and I can't talk or I'll miss my bus."

"Nick and I can drive you home." She reached out and grabbed my bad hand as I tried to go outside. "Seriously. You're worrying me. Why are you being weird?"

The doors closed. I looked at my feet and tried to think of good words. Leza was worried about me. I was worried about Mama Rush and my mom and my parents and everything. Just everything.

"I got another ribbon after you left. It was just a third place—a white one, but still. I'll get some blues next year." She squeezed my hand and grinned. "Why didn't you stay?"

Say something.

And don't say something stupid.

She was so pretty, even now that I knew she had Nick the honey-honey. I wished I still had muscles. I wished I knew how to fix muscles and Moms and broken presents. If I broke so much stuff, I should at least learn to glue them all back together again.

"Ghost book. I just—Mom and Dad, and purple shoe-laces." My head started to hurt all of a sudden. "Stuff is so broken. And cheerleaders peanuted me—and—and Todd was there, and our parents were broken, too."

Leza's eyebrows pulled together over her nose. Her eyes glazed over a little. "Um, okay. Maybe I'll figure all that out by tomorrow."

My head hurt worse. My face had to be turning red. More buses left. I thought about pulling my hand back, but I didn't want to be a Big Larry and break something else. I really didn't want to go driving around with Nick the muscleman either. I could think of lots of things I'd rather do than ride around with Nick. Like have all my teeth pulled. Like wear purple shoelaces to a funeral.

"Shoelaces."

Leza looked down. "Black ones." She sounded tired, or maybe like I was getting on her nerves. I was probably getting on her nerves. I was probably missing my bus.

I tugged my hand a little. "Bus. Ghost book. Shoelaces." Even though it nearly made my brain explode out of my stupid-marks, I managed to smile so she might let me go.

Leza shrugged. She dropped my hand. "Just—okay, if that's how you want it. Guess I'll see you tomorrow."

I was glad she didn't stick around to see me trip down the last two stairs and nearly bust my face. The bus almost left without me, but I got to the door just in time to bang on it.

The driver let me in. When I went by him, I thought I heard him say, "Freak."

But I could have imagined that part. I probably did, since it sounded like Todd. When my head hurt, I imagined lots of things. Maybe I imagined Leza being tired of me, but I didn't think so. Leza was getting tired of me. Her honey-honey probably thought I was a pain, like Todd did. Or maybe I was imagining everything. I wished I was.

All the way home, I kept my eyes closed. The sun was too bright again. I wondered if the sun could cook my eyeballs. It felt like it was cooking my eyeballs. There had to be some way to fix Mom, right? Things got better, then they got worse. I could make them better again if I tried. If I got Mom and Dad glued, other stuff would be easier to fix.

So I just needed to use my best pragmatics. No Big Larry talking, or breaking things, or acting weird at track meets. No looking in boxes. No upsetting her.

My eyeballs were definitely cooking.

At least my house wasn't too far. My stomach growled. I hoped I could find some chips or something. I needed to eat and read over my lists and figure out what to do to start fixing Mom. Shoelaces. I'd already forgotten the library and the ghost book, and I didn't want to forget anything else. If I forgot stuff I might freak out and if I freaked out, Mom might crack.

I thought about my clay dream all the way up our front steps, and the whole time I fought with the stupid door to get it open.

Inside, it was darker. Good. Darker was good. All dark and quiet, except—except—

Noises upstairs. Bangs and rustles.

Stop imagining.

I closed my eyes against the sharp pains in my head.

Stop, stop, stop. Nothing's there. Mom was at work. Dad was at work. J.B. was a ghost and he ran his mouth, but he didn't make bang-and-rustle noises, and besides, I was going to kill him first chance I got.

Something banged and rustled again.

My eyes popped open.

Not imagining.

Mom or Dad must have come home. Dad. Dad always banged around like that. He probably remembered my half

220

day and wanted to make me some awful lunch. That was it. That was all. No need to be a baby. No need to be a freak. Why did my head have to hurt so bad? Maybe I deserved it. But I wasn't going to deserve it anymore. No more ruining.

I put my memory book down on the first step and climbed up as carefully as I could. My headache made the hall seem too long, but I ignored that. That was imagining. Halls didn't get longer and shorter. The noon sunlight came out of rooms in weird ways, making patterns on the floor. I walked across the patterns. The gold in my shoelaces glittered.

When I got to my parents' room, I looked inside, mostly expecting to see Dad, but I didn't see Dad.

I saw Mom.

Shoelaces.

Mom was standing by their bed dressed in jeans and a black blouse. Her hair hung loose around her shoulders, all straggly and sweaty and out of place like she'd been working really hard. Stuff lay all over the bed—boxes, clothes, suitcases.

My head gave a bad stab and I had to shut my eyes for a second.

All that stuff. Mom, sweaty. She had been working hard making a great big mess. Was she looking for something? Was she upset like tearing-out-her-hair upset again? If she was, I had to help her. I had to start gluing instead of breaking.

When I opened my eyes again, Mom was still standing beside the bed. She reached down and grabbed something as I walked into the room.

Then she saw me and jumped. When she turned toward me, she got all still, like she was trying to turn back into ice.

"No," I whispered. "No ice. No breaking."

I was going to help her. Glue her.

Then I saw how her hands gripped a folded white shirt. She glanced from me to the boxes and open suitcases on her bed.

Throbbing. Throbbing. My brain was throbbing. My head hurt so much. I rubbed my stupid-mark and tried not to cry because of the throbbing. If I cried, I'd be breaking instead of gluing. Boxes. Boxes and that shirt and suitcases and what a big mess. "Suitcases," I mumbled. "You going somewhere?"

The bright sunshine through the open window blinds made stripes on Mom's face. She blinked too fast and swallowed a lot and held onto her shirt. "What are you doing here? School isn't out for hours."

"Half day. Teacher training stuff." My throat felt so tight I could barely talk, but the look on her face made me worry, so the words came out. "Did somebody die? Everybody's dead, though. I mean, Grandma and Grandpa and stuff. Shoelaces. Who died?"

Something like a smile changed Mom's lips, but it wasn't really a smile. My headache brain thought she was about to scream, and I winced. A scream would make my head blow up for sure. But Mom never screamed except when she found me holding guns. The sunlight-stripes blazed. Fire on her face. Fire in my head. Shoelaces. Sin. Probation officers. Please don't scream.

"You were such a special baby," Mom said quietly instead of screaming. Her lips moved weird again. She looked down at her shirt, then back up at me. "I still see that when I look at you. Did you know that?"

I didn't know what to say, so I rubbed the sides of my head.

Mom studied her shirt again. "Sometimes I don't even notice the scars."

Before I could stop myself, I touched them all. Every stupid-mark. They felt flat and smooth and hot, and not even like real skin. Something needed to be glued, but what? How?

Mom just stood there, talking more to her shirt than to me. "Sometimes, the scars are all I can see. The scars and how still you were when I opened that door. All that blood—and you were so, so still . . ."

Her voice trailed away to nothing.

I was the frozen one now, stuck in the bedroom doorway with my hand on the stupid-mark at my temple. When I pushed it, the pain in my head ran to my fingers and pushed back. Tears slid down my face. This needed a lot of glue, if I could fix it. I could fix it. I had to. Mom didn't need to be broken anymore.

But she looked all shattered, standing there with the sun and shadows striped across her face, and I couldn't move. I couldn't pick up any pieces.

"Sometimes I forget, and the day seems normal enough," she told the shirt in her hands. Her hands were shaking. "Then I remember, and all I can think about is checking on you, getting there sooner, getting there before it's too late this time."

Too late. Too late. Too late. I pushed the stupid-mark harder, harder. Maybe I'd pass out and not hear anything else. My head wouldn't hurt and my heart wouldn't hurt, as long as I didn't wake up.

"I can't live like that. Like this. Worrying every second, until I'm sick inside." Mom finally looked at me instead of the shirt. "I tried, Jersey. I really did. I hope you believe me."

Tried. Believe. She tried. She couldn't live like this. She tried. I wanted to throw up.

Mom put the shirt down in her suitcase.

She came over to where I was standing, and that's when I realized she was crying as much as me.

"You don't understand, do you? I never know for sure." Her hands shook and shook when she put them on my shoulders. Her eyes had big circles under them like they did when I first got home from the hospital. When she talked, her breath smelled bad, like she hadn't brushed her teeth in a long time.

I was supposed to understand something. Glue something. Her hands on my shoulders. The boxes and suitcases. Circles under her eyes. Understand. Understand. Believe. She tried.

"I was going to call you later." She let go of my shoulders to hug herself. "Give you my number."

Even through the hammer-hammer of my headache and my brain, I added *call you later* to phone number and suitcases and boxes. "How long? Is it for work? You're leaving for work, right?"

Big Larry. Selfish. Don't be a baby. Don't break things. It's okay if she goes somewhere for a few days. She'd stayed at work overnight before. But there were a lot of suitcases. Women took lots of suitcases sometimes. And boxes. And the mess. More tears leaked out of my eyes. Leaving. She tried. She couldn't live like this. She tried, but she was leaving. Leaving the room and the blood and how I looked all still in the blood. Leaving the house and Dad and being sick and me. Leaving me.

No.

Moms couldn't leave. Moms didn't leave.

"Moms don't leave." It popped out. Then it jumped out. "Moms don't leave!"

Mom's tears didn't leak anymore. They just plain ran. And her hands shook worse.

"You left me first, Jersey," she whispered.

She dug her fingers into her arms as she stared at me with those circles under her eyes and her hair everywhere. I thought about when she tore out her hair in my room, and my head hurt more, more. I was going to throw up. I really was.

I left her.

I left her first.

I broke everything.

"You left me like—like that." She pointed down the hall to my room. "And you didn't even try to talk to me first. You didn't say good-bye, you didn't pack a suitcase—and—and you left me to clean up the mess."

She sobbed and hugged herself harder. "I had your blood all over me. Later, I kept showering and showering, but it wouldn't come off."

More sobs.

The room spun and lurched. I closed my eyes. Opened them. Mom had blood all over her, just like she said. My blood. Smeared on her face, soaking her clothes, covering her hands. Her eyes, still like I had been still. Dead like I'd been dead. Almost, but not quite. Just a little life left. A few pieces, maybe big enough to glue, but only if they didn't break any more.

When I blinked, the blood went away, but I thought I could still see it. Like a scar on Mom. Like the scars I had, only deep under her skin where she could feel it and nobody else.

"I just need some time to myself," she said. "Can you understand that?"

Don't throw up. Can't throw up. All those suitcases. All that mess. How long? Where? How long? The room turned circles and my stomach turned with it. My fault. Not my fault. Her. She couldn't handle things. My fault. I broke Mom. She told me it was okay if I said stupid stuff, so I hadn't been trying. Not hard enough. Real Big Larry. Real selfish. I acted stupid at the track meet. I could be less stupid. And lots less selfish. Unselfish. Don't throw up. My fault. Handle things. She was leaving. Of course she was leaving. Why would she stay here with shoelaces and peanuts and losers like me? Time to herself. She was leaving for time. Time without me, without the blood, without Dad, without me, especially me.

"Time," I said even though I had my teeth clenched. My head hurt so bad I felt it in my teeth, my fingers. My stomach turned over and over and over.

"Time," Mom echoed. She looked like she wanted to touch me again. She took a step toward me.

"Don't. No!" I backed away from her, into the hall. "Cracks down the middle. Your arms might fall off. Dust. Clay and dust. I'll turn you into dust!"

She stared at me with those flat, broken eyes.

I turned around and stumbled down the hall. Away from her eyes. Away from her. To the bathroom. I shut the door, made it to the toilet, sort of fell toward it, and threw up. Then I sat there smelling acid and tasting bad, bitter stuff. It was dark with the door shut. The toilet seat felt cool on my cheek. Dark and cool. Cool and dark. Was I still crying? Still crying. But my eyes had dried up. All the tears cried up. Cracks. My mom had cracks down the middle. Her arms had fallen off. If I said anything else, if I went out there and bothered her, she'd just be dust. So I sat with my head hurting until all the tears were gone in the cool-dark for a long, long, long time.

Time. Time and dark.

By the time I got up and went out into the hall, the house was quiet again. Totally quiet.

Time and quiet.

The mess and the boxes and the suitcases were gone.

Time and gone.

So was my mother.

chapter 20

Dad and I counted days by breakfast, lunch, and dinner.

Slow. So slow. Even in my head, stuff was . . . slow.

Three meals equaled a day.

Slow.

The first breakfast-lunch-dinner, we didn't even put on real clothes, just stayed in our pajamas and robes. Slow. He didn't make me go to school. I didn't make him go to work. So, so slow. Nobody called us, not even Leza.

Mom's gone and it sucks, I wrote in my memory book. Then I wrote a whole page of *it sucks*.

Dad made bad oatmeal and good sandwiches and so-so frozen diners and borrowed my memory book. He wrote half a page of *it really sucks*, and *she'll come back soon*, and *we'll be okay*.

When Dad talked, he sounded slow.

He wrote slow, too.

He wanted me to stay in his room for a little while, until

he was sure about the *we'll be okay* part. The bed was big enough and he said he'd worry less if he could see me. Slow. Slower. Slowest. I didn't argue with him. At least that way I didn't have to listen to J.B. on top of everything else.

After our third lunch, we made each other take showers and get dressed, and after our third dinner, Dad tried to tell me that Mom leaving wasn't my fault.

He was sitting at the table when he said it. Fast, not slow. I was putting my dishes in the sink. Slow, not fast.

Dad cleared his throat. "You don't think it's your fault, do you? Because it isn't, Jersey."

I dropped my plate on top of my glass by accident, but it didn't break. "Don't, okay?" I said.

He leaned forward, like he could reach me to pat my back. "But you need to know—"

"I know!" I turned around fast not slow and I almost fell. Dad stood up to help me but I shook my head. Fast, fast. Not slow. He backed off and sat down as I pulled on the edge of the cabinet to stand straight. "Straight. Slow. I know. It's my fault."

"No. We had fights before you ever shot yourself. And while you were at the hospital, and since you've been home—"

"Have ears," I cut him off again, knocking my good hand against my ear. "They work better than my eyes. Please stop. Ears."

Dad closed his eyes. Opened them. Rubbed his hand over his beard-stubble. "I just don't want you to be upset."

Dad needed to shave. He needed to shut up.

That volcano-feeling started in me again, way down

deep, hot and hotter and hotter, moving up to my chest, down my arms to my fingers. They twitched. My ears burned. "Ears. Hurt myself. You don't want me upset because you think I'll hurt myself again. I know. Straight. I know. Slow. So does Mom."

"Jersey, she—"

"Found me! Needs more time!" Down, volcano, no blowing up but I have to blow up or my head will blow up, blow off. "Mom thinks I left her. I left Mom. Ears! I don't—I don't want to talk now, okay?"

Dad finally leaned back. He looked like he was giving up. Good. Glad. Ears. All the lava inside me went back down.

He let out a long breath. "She said in her note that she'd call tonight."

"Don't want to talk," I said so fast I messed up talk like *tawk*. "Tomorrow, school and stuff. I just need ears. I mean, school. Back to normal."

"Okay." Dad folded his hands and stared down at his fingers. "School tomorrow."

The bus was late. I was missing Algebra. And talking to Leza, if Leza would talk to me. She might be mad. She had called after the third dinner, but I didn't talk to her then. I told Dad to tell her "later." Mama Rush called from The Palace. Dad told her "later," too. Mom called. Dad didn't tell Mom "later." He just listened. She said she'd taken a week off from the bank, and she was at the beach. When she came back, she was checking into a hotel.

Maybe she'd stay at the beach. Maybe the beach fixed broken people. Or maybe the way I broke people, they couldn't ever be fixed. Ears. At least the bus finally came. At least no Algebra.

When I got off the bus, I saw the Wench standing by the front doors in a black dress with black shoes that didn't have any laces, not even black and gold springy ones like mine. She saw me and waved. I didn't wave back. As I went slow, slow, good boy, bad boy up the steps, the Wench just stood there with this weird smile and her hand up from when she waved.

Don't say ears. Don't say Santa Claus, and especially don't say devil. No devils. Ears would be better than devils. Slow, slow, slow.

The other kids from the bus banged past me. I felt hot down in my stomach, like the volcano was trying to grow again, or swell, or get bigger, or whatever volcanoes did. But I didn't even know why. Ears. The Wench hadn't moved. She wiggled her fingers at me one more time. Maybe if I waved back, she'd go away.

As I got to the top step, I tucked my memory book under my bad arm and sort of nodded to her. Not a wave, but better than nothing. She smiled and came toward me.

Ears.

All the other kids got inside before the Wench cut me off in front of the doors.

"Jersey," she said, all serious with that funeral face. "Your father called this morning. I'm sorry about your mother."

Tell her to drop dead.

Tell her to go away.

Tell her to go to a funeral or go inside or leave you alone or you don't want to talk. Tell her anything. Tell her to go away!

"You don't have any shoelaces," I said.

The Wench stared at me. "Okay, well, we wanted to see how you were doing."

We. We who? Teachers? Other kids? Ears? Did they have another assembly? Oh, look, the geek-freak's mom left. He'll probably put a bullet in the other side of his head. Ears. He'll probably screw everything up all over again. Hide all the live chickens. Don't say chickens. Don't say ears. Don't say devil. Don't tell this woman to jump off the highest football stadium bleacher and fly to Alaska or fall down some volcano. Don't blow up. Don't pull the trigger.

"Mom didn't die." I tried to shrug, but I felt too stiff to do it right. "Trigger. She's just at the beach. But, thanks. Ears. I need class. To get to class, I mean."

"We thought maybe I should stay with you today and—"

I walked around the Wench, went through the doors, and left her talking to herself.

She probably followed me. I didn't care. If the Wench followed me all day, I might hurt her. I thought about finding some paint to draw happy faces on her stupid black dress. My teeth hurt because I had them shut so hard. Scary red spots dotted the outside of everything I could see. Lava. Volcano. If I kept listening to the Wench, I'd get red spots and start talking back and I'd be a total Big Larry ruiner volcano and nobody would like what I said. Fast. Too fast. Slow down. Slower. Slower.

When I got to Civics, the teacher, one of our baseball coaches, looked up from his desk like he might ask me for a note. He saw it was me, and he didn't. Great. Did Dad call everybody? Thanks, Dad. Or maybe the Wench talked to everybody. Maybe everybody at school was "we." Whatever. Thanks, Wench.

The coach jerked his head toward an empty desk and put his finger on his lips. Everybody was writing like crazy.

A test.

It was all about presidents and electoral colleges and Supreme Courts and stuff. Definitions. True and false. Matching. Fill-in-the-blank. Short answer and an essay.

Define *republic*. And *democracy, monarchy, oligarchy, dictatorship* . . .

The words got all blurry when I looked at them. Fast. Reading too fast. Needed to slow down. Red spots showed up on some of the paper. I was clenching my teeth again. Red spots, like lava and blood and red, white, and blue. Was the Wench in the hall? I should have told the coach I couldn't take the test. Now if I said I couldn't do it, he'd get mad and I'd have to go to the office and the Wench would stick to me for sure. Red, red spots.

When does a new president get inaugurated?

How many electoral votes does California have?

Match the following Constitutional Amendments to their proper number.

Explain the difference between a federation and a republic.

Is an oligarchy better than a dictatorship? Support your position.

Support my position. Red spots. Ears. Could I even say *inaugurated* with my dumb half-a-mouth? I could barely write the answer even with my working five fingers. *A president gets inaugurated every four years.* Or did he mean the month? I scratched out the word *ears* I wrote by mistake and started to put down January, then tried to remember if it was January or February. Ears. When did a president get inaugurated? Maybe it was December. I knew this stuff Before. If Mom could see me taking the test, she'd cry, because I was all stupid and different and I had scars on the outside, and I couldn't say *inaugurated* even if I tried. January. February. I didn't know. Ears. Spots. Slow down. Stop the red. Stop the volcano.

I took a deep breath, and another, and one more. The red spots turned black, then gray. My eyes squinted. Test words got narrow and blurry. The inside of my head felt too big and stuffed all full, like my eyes might pop out, but I kept breathing, kept staring at the paper, and I didn't blow up even when I tried to explain two reasons for the separation of church and state.

When the bell rang, I was still trying to answer a question about true or false, the American flag is always higher than other flags. It looked true, but it might have been false. Most of the questions on my test were still blank. True or false, Jersey got a big fat "F" on this test. True or false, Jersey Hatch is a freak-geek moron with stupid-marks. Inauguration. Ears. January, February, and I didn't know the definition of *federation* or *oligarchy*, either. American flags. I needed to go to Earth Science. I needed to hide from the Wench in case she was waiting in the hall.

When I turned in my paper, the coach didn't look up from the book he was reading. Something about bulls and bears and the history of Wall Street. It looked boring but lots more interesting than oligarchies and red spots. Ears.

I followed two basketball players out, trying to keep right behind them so the Wench wouldn't catch me. Out of the corner of my good eye, I saw her hovering by the bathrooms, so I couldn't go there. Ears, ears, ears! I could hold it for one class. Just one more, to do without the Wench. I tried to get to Earth Science with the basketball players, only they turned down a different hall, so I tried not to limp too much with my bad leg and to walk fast like everybody else. The Wench was still looking at the Civics classroom door.

So far, so good.

I turned the corner to Earth Science and Todd's girl-friend almost opened her locker right into my face.

"Oh! Jersey. Sorry." She took a book out of her locker, slammed it, and gave me a twitchy smile. "You got here fast. Usually, I'm gone before you come by."

No Wench. I glanced back toward the corner. Still no Wench. Good. But . . . Maylynn knew where I walked? When I walked? Her smile kept twitching. Don't say "ears."

"Sorry I was fast," I said. "It's the Wench. After me."

"Ms. Wenchel?" Maylynn looked over my shoulder to-ward the corner. "Is she supposed to be your aide again today? Leza said that was over."

"It was, but I missed three days. Ears. Mom. Ears. I mean, the Wench and the school—Mom—it's okay." My smile probably twitched, too, at least the half that worked. Maylynn had really big dark eyes. She was pretty. Not as pretty as Leza, no, still not, but pretty enough.

People elbowed past us. Almost time for the bell. Mom was at the beach. Red spots and beaches and ears. There weren't any bells at the beach. Ears. Maylynn started to walk away, but I asked her to wait.

"Can you help me talk to Todd?" I took a step toward her, staring at the blue book in her hands. Red spots on blue. "I need ears. I mean, to know. Stuff. And I can't get him to talk. Neither can Leza. Will you help?"

Her mouth came open. "I—don't know. I need to go or I'll be late for class."

"Please? I see spots." I reached for her book, for the spots on her book.

She backed up fast, bumped into somebody, and let out a little shriek.

"What the—" The shout came out of nowhere.

Todd came out of nowhere.

When he grabbed my shoulder, I tried to turn around, but he pushed hard. I slammed against the lockers. Pain shot through my bad shoulder. When I bounced back, Todd caught me. All around, people fell all over the place getting out of the way.

"You stay out of her face," Todd growled. His black eyes burned as he glared at me and clenched his jaw. Sweat broke out on his forehead. He had me by the collar with one hand. The other hand made a big fist. "Man, don't you know when to leave *anything* alone?"

Lights out for Jersey. Big fat "F" for Jersey. Ears. Too fast, too fast. Spots and ears. My shoulder hurt. Ears. If he hit me I'd hit him back. If I could. Volcanoes. Hot inside. Way, way down inside, flying up, trying to get out. I'd hit him back. Hit him. Why didn't he hit me? People watching. So many kids in a big circle. See the geek? He'll get his head bitten clean off. Volcanoes. The biggest volcano ever.

"Spots," I muttered, then bit my lip. Stop the volcano. Stop it. But it's coming. It's blowing.

"It's my fault." Maylynn grabbed Todd's elbow. "Let's just go."

"Hit me," I said, quiet even though I felt so loud inside. "Don't care. My mother's at the beach." More hot, flying up, about to blow out, about to cover everything in red.

Todd's eyes got so narrow I couldn't see anything but lids. He pulled me closer, held me tighter. He could punch me even with his girlfriend hanging off his fist-arm.

"Todd," she said, louder this time.

"Hit me!" The words slammed up, up, and out, out. "Break my head more. Hit me. Hit me. Hit me, Todd. Ears. Hit me!"

From behind Todd, I heard someone start yelling. Leza.

Todd lurched forward and dropped me.

I stumbled back and banged into the lockers again, this time with my head. More spots. Black with red. Blue with red.

". . . Get suspended, you total idiots!" Leza was shouting. Todd yelled back but I barely heard him. Arms and legs brushed against me as everybody scattered.

The Wench was coming. I could hear her whining, "Ohdearohdearohdear . . ."

Leza pushed Todd again, harder than ever, pushed him down the hall away from me and away from the Wench. Maylynn ran after them.

I couldn't move. I needed to move, but I just couldn't. Too many spots. Too much hot. I turned around and kicked a locker. Almost fell down and had to grab at the lockers not to bust my face. Now my foot hurt, too. Spots. Why wouldn't they go away? Red spots. Black spots. Blue spots. I turned back around.

Time to go.

But the Wench got to me about the same time Leza got

237

back from pounding on Todd. Both of them cornered me against the lockers. Through my squint-eyes, the Wench had another weird smile on her face. When I turned my head, I could see Leza's teeth, but she wasn't smiling.

"Jersey," the Wench started, but Leza yelled like the woman hadn't even talked.

"What kind of moron are you? 'Hit me, hit me, Todd. Hit me.'" She balled up her fist. "I'm gonna do it!"

"Hit me." The red spots faded. Black and blue, too, and the heat went away faster than fast. All drained out. Blowing up was done. Empty and cold inside now. Shivering cold. No more volcanoes. Just ice. Ice like Mom, out on her beach, trying to get warm again. "Hit, hit, hit, ears, beach. Mom."

The bell rang.

Over that loud sound, the Wench made another try. "There won't be any hitting here!"

She sounded lots like the bell, all high and ear-hurting loud until it stopped. Only, I could still hear the bell and the Wench a little, ringing in the back of my brain.

Leza punched my shoulder, but not hard. Then she started to cry. "Your mom left—your mom—God!" She sobbed. "Now you're scaring girls you don't even know and daring my brother to hit you? I *swear*, Jersey, somebody should hit you." She wiped her eyes real fast with both hands. "Todd was *this* close to talking to you. If you'd just—oh, never mind. I'm done for now. I'm just done."

The Wench didn't even try to talk. Her face froze up worse than Mom's and she looked around a lot, like she hoped somebody else would show up and take me away.

Leza ignored the Wench. She wiped her eyes again, and I had a sudden picture in my head of Leza with her braids and Rollerblades and skinned knee, crying and not letting anybody see. She was tough. She could handle anything. Leza with her braids, turning to clay and breaking all apart, just like everyone else.

She looked down, then straight at me again. Tears. So many tears, slow, swelling up in her eyes, running down her cheeks. "I was glad you lived, you know? I felt so bad for what I did, and I always wanted to be your friend. I thought you'd be nicer now, but you're still just a big, self-ish moron idiot. God, I'm stupider than you are."

You're so self-centered I bet you think I'm mad at you.

Two voices in my head now. Mom's and Leza's. Maybe three. Maybe more. Faces. All those faces. Girls I didn't know.

You left me first . . .

I felt so bad for what I did . . .

But what did Leza do? What could she have done?

Leza was still crying. I started crying, too. I wanted to hug her. I reached for her, but she just shook her head, turned around, and walked off down the hall.

My insides banged around, then fell all the way to my toes. I hurt everywhere, like my heart was falling out. Why? What was wrong with me? I couldn't stand her walking away. It was too fast, too big, too much.

"Wait," I called after Leza. Tried to go after her, but the Wench grabbed my arm.

"Been there, did that," Leza shot back over her shoulder. "And I don't even know why."

"Let her go," said the Wench. "She just needs a little time."

"Everybody needs time!" I jerked my arm away, banged a

locker with my elbow, then sat down in the dirty hall. Leza turned the corner. Gone. All gone. I shut my eyes. Ears. Selfish, selfish ears. Maybe when I opened my eyes, I'd wake up, and I'd still be at home, and Mom wouldn't be at the beach, and Dad would be there, and everything would be okay. I didn't care if I had scars. I didn't care if I was stupid, as long as this was the dream. Let it be a dream. Ears, ears, ears.

I opened my eyes.

Dirty halls. Lockers. The Wench.

Fast like a finger-snap, everything went away. Snap. Poof. No insides, no outsides. No hurts or happy or tears or anything. Just nothing. Empty and cold and ice and nothing.

No wonder Mom went to the beach. Anything was better than ice and nothing. Anything was better than here.

"Wench. Halls. Ears." I banged my head on the locker behind me. The hurt helped a little, but it went away too fast. Back to ice and nothing. I banged my head again, harder. More hurt. I could think some when I hurt. "I want to go home, okay? Mom's at the beach and we haven't been to the police station, and I want to go home. Ears. Police station. Mom's at the beach. I'm not. I'm cold. I'm ice. Take me home."

chapter 21

Home. Nobody. Nobody but me. Nobody home. Quiet, cold empty, inside and out. The Wench brought me here herself. I think she was glad I wanted to leave school.

I'll make sure to get your assignments . . .

I've left a message for your father . . .

You get some rest . . .

She even tried to buy me a snack first, but I wouldn't let her. Plenty of food at my house. At my empty house, with nobody home. Nobody, nobody.

I walked into the kitchen carrying my memory book. Walked straight to the trash can, to the oatmeal paper towels and crumpled up bread wrapper, and I threw the memory book away. Sick of carrying it, looking at it with its white cover and smeared letters and pen on a dirty string. Sick of writing in it, reading it. I didn't want to remember anything, anyway. Good-bye. Go away. Nobody.

Now it was me, just me with no memory book, and I sat down at the kitchen table alone. The kitchen table was good.

The kitchen table was safe. Sitting to stay away from up-stairs. I needed to stay at the table. We hadn't been to the po-lice station. Upstairs, the gun was waiting. The police kept the bullets, but I knew my dad. He kept everything. He for-got lots of stuff. Somewhere in some box or corner or drawer, there were bullets. I just had to look. But I didn't really want to look, only I did want to look. I wanted the gun and the bullets, but I didn't want to hurt myself, only I did want to hurt myself. Bullets. But not really. I really wanted to be able to stop. Just . . . stop. Quit worrying and trying and screwing things up. Quit everything. Be still in my head.

I wanted to think right. I wanted to feel right and walk right and talk right and smile right, only I ruined all that. I blew it all away. I blew me away. Bullets. I could blow it all away better. Do it right. Not mess it up this time and really die and I wouldn't be a geek-freak anymore, and I would be still, and people could live without me lots easier than with me. Bullets. Nobody, nobody. I was nobody. Nobody home.

Mom gone. Leza. And Todd, and I didn't even know where Dad was. Mama Rush—she didn't want to talk to me anymore. Nobody. Nobody home. My stomach twisted up. For one second, I felt something more than cold empty. Then it was gone. I put my head down. The table felt hard and cold empty under my cheek. It was still, quiet, so quiet. Inside and outside. Cold empty. Quiet. Bullets. Maybe I could sleep. But if I slept, I'd have to wake up. If I woke up, everything would start all over again.

Was it like this?

I blinked.

Maybe I wasn't mad and upset when I shot myself.

Maybe I was tired and quiet, tired of the quiet, tired of the cold empty. Maybe I just felt tired when I pulled that trigger. Bullets. Maybe I didn't feel anything at all. God, I was sick of thinking about the gun, about shooting myself, and Before and now and everything, everything, everything. Elana was the last thing on my list. I'd messed up with her last. And messing up with her messed me up with Todd and Leza and the Wench and school. Messing up. Up and forward. All the rehab didn't help much, did it? So I could walk and talk and be stupid even bigger and better. Bullets. Bullets were upstairs. Bullets and the gun and I could do it right this time.

I covered up my head with my good arm. Tried to think about other stuff. When I thought about school I thought about Todd and Leza. When I thought about home, there was J.B., Dad, and Mom. No Mom. When I thought about Mama Rush, there was The Palace, Romeo man, taxis, broken presents, and she didn't want to see me much anymore. When I thought about Before—no. Then I stopped. No Before. Before made me think about now. Now made me tired.

"Stop it." I sat up.

The table rattled when I banged it with my fist. My hand throbbed. It felt good and bad at the same time. Something different from cold empty.

The hurt made me move. When I hurt, I felt less tired. When I moved, I felt something, at least. So I got up and didn't think about Before or now or Leza or Mama Rush or Mom or anybody else.

I just went upstairs.

J.B.'s voice caught me as I limped by my closed bedroom door. *Hey. Moron. What are you doing?*

For some idiot reason, I stopped. I felt like killing something. Maybe I could finally kill the ghost. "Shut up. You want me dead, anyway. Bullets. Die, die, die."

Stupid. I never wanted you dead. I never hurt you.

"You shot me." I banged on the closed door with my fist. It hurt, and that felt good, and the door rattled. "You ruined everything!"

But . . . when I tried to lower my arm, I couldn't. My hand just stayed stuck against the door wood, fingers all curled up to make a fist.

"You shot me," I said to the hand and the door and J.B., but not as loud this time. I felt a little hot instead of cold. Wrong and upside down inside. The door looked funny. My hand looked even funnier.

You're an idiot and a moron and a ruiner and a Big Larry. You're selfish and self-centered and I bet you think I'm mad at you. Shoelaces. Bullets. Ears. Peanuts. Cheerleaders. Up and forward. You threw away your memory book. You threw everything away.

J.B.'s snarl made me want to snarl back, but I still couldn't move my hand. I kicked the door. My hand didn't come loose.

"Let me go." Whispering now, but I didn't know why.

You let me go, J.B. shot back. *It's you, not me.*

My hand got bigger in my brain, like some kind of giant's fist. I stopped trying to move. It was me. It was always me. My hand. I shot myself with the hand stuck to my door. The giant, giant hand. It was always me. Nobody. Nobody home.

That upside down feeling got lots worse. I felt dizzy, then sick, then all of a sudden, nothing again. Cold empty. Quiet empty.

And I knew.

Oh, no. Please. Please?

"Don't go away," I whispered to J.B.

Nothing.

I jerked my giant shooting hand back so hard I almost fell, then I used it to open my door.

Sunlight lit up dancing dust all around my bed with the green bedspread. The football rug lay neatly on the floor. Nothing sparkled. No shadows waited in the corners.

"Don't go away," I whispered again, then I yelled it until my throat hurt. But it was too late.

J.B. was gone, too. He left because he hadn't ever been there, not really.

Please. Not really. Gone. Gone. Nobody home. Nobody. I shot myself, and there was nobody here but me. I did this. I did it all. Bullets. Bullets. Bullets.

I couldn't be crying. J.B. wasn't real. But he sort of was, and he talked, and when I saw him in my head, he looked at me. He didn't count my stupid-marks and look away. But it was always me.

When I shut the door, I felt emptier than ever. Cold empty. Quiet empty. And really, really tired, way down deep, where the volcano used to be. Where it blew up and left me here with nothing inside.

It was easy. Really easy.

Gun in the bedside table—Dad was Dad.

Bullets in a junk box way in the back of the closet—Dad was Dad.

We needed to go to the police station, but we never had

time. There was never any time. Our family ran out of time, or something. No way to buy more or work for more or find more. Now we hadn't gone to the police station, and I still had the gun, and I was glad. Bullets. I had bullets, too.

Made a mess getting them, but I got them, and I left the mess. Didn't care as I put the bullets in the holes. Wasn't easy with one hand, but up and forward, up and forward. Left the box and extra bullets on the bed. Then I took the gun back downstairs and put it on the kitchen table.

When I sat down, I felt better. I wasn't alone now. I had the gun, and it had bullets, and if I got too tired or too mad or too cold empty, then I could have another blowout and just be finished. Being finished didn't seem too bad. I wouldn't screw it up. Not this time.

"What are you doing, moron?"

I kept asking myself that, since J.B. was gone now, and he wasn't there to ask me anymore. "What are you doing, moron? What are you doing? What, what, what?"

Looking at the gun, that's what.

Feeling tired, but not so tired.

Feeling scared, but not so scared.

A little mad. A little hot-cold.

But feeling something, at least. Something was better than nothing. Something wasn't so awful.

"What are you doing, moron?"

My eyes went back to the trash can, to the memory book, to the oatmeal paper towels and crumpled bread wrapper. Dad made me breakfast this morning. Bad, bad, bad oatmeal. But he made it for me. If I shot myself, I needed to keep it clean this time. No me-mess at the table. No me-mess in the house. No me-mess anywhere.

This time, I'd go over to Lake Raven, to the place where the benches faced the little fence. I'd climb the fence and do it there, so I'd just fall in the lake. Bullets. The lake would cover up everything. No me-mess at all.

"What are you doing, moron?"

I picked up the gun, fumbled to open it. One at a time, I took out all the bullets. Dropped some on the floor, picked them up. Then I tucked the gun in my pants and put the bullets in one of my pockets. It took a while, with just one hand. But now I couldn't shoot and I couldn't see the gun. Good. Right? Or bad. Maybe?

My breath came out fast, all at once.

Did that feel better or worse?

Stupid, stupid, stupid.

My insides were breathing now, in and out, in and out. Breathing wasn't so bad. The gun pressed against my belly wasn't so bad. I didn't feel blank, but I didn't feel sick. Not so bad. Sunshine came through the kitchen window. Afternoon sun. My memory book was in the trash on top of oatmeal. Dad made me oatmeal.

"Oatmeal."

Was Dad at his desk? I could try to call him. Mom's number at the beach was somewhere. And Mama Rush. I could call any of them. When Leza came home, I could call her, too, and say I was sorry about Todd and stuff.

If J.B. were still here, he'd tell me none of that mattered. He'd tell me they'd all be mad and hate me. But he didn't have to be here, because he wasn't real, and I told myself that stuff. Only not so much this time.

Breathing, breathing, breathing.

If the bullets stayed out of the gun and I stayed at the

table, everything would be okay, wouldn't it? Sooner or later, everything might be okay. It could happen, like the sunshine in the afternoon and how I felt a little better now. Good things could happen, right?

They could. Bullets. Really. I'd killed a ghost, even if he wasn't a ghost. That was something. It had to be something.

The phone rang.

I jumped so bad the gun in my pants banged the table. The phone rang again before I could get up, and another time before I got to it and punched it on.

"Dad?" I said, holding onto the counter.

"Uh, no. It's me. Todd." A roar-noise in the background made it hard to hear him.

When I didn't answer, he said, "You there? I'm in the car, so talk loud."

"Yeah," I said, well, sort of yelled so he would hear me.

"Mama Rush is sick and they took her to the hospital. She's got pneumonia. I—I thought somebody should tell you."

No. No. No way. No way! My insides stopped breathing again. I wanted to climb out of my own skin and run. Just run.

"Where?" I yelled. "They took her—where?"

"Mercy East. We're going there now."

Now. Go. Bullets. Mama Rush! No, no, no. No!

"I'll come. I'll—I don't have a ride." Slow down. Make sense. Think. Think and breathe. Bullets. Don't say bullets. "I'll call Dad. I'll come! I can come, right?" My fingers got tight, tight on the phone.

"Hold on." He covered up on his end and said something. I heard him say something again, heard yelling. Then Todd again. "I'll call you back."

He hung up.

I hung up.

God!

Really fast, I dialed Dad. His voice mail answered. No!

"Dad, come home!" I yelled. "Where are you? Come home now!"

I hung up. Tried Mom's number at the beach. It rang until the hotel picked up. I didn't leave a message.

Who else could I call? I had to get a ride. I could get a cab, but I didn't have the money. Mercy East. It was a few miles away. Mercy East. I'd been there first, after I shot myself. Mama Rush was there now. I didn't die there. Maybe it was a good hospital. I had to get there. Useless. If I could drive, I'd drive fast. I'd already be there. Ruined that.

"Mama Rush!" I banged the phone on the counter. It broke open. The battery went flying. Then I threw the rest of it against the refrigerator. It broke into two more pieces. Phone pieces. Mama Rush, Mama Rush. I crammed my good hand in my pocket and felt the bullets. Bullets in my pocket. Bullets were there. Mama Rush.

Tears swelled up in my eyes, popped out, ran down my face. I could walk. I'd have to walk. I had to get to Mercy East. I couldn't just sit here. Bullets. I couldn't just wait. I closed my eyes. Slow down. Try to breathe. Try to think. Figure something out. Come on. Figure it out.

But I couldn't. Nothing to figure.

No Mom, no Dad, no driving. No car, no keys. Was a phone ringing? I thought I heard one, but I couldn't tell. I shut my eyes tighter. Figure something out. Bullets. Figure it out.

Ringing.

Ringing.

Upside down.

Dizzy, dizzy, dizzy.

Banging on the door. Somebody was banging on the front door.

Somehow, I moved my feet. Moved my body and the gun and the bullets to the door.

"Jersey!" Lots of banging. "Hey."

A guy. Todd?

I opened the door. Todd had his phone in one hand and the other hand still up in the air to bang. "I said I was calling you back! What the hell?"

"Sorry. I—"

A horn honked. Honked again. Kept honking.

"Come on." Todd grabbed me by my good arm and jerked me out of the house. "We'll give you a ride."

The two of us lurched down my front steps and across my yard. The horn stopped. Todd's car in the driveway, a blue mustang. Leza in the passenger seat. Me and the gun in my pants and the bullets in my pocket got in the back. Todd slammed the door behind me. Leza didn't turn around.

"Don't be a pain in the butt because I can't take it right now," she said before Todd even got to his door. "Do me a favor and shut up. Don't even open your mouth."

I covered up my mouth with both hands.

Todd got in, revved the engine, and we roared out of my driveway.

chapter 22

Todd used his phone and found out Mama Rush was in the Critical Care Unit. CCU. My mind kept saying, Sissy-U. Sissy-U. Mama Rush would lay an egg if I told her she was in Sissy-U. I couldn't say Sissy-U. Todd talked to the care station in Sissy-U, though, then hung up.

"Nurses sounded a little mad," he said to Leza as he parked his car in the hospital garage.

Leza grunted and bit at her thumb.

I didn't say anything. I still had my hands over my mouth, singing the alphabet in my head so I wouldn't say Sissy-U. The gun felt hot and sweaty against my belly, but I tried to ignore it. I tried to ignore the bullets in my pocket, too.

When we got inside, we found out we beat Mr. and Mrs. Rush to the hospital, and we weren't supposed to go into the Sissy-U together—only one at a time. A-B-C-D-E-F-G . . . But we didn't see any police at the door, and the nurses were busy, so we all slipped in and walked toward

Room 3. Sissy-U.

Beep, click, hissss.

A-B. A-B-C. I wanted to sing it out loud. My heart banged against my ribs. The whole place smelled like alcohol and . . . other stuff, not as nice. Beep, click, hissss. The sound came from everywhere. I pushed at the mark on my throat and tried not to sniff or swallow or look left or right. Sissy-U. Sissy-U. Not for sissies. Definitely not. Sissy. Sissy. Beep, click, hissss.

"A-B-C," I whispered to make the sounds stop.

Leza elbowed me so hard I almost fell into Room 2.

Right about then, we heard a lot of swearing from Room 3, and, "Oh no you will *not* be sticking that tube down my throat," followed by a big bunch of coughing, and a crash.

Beep, click, hissss.

Leza closed her eyes. "Crap."

"A-B-C," I said nervously, rubbing the butt of the gun through my shirt.

"D-E-F-G," Todd said, sounding just as nervous.

"Sissy-U," I added.

Leza hit Todd instead of me. Then she leaned toward Room 3. The curtains were pulled so we couldn't see inside. "What's she doing?"

Beep, click, hissss.

Another crash. More swearing. Not just Mama Rush, either. A-B-C-D-E-F-G.

"What's she *doing*?" Leza repeated.

"Throwing a fit, sounds like," Todd said as three nurses marched out carrying a tray, some silver things like scissors, and a torn-up plastic tube. I stared at the tube as two of the nurses brushed past us. Did I have a tube like that

252

when I was in the hospital? A-B-C. H-I-J.

Beep, click, hissss. Sissy-U. Sissy.

The third nurse stopped and held up the plastic tube. He pointed it at us. "Too many," he said. "Who are you here to see, anyway?"

All three of us just stood there with our mouths open.

After a second, I blurted, "A-B-C-D. Tube. Sissy!"

"That stubborn old witch," Leza said at the same time Todd said, "Mama Rush."

The nurse stared at us.

Beep, click, hissss. Beep, click, hissss.

"Those are my grandchildren!" Mama Rush yelled, then coughed, then kept yelling. "Get out of the way and let them in here. I mean it!"

Nurses weren't supposed to kill people, but this nurse looked like he could have used that piece of tube to murder something. Us. Mama Rush. Sissy. A-B-C-D. He couldn't make up his mind who to murder. I could tell.

Beep, click, hissss. Beep, click, hissss.

Instead of using the tube to do bad things, the nurse shook his head, mumbled under his breath, and left us standing there.

Leza looked at Todd. Todd looked at me.

"Tube," I said. "Sissy."

We went inside.

Leza and Todd walked straight up to Mama Rush's bed. I stopped at the door.

Mama Rush . . .

It was her, but, but tube. Sissy. She was kind of dusky-pale. Skinnier. Wheezing. Frowning. Skinny djinni without her cigarette. A-B-C. Her gown was white and hospital-like, no real color. She didn't look like herself at all. No. Tube. Tube-sissy. Sissy-U.

I tried not to stare, but I couldn't help staring. D-E-F-G. Leza and Todd were talking. Todd had hold of Mama Rush's hand. She was telling them not to worry, in between coughing fits.

Beep-click-hissss.

Beep-click-hissss.

I could hear that noise coming from other rooms. Didn't want to hear it, but I did. Tube. The sounds made me sweat. Skinny, wheezing Mama Rush made me sweat. Tube. Sissy. How could she be sick? She was really sick. I thought she didn't want to talk to me, but all the time, she was getting skinny and wheezy and sicker. L-M-N-O-P. Self-centered. Didn't need J.B. to remind me. So self-centered, I thought she was mad at me. Mad at *me*. Self-centered. Tube. I had a gun. The gun. And bullets. Sissy. Sissy-U. But I didn't want to think about the gun and bullets. Not around Mama Rush.

She would . . . know.

"Jersey Hatch," she wheezed.

I jumped.

She motioned to me. "Get over here. Now." To Todd and Leza, she said, "You two move for a minute. On second thought, go on outside and see if your parents got here yet." She coughed and shooed Todd and Leza with both hands, all at the same time. "Tell them I'm fine."

Todd didn't argue. Neither did Leza, which sort of made me more nervous. They just glanced at me, nodded, and left. Tube. Tube sissy. Did she know about the gun? Did she know about the bullets? How could she already know? Mama Rush really was a djinni. Skinny djinni no cigarette no color. She was sick. So sick.

"I said get over here," Mama Rush snapped. Coughed. Frowned at me. "Got some things to talk about just between you and me."

I got over there. Close to the bed. Tube. Sissy. Close enough she could reach me and touch the gun. Touch my pocket and find the bullets. Sissy. Her hand—the one without needles and tubes—shot out. She grabbed my good hand and held on tight. Coughed so hard her whole skinny djinni body shook.

"God, I hate hospitals. Okay, okay, go on. I can tell you need to say something first."

"What?"

"Whatever nonsense you're holding in. Loosen up. Let it out."

"Oh." I let out a breath. "Tube. Like tube? And machines make that beep, click, hissss I hate. Sissy. Sissy-U. I shot myself with a gun that had bullets. Beep, click, hissss. You're skinny."

Mama Rush kept hold of my hand. She looked down at herself. Coughed. One of her eyebrows lifted up. "Think I've lost some weight?"

"Yeah. Skinny djinni no cigarette. Tube. Sissy." Her fingers felt hot and dry against my skin. She coughed a long time. I started to sweat more. I had tears, too, but I was keeping them for now. Tube. At least I could do that much. The gun was a few inches from her hand. The bullets even closer. She'd find them. She'd know. Sissy. Tube. She'd probably shoot me and everything would be over. Beep, click, hissss, bang. Maybe she'd shoot the nurse bang, or save it all for Romeo man. Or maybe she'd just be upset and disappointed and I'd want to die instead of see that look on her face. Tube.

"Quit fidgeting," Mama Rush instructed between coughs. Beep, click, hissss from a room close by. Probably 2. Or maybe 1, or 4. I stood still. Hoped the gun didn't show through my shirt. Sissy-U. Sissy-U.

"You working on your list still?" she asked.

I nodded once and tried not to fidget. Didn't want to tell her I threw away the book. Not that. Not now. I threw it away, but I remembered. "Still got two things left. Did something awful, and Elana Arroyo—ask Todd, only I can't ask Todd, or I haven't yet."

"That list, it was a good place to start, like I said." More coughing. "But not everything fits on a list, Jersey." She stopped to take a breath. It sounded so bad I felt pain in my chest. Pain like I thought she felt. "Not everything gets its separate little number and its neat little place." Cough. "There's more than one way to look at stuff."

She had to work to breathe. No fidgeting. Don't fidget. I wanted to fidget. I wanted to say something so she wouldn't keep talking and making herself cough. Don't fidget.

"Things in the real world get messy," Mama Rush muttered.

"Real world," I said in a hurry. "Things are harder in the real world."

"Yeah. No kidding." Her eyes fixed on mine. "Listen, I'm asking you this because you've been here before. Sort of. A minute ago, you said 'sissy' and 'tube.' You think I'm a sissy for not wanting that tube down my throat?"

They wanted to put a tube down Mama Rush's throat?

They wanted to make her beep, click, hissss? Some of my tears got away. "No!" I said. Then, "Yes. I mean, you need it? I had a tube. I went beep, click, hissss."

Best I could, I lifted my weak hand and scrubbed the bent fingers against the stupid-mark on my throat. "Tube wasn't enough. Ventilator. Gave me a hole, remember? Sissy. Sissy-U. Tube."

Mama Rush coughed, then let go of my hand and sighed. "Doctor said it'd just be temporary, but that scares me. What if they never take it out again? I don't want to croak with some stupid tube sticking out of my mouth—or worse yet, inserted in my throat like yours was. I wouldn't even be able to say any brilliant last words."

Her stare burned holes in my face.

I was supposed to say something. Tube. Brilliant last words. You aren't going to die. Don't say you're going to die. But she might die. Tube. She needed a tube. She needed the beep, click, hissss. I had to say the right thing. How could I say the right thing? My eyes wouldn't stop blinking. All of my fingers curled. It was hard to breathe, and I didn't need to cough or anything. Sissy. Sissy-U. Beep, click, hissss.

"They—they took out my tube." I bumped the stupid-mark with my bent fingers again. "They took out my ventilator, too. Beep, click, hissss. I went home, and—and stuff. Tube."

She stared *so* hard, and her eyes—big with water at the bottom, like she was keeping her tears, too. "Did it hurt?"

"Don't remember. It doesn't hurt now."

Mama Rush finally quit staring. She rubbed her throat where she'd get a stupid-mark if she had to have a ventila-

257

tor. But she might not need a ventilator if she let them do the tube. Sissy-U. She might get better and she wouldn't need any last words.

"Brilliant last words," I blurted. "Sorry. I mean, you don't need those."

"Speak for yourself," she grumbled as she turned her head and stared at the wall on her other side.

I watched her chest go up and down. It wasn't easy for her to breathe. Sissy-U. She needed that tube.

"Guess I have a choice to make," she finally said, her voice all quiet.

"Yeah. Tube. Sissy-U. Choice."

"Seems like you got a choice to make, too, Jersey." Mama Rush coughed. She still wasn't looking at me.

Heat rushed up and down and all around me. My good hand flew up to the gun-lump. I felt like I wanted to pee. My teeth clamped together. I touched the hard metal through my shirt, then moved my fingers away fast. To the bullets. Away from them. Tube. She knew. I knew she'd know. Tube. What should I say? Right thing? Wrong? Brilliant last words. Sissy-U.

"Wish I could make the choice for you," she whispered. Coughed again. Maybe she wasn't keeping all of her tears, either. "But I'm old, and I know a few things. If I made your choice for you, if I got in your way, it wouldn't stick. You'd just come back to having to make the same choice again. Likely sometime when I wouldn't be there to get in your way."

"You'll be here," I said, fast, fast, losing my tears just as fast, fast. Both my hands, shaking. My insides, shaking. "You'll get in my way. You always get in my way—I mean, you can. It's okay. Brilliant last words. Tube. You'll always be here and you can get in my way. Tube. Beep, click, hissss."

"Sissy-U," she said before I could say it. "CCU *does* sound like that."

All of a sudden, I wanted her to look at me instead of the wall, but she didn't. She wouldn't. I knew it. Tube. It was time to go now. She had to make her choice. I had to make my choice. Nobody in the way. Brilliant last words. Tube, tube, tube.

I needed to run.

"Hey, boy!" she called after me as I lurched out of Room 3. "Send in that nurse. You know—the male nurse with the big attitude. Tell Mr. Sissy-U I want to talk. Todd and Leza, too."

chapter 23

Mama Rush needed a tube. She needed brilliant last words. She knew about the gun.

I couldn't stay. I wanted to get away, but I had to tell the nurse and Todd and Leza that Mama Rush wanted to see them and I had to go after that. Had to go. Out. Away.

The nurse went past me into Mama Rush's room before I could say anything. Tube. Maybe he'd put the tube in. Maybe he'd do it now. Last words. No last words. I needed to quit crying. Baby. Baby in the Sissy-U. I pushed through the doors into the hall.

Waiting room to the right. Glass walls. Glass doors. A bunch of orange chairs and a table in the middle with magazines and a phone on top. Todd and Leza standing by the table. Baby. Sissy-U. I'd been in a Sissy-U. I had been here in this hospital. Did Todd and Leza and Mom and Dad and Mama Rush stand around the table with the magazines? Orange chairs.

When I stumbled inside, Leza said, "Oh, God. What

happened?"

"Tube." I wiped my tears with my good hand. "Sissy-U."

"What happened?" Leza pulled at her hair with one hand and flapped her other hand up and down. Tears ran down her cheeks. "Did she get worse? Is she—"

"Tube." I closed my eyes and squished out tears. Took a fast breath. Do this right. Slow down. Don't think about the gun. Slow down. "Needs . . . a . . . tube. Like me." I pointed to the stupid-mark. "Beep-click-hissss. Tube."

Sobbing, Leza ran out of the waiting room and straight through the doors into the Sissy-U. Todd started after her, but I couldn't let him just go. Again. I couldn't.

I grabbed his arm.

"Sorry." God, quit blubbering. Baby. Sissy-U. Sissy. "About all I did. Whatever. All of it. Sorry about being self-ish. Big Larry. Freak."

"Knock it off." Todd tried to pull his arm away, but I held on.

"Sorry. Tube. You're so self-centered—no, wait. Not you. Me. Freak."

Todd shook his arm, but not hard like he wanted to hit me or hurt me or bash me into the wall. "You've got prob-lems. Turn me loose."

His eyes looked funny. Half-closed. Wet. His jaw popped. Grinding his teeth. Todd always used to do that when he was nervous. I remembered that. Todd from Before.

"Elana—I made you hate me over her. Sissy. Sissy-U. Don't remember—doesn't matter. I'm sorry. Sorry, sorry, sorry."

Pop-pop. Todd's jaw. His eyes opened a little wider. Then tightened again. He showed his teeth. Blew out some air.

Todd from After.

When he finally said something, his voice sounded rumbly like thunder before a bad storm. "You think I hate you over Elana Arroyo?"

He jerked his arm out of my grip and made me stumble. Caught me. By the shirt. Face to face. Inches from him. Any closer, he'd touch the gun.

"You think that's it, Jersey? You think that's *all*?"

"Tube. List. Sissy. It's on the list. Number Six. Elana Arroyo. Ask Todd."

"I can't believe you." More rumbling. Lightning in his eyes. "You—you're a—a—"

"Freak. Yeah. Freak. Did I hit her? Maybe? Get her pregnant?" I pushed back to keep him off the gun. "What? Freak. Pregnant. Tell me."

Thunder. Lightning. Todd's face got stormier. "You stole her! You took her away even though you knew I liked her. She was my girl, and you took her, and you cheated on her, and treated her like trash!"

I opened my mouth, but all that came out was, "Stole. Cheated. Trash."

Todd jerked me higher. Closer. Back toward the gun. Thunder. Thunder! "Everything was trash to you back then. Big bad Jersey. You took my starting spot on the football team. You tried to take my spot on the golf team, but you blew that running your smart mouth to Coach."

"Big mouth. Bad Jersey. I took your spot?" I was standing on my toes now, but I didn't care, except for the gun. Don't let him touch the gun. "So that's why you hate me. Selfish. Big Larry. I was a jerk. So self-centered I bet you think I'm mad at you. I mean, me."

"Quit saying that." He tightened his grip. Words through his teeth, but still thunder. More flashing in his eyes. Closer to the gun. Closer.

Thunder. Lightning. I barely touched the floor with the end of my toes. I grabbed his wrist to keep from falling into him. "Thunder. Thunder. Quit saying that. Saying what?"

"You're so self-centered I bet you think I'm mad at *you*." Thunder. Loud. Thunder. Did the windows rattle?

"Elana—"

"Shut up!" His teeth came apart. Spit hit my face. "I didn't say that because of her. I said it because I was mad at myself for giving you another chance."

"Thunder. You—*you* said that." Lightning. Thunder and more thunder. It couldn't have been Todd. It was a girl. A girl in my memory. But it wasn't my memory, was it? Just what I thought. Just something I stuffed inside the holes in my head. Stupid. Stupid. Thunder. "You said that. You."

"The day you did it." Todd was shaking now. I shook with him, on my toes. "I tried to talk sense to you and just got the same shit back about how you sucked and weren't good enough and wanted to blow your head off and die. How was I supposed to know you were serious? That you'd do it? You freak!"

He let go of me then. Just sort of dropped me onto the floor, right on my butt. The gun jabbed into my belly, but I didn't really feel it. I didn't move.

"We were getting over stuff." Quiet thunder. Rain running down his face. "But you wouldn't ease up. You wouldn't sleep. You wouldn't eat. You just kept getting weird, and more weird." He shook his head. "Then you messed her up. I messed her up. *We* messed her up, man!"

"I messed up Elana."

"No!" The word exploded through my head. My ears buzzed, it sounded so loud.

Todd leaned down fast, grabbed my shirt, and pulled back his fist, but he was still shaking and he wouldn't look at me, not in the eyes. "We messed Leza up bad."

All the noise in my head stopped. Like somebody turned off a switch. Nothing moved inside. Nothing moved outside. Stuck to the floor. Stuck to the gun.

Leza.

Leza?

"She heard it," Todd whispered. His fist dropped. "She was standing on your front porch because I called her. I sent my baby sister to see about your worthless ass, and she *heard* you shoot yourself."

I wished I was an orange chair. I wished I was part of the floor. My lips started moving and I heard myself say, "Heard it. Heard. Heard it."

Todd let me go and stood up. He rubbed his arm across his face and still didn't look at me. "She freaked out and called your mom instead of 9-1-1. Your mom was on her way home from work, so she got right there—and Leza was standing outside when your mom started screaming."

Now he looked at me, and I wished he wouldn't. I wished I didn't have eyes or ears. I wished I had died when I shot myself, but I didn't die, and I was hearing this and I couldn't stop it.

"She thought she should have gotten there sooner, or gone in—maybe stopped you. And later, she thought it was her fault your mom got so messed up."

"Messed up. Stopped. Stop. Heard. Stop." Shut up! Why

264

couldn't I shut up?

"Messed her *up*. And why?" Todd laughed, but not happy. More like a bark, or almost throwing up. "Because you didn't do good in a football game. Because you got suspended from golf for backtalking Coach. Because you made some sucky grades and pissed off your parents and your R.O.T.C. commander. You wouldn't listen to anybody and you wasted yourself and messed her up over a whole bunch of *nothing*."

That made me stop talking. I couldn't move again. I couldn't do anything but look at Todd as he backed away from me.

"That's why I can't stand you." Past the table now, almost to the door. Still backing away. "That's why I don't want to look at you."

At the door. Opening the door.

"You used to be my best friend, man."

And Todd was gone, and I was there on the floor and all I could think about was Leza and messing her up and tearing up that stupid list because it was nothing.

It was all nothing.

I killed myself over nothing at all.

Later, maybe minutes, maybe an hour, I stumbled out of Mercy East, out to the sidewalk, It was almost dark and a little cold.

Nothing.

Nothing at all.

Where was I going? Not home. Not to Dad. Not to the house and Mom at the beach and J.B. gone. Not to nothing.

Not to the green bedspread and the football rug. Not to Before, or After, or any of it. None of it. Nothing. Home was a long way, anyway. School was closer. In between me and Lake Raven.

I messed Leza up. I did it for nothing. I broke Mom. I did it for nothing. I broke Dad—nothing. Nothing. Little stuff. Little now. I made little stuff big and I messed up Leza and ruined everybody and ruined me over *nothing*.

Nowhere to go.

Nothing, nowhere, nobody.

Maybe I could think at school. Up in the stadium. Up in the bleachers. Nobody would be there at night. No girls running races, no cheerleaders, nobody to get in my way. My face felt wet. I was still crying a little. Walking, and thinking, and crying.

By the time I got to the school, by the time I got to the bleachers, I coughed like Mama Rush. I needed tubes. I needed to sit down. Everything burned, especially my legs. Wet all over. Sweat and tears. My eyes burned and I rubbed them as I climbed up into the bleachers. Good boy, bad boy. Bad boy dragging, dragging. My bad arm felt numb. Everything hurt. It was dark. Cool dark. Dark empty. Nothing. Except it didn't smell so good. A little like sweat and old water.

"Slow down," I said out loud as I flopped down and lay still. The hard metal felt hot through my shirt. The sweaty gun pushed at my gut under my shirt. This was the same seat where I watched Leza run before I met her honey-honey. Cough. Breathe. Slow down.

The same seat where I cheered with cheerleaders and thought lots about peanuts. Peanuts and cheerleaders just

266

seemed to go together. Breathe, breathe. Slow, slow.

But I could never be a cheerleader. I could sit with cheer-leaders, they could be nice to me, but I couldn't be one of them. I wouldn't be running on the track, either. Or doing any of the stuff from Before. I could like Leza as more than a friend, but she wouldn't like me that way. She had a honey-honey. I had stupid-marks. I messed her up. I messed it all up. For nothing.

Was Mama Rush getting her tube?

Mom was gone. Dad was broken. School had the Wench and Algebra and I got peed on and upset everybody. J.B. was gone. I didn't have my memory book. I felt like I should have it, but I threw it away. Now it was in the trash. Lots of stuff in the trash.

When I could breathe enough, I sat up and pulled the gun out of my pants. I laid it on the bench beside me. Bright in the moon. Trash. The gunmetal looked shiny. It would taste oily if I put it in my mouth. I couldn't do that. But I could put the bullets in it.

Took forever to get them out of my pocket. I dropped some. Took forever to pick those up. Only found three. Trash.

After I got the gun open, not easy with one hand, I put them in.

If I shot the gun, would it fire? Trash. It might be on an empty space. I wasn't sweating now.

Maybe I should wait here until it was school again and shoot the guys who peed on me. If I shot Mr. Sabon, nobody would have to do Algebra for a while. 3x - math teacher = nothing. But Mr. Sabon looked like Santa Claus and he was pretty nice. Trash.

The guys who peed on me used to be nice, too, Before.

Did I make them mean? Did I mess them up, too?

I thought about the clay people in my dreams breaking all apart. I thought about Mom at the beach. Waves and water.

Why couldn't Lake Raven be an ocean with a beach?

When I thought about Lake Raven, I thought about the place where the benches faced the little fence. Beaches. Everybody needed beaches. I thought about how I could climb the fence and do it and fall in the lake with no me-mess at all for anybody to find. Would that fix things? Beaches. It would for me.

You're so self-centered I bet you think I'm mad at you.

"Todd said it!" I yelled. Then I started losing tears and I picked up the gun and pointed it toward the school and pulled the trigger.

It clicked.

Empty space. Three bullets. Two holes left. Would the bullet be next if I pulled the trigger again? Triggered. I was triggering. I triggered stuff.

"I'm self-centered," I whispered. "Faces. Leza. Mom. Todd. I'm self-centered. They say so. I say so." Put the gun on the bench. On the metal. Felt the gunmetal and the bleacher metal with my fingers. Even though it was hard, I opened the gun back up, found the three bullets, and took them out again.

For a second, I felt better. I lost tears, and breathed hard, but I felt better. Beaches. Self-centered. Mama Rush couldn't die, and I needed brilliant last words. What would I say?

So long.

Good-bye.

The geek-freak choked on a chicken head.

Beaches. Peanuts. Tube. Cheerleaders. Sissy-U. Come home, Mom, it's all safe now. Jersey's gone. Beaches.

"So long. Good-bye."

Was this how it was Before?

"So long. Good-bye."

Did I just sit on the bed and try to decide and all of a sudden shoot myself?

Tube.

Over nothing.

It couldn't have been like that. I had to have a reason. Good reason. Or lots of reasons. Reasons that mattered. But they were nothing.

"So long. Good-bye."

My stomach started hurting. My breathing got faster and faster. My chest started hurting, too. And my head. The fingers on my bad hand curled up. Bullets in the gun. Tube. I had to put the bullets back. So, I did. One bullet. Two bullets. Three. Back in the gun. And I felt better again. For a second. Maybe a minute.

In and out, with my good hand and my stupid curled fingers. Bullets in, bullets out. I did it over, and over, and over. Cold. Teeth chattering. So long. Good-bye. There had to be reasons that mattered, but there weren't any reasons that mattered. Now and Before. I was tired of thinking about Before. Tired of thinking about everything.

"Tube. So long. Good-bye." Bullets out. Bullets in. I dropped another one and let it roll. Two bullets now. Two was plenty, because I didn't really want to shoot anyone else. I only needed one bullet at Lake Raven. Just one. In and out. In and out. As fast as I could.

So long. Good-bye. Cold. Cold and tired. Bullets in. I tucked the gun in my pants again and lay back down. Just a minute of rest. Just a little rest would help. I closed my eyes.

Brilliant last words. I'd find some. I would. Mama Rush wouldn't need them. I'd find brilliant last words, and fix everything.

"So long. Tube. Good-bye."

chapter 24

I have this dream where I'm walking through a desert made of dust and broken clay. The sun burns my face as I get to my school. I keep walking, back, back behind, to the bleachers. I climb some steps and sit on a hard metal seat, and I pull the gun out of my pants. It has bullets. One, maybe two. Enough to do what I have to do. It's over. No more pain. It's time to be gone. It's time to rest. It's finally time to rest. I don't even try the mouth this time, because I know I can't do it in my mouth. I'm not even shaking when I lift the barrel to the side of my head—the side without any scars. When I squeeze the trigger, I'll go blank and fall into nothing, and I don't care who finds me, and I don't care who cares. It's time to be dust. Dust and clay and ashes and sand. It's time. My finger's on the trigger. I squeeze and squeeze, a little more, a little more, and—

Shaking.
 Hurting.

Shouting.

I woke up jerking and making lots of noise. Clay and ashes. My throat was so dry. Parched. Morning. Morning sun burned my face, just like in my dream. It was burning my skin pink and my scars brighter red. Clay and ashes. I was in the school bleachers, and I'd slept all night, and it was morning, and I still had the gun with the bullets inside tucked in my pants.

Was I still alive?

I rubbed my throat as I sat up. Then I shook my head and rubbed my curled-up fingers with the fingers that still worked. Yeah. Alive. Burned pink, hot, thirsty, but alive. Alive with the gun. Ashes, ashes, ashes. Hell of a dream. It made me sick down inside. It made me want to yell some more.

Mostly, though, it made me make up my mind.

I knew where I had to go, what I had to do. No more questions left. Ashes. Ashes and clay. Dust and ashes.

My legs ached as I went bad boy, good boy down the bleacher steps, barely keeping upright with the rail. The sun—so bright. My head was already trying to hurt. My cheeks felt all hot and tight. I wished I had some water, some ice. I was so hot, but it had been cold last night. I remembered the cold. I remembered the clay and ashes. I remembered in the dream how I didn't care about anything. Dust. I was just dust in the dream. Maybe everything was dust.

I took an old path away from the bleachers. I knew it from Before, when Todd and I used to walk home. It led into a bunch of trees, then to a little road, and all the way to Lake Raven on the big end, near where the benches faced the little fence. Ashes. Clay.

My feet worked funny, but I was moving, into the trees, not sweating. At least it would be shady in the woods. It smelled better than the bleachers, like pines and wet dirt. Fresh dirt. Not sour dirt. Not clay. Clay or dust or ashes.

I still didn't remember shooting myself. Dust. Dust. I didn't know, not really, only I did a little. I knew about tired. I knew about cold empty, and mad, and now I knew how everything seemed like it got too big and bigger and I made nothing huge until I pulled the trigger.

Clay and dust.

Ashes and clay.

Bullets in. Bullets out.

Nothing made me feel better for longer than a second or a minute.

Ashes. Dust. Clay.

"Ashes, dust, clay," I muttered out loud. The sound of it helped me walk faster. Through the woods, to the road. "Ashes, dust, clay." I was walking. Walking to Lake Raven. Ashes, dust, clay. To the benches and the little fence. Ashes, dust, clay.

On the road, my face got hotter and hotter. I tried to keep my head down so my nose wouldn't keep burning, but I kept tripping forward.

"Nose," I said the third time I did it.

For a while, I walked with my hand over my nose, so my fingers got hot. It sounded funny when I said, "Ashes, dust, clay," under my hand. Like it was from a speaker somewhere. Like I was on the radio. "Radio. Nose. Ashes, dust, clay."

The road was lots longer than I remembered.

"Radio. Nose." I put my hand down and wondered how far I was from the lake. Far enough. Too far.

It was my fault. Mine. Jersey Hatch.

Only, I didn't feel like calling myself Big Larry and ruiner and loser and geek-freak. None of that. Nose. Radio-nose. I was Jersey Hatch, and I was self-centered. I was Jersey Hatch, and I wasn't so nice Before. I was Jersey Hatch, and my life was my fault. Clay and dust and ashes. Lots of other things were my fault, too, but I didn't feel like making that list. My nose burned and burned.

"Nose."

I'd have a really red nose.

I was Jersey Hatch. I had stupid-marks and a half-a-mouth smile and a weak hand and a weak leg and a big mouth and a big red nose. I sucked at Algebra. I wasn't so good at Civics or Earth Science or any class, and I didn't like the Wench. Red radio-nose. I was Jersey Hatch and I said lots of stupid stuff. My mom was at the beach and my dad made bad oatmeal. Todd didn't like me, and Leza was tired of me, and guys I used to know wanted to pee on me.

Mama Rush.

Mama Rush was sick and she needed a tube, and she knew I had a choice to make. Mama Rush didn't get in my way. Skinny djinni. I hoped she got to smoke another cigarette. Tube. She liked her cigarettes even though they were bad for her.

Breathing harder, hard, hard. My legs burned like my nose, only not from heat. The gun rubbed on my belly. I had sweat there, but not on my face. Nose. Radio. Tube. A sign. The lake. Lake Raven just ahead. The benches. The little fence.

I probably came here with Todd and lots of people Before. Even the guys who peed on me. We probably walked just like I did, off the road, across a stretch of dirt, through a little patch of woods, and out again, to grass. Lots of grass, stretching everywhere. Up and back, right and left. Green grass covering a really big, wide hill, and down, on the other side of the hill, Lake Raven. Blue water in the summer and fall. Black water in the winter and spring. The benches and the little fence. I could see them now. Radio-nose. See them, head for them. Almost there. Almost finished.

Sun burned my nose. Sun blazed off the little waves on Lake Raven. Blue black water. Lots of ripples. Little white-top waves. A breeze hit my face and cooled it some.

"Nose," I muttered. "Nose and radio. Clay and dust and ashes."

Almost there. Almost. Almost.

At the benches now.

To the fence.

Beyond the fence, the hill dropped away, straight down to the lake. Nose. Good thing there was a fence, or people would fall in all the time. Radio. All the time.

I stopped at the fence to catch my breath and stared out across the water. The sun was so bright I had to make my eyes squint. Lake Raven was big, but I could see the beach on the other side. A little beach, nothing like the ocean. Little waves, nothing like the ocean. But people still came to Lake Raven and the little beach when it was warm. We came here lots when I was little. Mama Rush used to bring

Todd and Leza and me, too, to that little beach on the other side. Sometimes people swam, or floated on floats, or floated in little boats pretending to fish. Nose. That's what Dad said they were doing. Pretending to fish.

Lake Raven wasn't too big to see the other side. But it was deep. I knew it was deep. If something fell in Lake Raven and sank, it would sink forever, down in the blue black, all the way down to cold empty nothing. Radio. Radio-nose.

"What are you doing, moron?"

The question popped out, sounding so much like J.B. I guess it was J.B.

"What are you doing?"

I thought about Leza in the hospital, talking about Mama Rush.

What's she doing?

I hoped Leza was doing really good. I hoped Mama Rush was okay, and Todd, and the cheerleaders, and my dad and my mom. I even hoped the Wench was okay, and Mr. Sabon and the other teachers, but I didn't much care about the guys who peed on me, and I didn't like Romeo man or Leza's honey-honey. If they weren't okay, well, whatever. Nose. They could be un-okay, and that would be okay with me.

Still breathing hard, but not so hard, I bent down, used my good hand to hold onto the fence, and crawled through it. Through the fence. On the other side now. On the lake side. I stood up slow, slow, not too fast. Radio. I didn't want to go falling in the lake. No falling. Slow, slow. Rudolph nose.

Burning nose. Burning eyes. The water was so blue black

bright, and deep, deep, deep. I was standing on the hill now, in front of the benches, on the other side of the little fence. Nose.

I took out the gun.

It felt heavy and hot and sweaty.

Sun bounced off the metal like it bounced off the blue black water. The metal looked blue black, too. The gun had two bullets and four empty places. I felt like it was glued to my hand. Nose.

"Have to do this. Enough's enough." I tried to move, but glue. Really. It was glued. Nose. I tried to lift it but I barely made my arm twitch. Radio nose. Burning sun. Bright light on the water. Time. Time. It was time, and I couldn't move.

If I had brilliant last words, I knew what they'd be. Deserts. Up and forward. Big Larry. Romeo man and Sissy-U and skinny djinni. I'd say all of it. I'd shout it. Everything that clogged up my head and fell out of my mouth. Selfish. Self-centered. I bet you think I'm mad at you.

"Peanuts and shoelaces," I yelled. "Hoochie-mamas. Frog farts! Yeah. Frog farts!"

I still couldn't move.

"Frog farts!" I yelled again. "Nose and radio and devil and Santa Claus. Wench. Wench. Brilliant last words. Tube. Socks. Peeeaaaaanuts!"

My jaw clenched. I ground my teeth loud enough to hear them over the soft rush of the breeze making waves on Lake Raven. Nose. Radio. Enough. Enough! I glared at the gun and didn't squint my eyes even though the sun-glare hurt.

"Enough."

In my head, the gun answered me like J.B.

Never enough until it's over. Never, ever enough. More. Always more. Always one more time.

"Over now."

I lifted it a little. A little more. Even with my shoulder. My neck.

"Enough!"

The gun slipped and slid. Not glued anymore. I had to hold it tight.

Never enough until it's over. Never, ever enough . . .

Even with my ear, my nose. Nose. My eyes. I could see it there in my fist, blue black like the water. Oily and metal and waiting.

Never enough until it's over . . .

Even with the top of my head. Higher. Higher. All the way up. High as it would go, high as I could get it. Hold it tight. Hold it. Hold it.

Never enough . . .

I leaned back, back, then swung forward and threw that gun as far as I could throw it.

It sailed out of my hand. Unglued. It flew. Unglued. Nose. Radio. Peanuts. It flew! And it fell. It turned over and over and fell straight into the blue black ripples with a big spray-splash.

I was hopping, trying to get my balance and stand up, trying not to fall down the hill. Almost to the edge. Almost over and gone. I fell sideways to keep from pitching into Lake Raven. Nose. I fell hard. Facedown in the grass. On the hill. Nose. Burned nose. Mashed nose. But I didn't care. My heart thumped. My breath jerked in my chest as I sat up and looked down at the lake.

The gun was gone, gone forever and sinking, sinking

into the cold black empty, with its two bullets, with its four empty places—but without me. Nose. Without me or my nose. Or my shoelaces or my peanuts or anything else.

I started laughing. Then I started crying. I put my hands over my face and sat there and cried and I didn't keep any tears at all.

The police brought lots of cars with flashing lights, an ambulance, and a fire truck. Maybe two fire trucks. Lots of noise and lots of people. Lights, noise, and lights.

They brought a big man in a uniform who crawled over the fence and fell down on the other side. Lights and noise. He got up and kept coming until he got his hands on my shoulders and said, "Son, are you all right?"

He didn't let me go. He helped me get back to the fence, get back through, get to the benches on the other side. As I stumbled toward the lights and noise, noise and lights, I saw him. He was standing with some policemen with his hands in his pockets. He was looking at me.

Todd.

A policeman brought me water and a blanket, and the guys in the fire engine ran out to check me over. They started putting something white and cool and nice all over my nose and my cheeks and my stupid-marks.

"Todd," I called, but my voice was too quiet. Besides, he was turning around. Getting in a police car. Then he was riding away, away. I wanted to run and catch the car and tell him about the gun, about how I threw it away and how I threw away dying forever until it was my time to die. I threw it into the lake, the gun and the nothing and the dying. But

Todd couldn't see me waving and I'd never be able to catch that police car.

Maybe I could tell him later. I'd tell him later. Maybe he'd listen.

It was afternoon, the police said. I'd been gone almost a day. And Todd helped them find me. Noise. Lights. Nose. Only my nose was white now, and it wasn't burning. Then another car came, and I could see who was driving.

My dad.

When the police let him through, he ran straight to me and grabbed me off the bench, blanket and all, and started hugging me.

"Nose," I said.

Dad didn't stop hugging me.

"I threw it away, okay?" I hoped he wasn't too mad at me. "Nose. I threw it in the lake. Bullets, too. The gun. I threw it away forever."

Dad still didn't stop hugging me.

He didn't stop for a long time, but that was okay. That was just fine.

I didn't mind at all.

chapter 25

"Did you talk to Leza?" Mama Rush sat across from me at our outside Palace table, only my clay ashtray wasn't in front of her. She had a plastic tube stuck in her nose and an oxygen tank beside her and a sucker crammed in her mouth.

"Yes," I said. "Sucker. A bunch of times."

I didn't have a sucker because I didn't want to drool. Mama Rush's sucker was sour apple. Drool. Probably why her face looked all puckered up and way past mad. And she was wearing a green robe sort of the same color as the oxygen tank and the sucker. Mama Rush was having a green day on her purple scooter. Drool. Sucker.

"Quit staring at me, boy," she growled around her sucker stick. "I'm not going anywhere."

"Green drool," I said. It was nice to talk without my face hurting. My sunburn was finally gone after three weeks. Three weeks since the gun took its last swim. Three weeks of being with happy Dad who got us breakfast from fast-food places and restaurants and promised no more oatmeal ever. And now, Mama Rush was out of the hospital and better and taking visitors. Taking me, at least.

"Drool." I sighed and didn't stare at her oxygen tank. No staring. Don't say tank. "Sucker. Green drool."

With her right hand, Mama Rush tugged at the pocket where her cigarettes used to be. The pocket was ripped all the way down one side, but she tugged at it, anyway. "Don't talk about drool, Jersey. It's disgusting. Talk about socks or shoelaces or something."

"Frog farts."

She glared at me and bit on her sucker and ripped at her pocket. "Kids. I swear. You'll be shouting about farts in public—somewhere you shouldn't. Mark my words."

"Frog farts," I said. "I do. Shout it, I mean. Frog farts. A lot. Mr. Sabon sent me to the office for frog farts."

"Yeah, well, old Sabon needs to get the stick out from up his ass. Anyway, I'm glad Leza talked it out with you. I was worried she wouldn't tell you what she went through that day, hearing everything, and calling your mom instead of the police. She still has bad dreams, and I think she still blames herself for your mom being—well, like she is now."

"Told her no," I muttered, wondering if I should try a sucker. "Leza. That it's my fault. I told her I was sorry until she made me shut up."

Mama Rush grunted and chewed through her sucker with a loud crack. "Tell her some more tomorrow. And next week. Keep telling her."

"Drool. I mean, frog farts. I mean, I will."

More sucker crunching. More tugging on her pocket.

Then, "You got it all figured out now? About why you pulled the trigger?"

"Trigger." I sat up a little straighter, and I didn't say "drool." "Too much pressure. Too much perfect. I got all flat and dead inside, and I made little things too big. I made nothing too much."

"And you got depressed," Mama Rush added.

"Depressed. Yeah." I nodded. "Frog farts."

My stomach hurt just thinking about it, but I figured I deserved that. Trigger. Trigger drool.

Mama Rush told me she'd gotten a "condensed version" of what happened at the hospital, so I told her about the gun and throwing it away, and how it was gone forever. I told her how I'd never pull the trigger again, how I wouldn't die until I died. I promised her. After that, I said I was sorry until she told me to shut up just like Leza had.

Then I said, "I thought there would be a big reason, you know? Drool. One big reason. Some huge secret. All simple. All neat. Just one reason. Socks."

"Yeah. Socks." Mama Rush stopped talking and started a new sucker. It was quiet outside, except for that cool little breeze and her oxygen and loud breathing and sucker-crunching.

Finally, she put her sucker stick on the table. "Thinking about all this upset you, Jersey?"

I nodded.

"Good. You should be upset. But you promised you'd never hurt yourself again, upset or not."

I nodded my head hard.

"Good boy. That's a start. Now walk me back to my room. I have something for you."

Before I could even stand up, Mama Rush picked up her oxygen tank and swung her scooter away from the table— all at the same time. She dropped a bunch of suckers and they crunched under the wheels.

As she motored toward the door, Attila the Red came out and had to jump to the side.

Mama Rush gave her a wicked glare.

As I lurched past Meki Shansu, I swear I heard her say, "Same to you, old woman."

But I probably imagined that. I didn't imagine how fast Mama Rush was driving. I nearly fell trying to keep up. And I nearly fell on top of her when she stopped even faster near her room to flip off Romeo man and mumble a bunch of stuff I was glad I couldn't hear. Romeo man—who must have gotten a little smarter since I saw him the first time— turned around and sort of ran away down another hall.

"I really should move back home," Mama Rush said as she found her key and opened her door. "Seeing that man just pisses me off. Even teenagers aren't worse than he is."

She whizzed in.

Drool. The door almost shut in my face before I caught it, but I caught it and got in and followed Mama Rush back to her bedroom.

Right away, I saw a wrapped box. Wrapped with green paper with a green bow. Mama Rush's green day, I swear. Drool. Next to the present was the ashtray—she'd put safety pins in it. And next to that, the trivet and ceramic flowerpot, and the funny-looking piggy bank. All the other mess was gone. Cleaned off nice and neat. Drool. Guess there were some things she couldn't fix.

She leaned back and nudged me just as I finished thinking that, and pointed to her window.

There was a mobile hanging there. Lots of little colored bottles. Tiny bottles on metal hangers, all floating around. Green and blue and yellow and red. Lots of green, too. Lots. Floating. They had dust inside. Only, I knew it wasn't really dust. It was clay. Bits and pieces and piles of clay dust. The rest of the presents, drifting back and forth in little colored bottles.

"See? I told you." Mama Rush motored a little ways toward the mobile and gazed up at it. The colors danced around the room. Bottles. They danced around her. "Lots of ways to look at stuff. And you can always make something out of something—if you try."

She gave me a look over her shoulder. "Go on. Open your present."

I had another present? Other than the floating bottles full of clay? Bottles. Green day. Good day. Bottles. So pretty. I had to make myself look away, make myself pick up the package and tear the paper.

Mama Rush motored back over. Inside the paper I found a box, and inside the box, I found the coolest notebook ever.

Camouflage green cloth on the outside, with a black leather binding and leather edges, and my name wasn't on the outside. I opened the cover. Written in Mama Rush's squiggly printing on the inside cover was my name, telephone number, and address. Right under that, she had written, *If you aren't Jersey, that's all you need to know. Stay the hell out of his notebook and give it back to him before I have to hurt you.* Then she had signed her name and put her phone number underneath that.

"Green day," I said. "Good day. Bottles. This—this is great. It's great."

"There's a pen holder in the back. I put in some black and blue ballpoints, and a couple of red ones." She leaned back. "I don't want you to start thinking everything's simple and neat again, but you need a new memory book. Been looking naked without one."

My new memory book had lots of paper, and some dividers. And on the first page, squiggled by Mama Rush, was a list.

1. ~~See Mama Rush and give her all the presents I made her.~~
2. ~~Talk to Todd and find out why he hates me.~~
3. *Pass the adaptive driver's evaluation.*
4. *Make decent grades.*
5. *Take the ACT.*
6. *Get a girlfriend.*

I looked up at her. "Green day. Good day?"

She tugged at her oxygen tube and fiddled with her torn pocket, then smiled. "Well, some things might be a little simple and neat. Besides, it seemed like a good list to tackle next. You better get busy, because that's a lot to do."

"I love you," I said, and I put down the cool new memory book and hugged her.

She hugged me back. "Would you add something for me? To that list?"

"Bottles. Sure." I stepped back, found the pen holder, took out a pen, and got ready.

Mama Rush's smile turned kind of wicked. "Put down, 'Throw Carl into Lake Raven for Mama Rush.' Can you handle that for me, Jersey?"

Bottles. I wasn't stupid.

I wrote that down in a hurry.

When I got to my house, Leza was in her yard looking prettier than ever. She came over to the cab and helped me carry in the Chinese food I got for dinner. I didn't say drool.

We put it on the kitchen table. Dad would be surprised—and happy. He was pretty sick of hamburgers, I figured. Hamburgers. Bottles. Bottles and hamburgers. I was sick of them, too.

Leza and I set up the food, even got out the silverware, and paper napkins instead of paper towels, and I still didn't say drool.

"Hamburgers." I looked at the table. "Lots better than hamburgers. Bottles."

"Yeah. For sure." Leza dusted off her hands.

I walked her to the door and opened it. She stopped on her way out and gave me a quick hug.

"Thanks," I said. No drool. No drool.

"Welcome." She pulled back and stared at me just like Mama Rush does. "Todd's a little better, I think. If you'll just give him—"

"Some time. I know. Drool." I did my best to smile with both sides of my mouth, but it didn't work. "It's okay."

She kissed me on the cheek.

I didn't pass out. Pretty good, for me.

Then I watched her as she ran home.

She sure was pretty.

Well? I could like her if I wanted to. Bottles. I had to like her. Who wouldn't?

The phone rang.

I shut the door and went to answer it. Took me a second, but I got there. It was time for Mom. And it was Mom. Mom in her hotel. She called every night, same time. And I talked to her every night, same time.

"How are you?" she asked right away, just like she did every night, same time.

"I'm fine. Green day. Good day. Bottles. Hamburgers. Slow down." I took a deep breath. "Went . . . to see Mama Rush. Got dinner for Dad, and stuff. He'll be glad. No hamburgers."

"You got dinner?" Definitely surprised, Mom was. Good. Dad would be surprised, too, for sure.

"Leza helped set the table," I said.

"Taking initiative. I'm proud of you, honey."

I couldn't help it. I laughed. Then I covered my mouth and laughed some more.

Mom went all quiet.

When I finally stopped, I thought I heard Mom laugh, too. "I guess I say that a lot, huh?"

"Yeah. Kind of. Bottles." I bit my lip to keep from laughing again.

"I'll try not to say 'I'm proud of you' so much."

"Slow down, slow down." Deep breath. "It's okay. Proud is good."

"I *am* proud of you, you know? Really." Something

rustled, and I imagined Mom sitting back in her chair at the hotel. Bottles. Probably a chair with a desk so she could work but also call me.

"Hamburgers. Thanks. Mama Rush gave me a new memory book. Bottles. It's green."

"Better than that white piece of junk?"

"Way better."

"You won't throw it away?"

"No." I touched the memory book. No way was I throwing it away. Too cool. And it had a new list, with stuff already crossed off.

"Is Mama Rush still laying off the cigarettes, Jersey?"

"Yes. Bottles. She is for now, but she eats lots of green suckers. Green apple. Hamburgers. Makes her face pucker all up and stuff. And she wants me to throw Carl in Lake Raven."

"The guy who fooled around on her. Yeah. I'll help you. We'll set a date."

"Mom—about school. Bottles." I played with the bottom of the phone, the little places where it sat on the charger. "If I don't do better by Christmas, what about a G.E.D.? Less pressure. Hamburgers. Dad said 'maybe.'"

Mom didn't say anything for a second. Then, "Maybe is good. Let's leave it at maybe and think about that closer to Christmas, okay?"

"Okay. Bottles. Hamburgers. Green day."

"Want to have dinner with me next week? Maybe we can get—um—something other than hamburgers. Monday night?"

"Good day. Good! Yes. Thanks. Hamburgers. I mean,

not hamburgers." I got excited so I almost dropped the phone. Fumbled it. Caught it. Got it back to my ear.

"—Tell your dad to call me," Mom was saying. "I'd like to have dinner with him another night, if you're all right with that."

"Very all right. Hamburgers. Bottles. Green day."

"Okay, honey. Well, I love you, and I'll talk to you later."

"Bottles. Love you, too, Mom."

I hung up smiling my half-smile and not even caring that much. Hamburgers. It felt okay, half a smile. Bottles. It felt fine. Dad and I had a fine dinner, too. Later, I got into my new bed in my new room down the hall. I left the green bedspread and the football rug in the old room, at least for now. They were in a good place. Green day. A very good place for now.

acknowledgments

The journey to this book became a quest, and finally an odyssey, with many, many helpers along the way. Thanks to Kathleen Duey, who sat in the conference lobby at the 2001 SCBWI National Conference, patiently listening to a nervous, unpublished author rattling off an ambitious idea. Your interest helped me believe others might be interested. Thanks to Melissa Haber, who made a huge difference with a single critique comment. Thanks to Christine Taylor-Butler, who understood things nobody else did, and made me laugh when I wanted to scream. Thanks to Melissa Neal-Lunsford, who told me it was creepy. Huge, endless thanks to my critique warriors Debbie Federici, Sheri Gilbert, and my family, who screamed at me to finish this, read it at least one thousand times (Debbie probably double that much), told me the truth, and swore at me for making them cry.

I cannot offer enough gratitude to my agent, Erin Murphy, for helping me grow as a writer so I could write this, believing in the book, and helping me polish it. I would also like to announce to the world that my editor, Victoria Arms, is simply brilliant, and I so appreciate her becoming *Blowout*'s champion and working through the manuscript with such a deft, gentle hand. Thanks also to Donna Mark and Jonathan Barkat for a beautiful cover, and to Stacy Cantor, Ele Fountain, Melanie Cecka, Diana Blough, and Deb Shapiro who fell in love with *Blowout* and helped make the book a reality.

Finally, I offer a humble thank you to every teen and young adult who trusted me enough to share their fears, pains, sorrows, and dreams. In the end, Jersey exists for all of you.

resources

Suicide is one of the leading causes of death for young people in the United States and the UK. For every young person who dies from suicide, many more make attempts. Many of those young people will suffer permanent injuries ranging from scarring to severe brain damage. Triggering events can seem trivial—fights with friends or parents, loss of romantic relationships, or even a bad mark. Often, young people who attempt suicide have underlying issues such as major depression, bipolar disorder, family conflict, recent losses, a history of abuse, a history of suicide in friends or family, or problems with substance abuse. Often . . . but not always. So what's the bottom line? What can you do? The answer has two parts.

First, know the more common warning signs:

- Withdrawing from friends, family, and typical activities
- Signs of depression, such as major changes in eating and sleeping habits, sadness, crying, hopelessness, boredom, low energy, irritability or anger, guilt, low self-esteem, poor concentration, and frequent complaints of physical symptoms like stomachache or headache
- Signs of mania or psychosis, such as hearing things, very unusual or magical thinking, rapid and pressured speech, agitation or very high activity level with little

to no sleep, risk taking (acting "bulletproof"), and extreme suspicion

- Disruptive emotional behaviours, such as running away or violent outbursts
- Deterioration in personal hygiene and/or appearance
- Significant personality change
- Throwing away, giving away, or abandoning important possessions
- Statements about feeling awful, feeling like a bad person, feeling dead or ruined inside
- Focusing on death or wanting to die in talking, writing, or art
- Indirect statements like *Everything will be okay soon; Nothing matters; It's no use; Everything's over; I have no future; I'll be out of everybody's way soon*

Second, take action. If you're a young person thinking about suicide or have a friend thinking about suicide, tell a trusted adult or use the resources below. If you're a parent, educator, practitioner, or just an adult friend, get help for the young person. ***Don't wait***. There are many options and resources for immediate help, such as the following:

- If you believe an attempt is in progress, the police or 999
- If you believe the situation is imminent or urgent, your local Accident and Emergency
- Your GP, who often can a) see patients on an emergency basis faster than anyone else, b) make initial assessments of risk, c) arrange for hospitalization if needed, d) match a young person to a counsellor or psychiatrist quickly, and e) access or provide other medical help faster and more efficiently than a layperson

- A therapist or counsellor, or local community health centre, if the young person is already involved in such services
- National 24-hour crisis hotlines with provisions for teens, including:

ChildLine – 0800 1111
Samaritans – 0845 790 9090
SANELINE – 0845 767 8000

If the situation isn't immediately life threatening, be a friend and support—or find friends and supports for yourself. Seek information from suicide prevention organizations with a focus on young people, such as the following:

- PAPYRUS (http://www.papyrus-uk.org)
- YoungMinds (http://www.youngminds.org.uk)
- Teen Advice Online (http://www.teenadviceonline.org)
- The Jason Foundation (www.thejasonfoundation.com)
- Yellow Ribbon International Suicide Prevention (www. yellowribbon.org)
- Metanoia (www.metanoia.org)
- Suicide Awareness Voices of Education (www.save.org)

To explore choosing mental health services for yourself or a young person you're helping, seek information from organizations such as the following:

- YoungMinds (http://www.youngminds.org.uk)
- Mind (http://www.mind.org.uk)
- SANE (http://www.sane.org.uk)
- British Psychological Society (www.bps.org.uk)
- Royal College of Psychiatrists (http:// www.rcpsych.ac.uk)

For more information about this book, the author, the subject of teenage suicide, and choosing and working with counsellors visit www.susanvaught.com.